MEANTIME

MEANTIME

FRANKIE BOYLE

BASKERVILLE

An imprint of JOHN MURRAY

First published in Great Britain in 2022 by Baskerville
An imprint of John Murray (Publishers)
An Hachette UK company

1

A CIP catalogue record for this title is available from the British Library

Hardback ISBN 978-1-399-80115-7
Exclusive hardback ISBN 978-1-399-80191-1
Trade Paperback ISBN 978-1-399-80116-4
eBook ISBN 978-1-399-80118-8

Typeset in Perpetua by Palimpsest Book Production Ltd, Falkirk, Stirlingshire

Printed and bound in Great Britain by Clays Ltd, Elcograf S.p.A.

John Murray policy is to use papers that are natural, renewable and
recyclable products and made from wood grown in sustainable forests.
The logging and manufacturing processes are expected to conform
to the environmental regulations of the country of origin.

Baskerville, an imprint of John Murray
Carmelite House
50 Victoria Embankment
London EC4Y 0DZ

www.johnmurraypress.co.uk

For my daughter and son,
the glorious, hilarious little legends.

I am astonished, disappointed, pleased with
myself. I am distressed, depressed, rapturous.
I am all these things at once and cannot add up
the sum. I am incapable of determining ultimate
worth or worthlessness; I have no judgement
about myself and my life. There is nothing I am
quite sure about. I have no definite convictions
– not about anything, really.

Carl Jung,
Memories, Dreams, Reflections: An Autobiography

1

At first I was worried that I might still be tripping but no, there was definitely a policeman standing at the side of the bed holding my hand.

'Morning,' I guessed, and he let my arm drop heavily back onto the mattress.

'I was checking your pulse . . . you looked dead.'

Possibly he had been yelling loudly before I woke up, and it hadn't been me after all. I struggled to bring order to my thoughts. 'Why are you in my house? I mean . . . what the fuck?'

He bawled something out through the bedroom door and an older man in a sad brown suit stalked in. I tried to get up, but my body didn't seem to be receiving the message. Perhaps the message itself was equivocal.

'Maybe you'd like to get up and answer some questions, sir.'

Sensing that my supine position might give me some kind of power, I demurred wordlessly with a little wave of the wrists. He stared at me with confusion, or possibly outrage, and I decided to swing uneasily into a sitting position.

'How can I help you . . .' I tried to remember what you call a policeman '. . . officer?'

The fact that I knew the place was clean, that I had dropped the acid and the last of the Vallies last night, that I had searched every crack in the floorboards for crumbs of hash with a butter knife for nearly a week now, made me feel a sudden euphoric confidence.

I can do this thing where I take a big gulp of air in and kind of block up my ears. Looks like I'm sniffing pretty hard when I do it – basically gives me a cushion of air behind the ears – and in the absence of any opiates between me and this potentially harrowing encounter, I was trying to block them pretty hard.

'Are you okay?' he said, and then something after that, which I couldn't quite hear. He bent down towards me and I found that without sound I could concentrate on the beauty of his face. Not beautiful like a beautiful girl, but like an old baseball mitt. The burst veins on his nose, the surprisingly white teeth click-clacking away. The folds on his forehead, crumpling as the teeth moved quicker, forming into an angry frown. And it bummed me out a bit, I suppose. Perhaps it was the tail end of last night's trip too, but I realised that maybe I should be listening to him.

'You both having a good day?' I asked, maybe a bit too loudly.

There was a very one-sided scuffle, then I was sitting at the kitchen table. The Referendum had been months ago but I still had a big Yes poster up over the window, and in the mornings it gave the kitchen the blue glow of a computer screen. I tried to focus.

'Are we boring you?' asked the older one peremptorily, as I yawned frantically to unblock my ears.

'Oh, no, no, no. Please, fire away!' I yawned.

'Where were you last night?' the crumpled suit asked, leaning meaningfully across my crumb-covered plastic table-cloth.

'I was here . . . officer . . . What is this?'

'Do you have anyone to vouch for your whereabouts last night?'

'No . . .' I vaguely remembered talking to someone, making a phone call, then remembered it was to Iron Man in a dream. I'd been having a lot of dreams about Iron Man, but this wasn't the place to get into that. Perhaps there was no place to get into it. I let the silence hang.

'Do you know a Marina Katos? She worked at . . .'

'At the Go-Go, I know.'

The Go-Go was a sort of Mexican bar I went to, but only after hours. I'd worked in a chain bar a few years ago. The work was dull, but I enjoyed the lock-ins, and relentless dope smoking. It got pretty boring after a bit, or possibly we'd all just fucked each other. A couple of us had this kind of epiphany one night that we didn't need to do this in our place of work, probably we could do it in any bar if we just hung around enough. So we all started going to this Mexican-themed bar-restaurant thing called the Go-Go staffed by students and a group of second-generation Mexicans, related to the owners. They were a bit nonplussed

3

at first but we hung around so often that eventually we'd have lock-ins just like at the old place. In fact, it was exactly the same except we got to eat nachos. I lost my job by the end of the summer and then for a while I was just a guy who drank with Mexicans.

I suddenly thought that, what with the way you should play it cagey with the police, I shouldn't be saying any of this out loud.

'Mexicans?' asked the uniform, in the appalled tone of someone who thinks you've made up a word in Scrabble.

'What do I look like to you? Do I look like someone you can fuck around with?' the brown suit shrieked.

I had learned over the course of the previous minute not to answer anything honestly without careful consideration. My honest answer would be that he looked like he had a skincare routine and went down on his middle-aged wife twice a week with a ferocious sense of duty that passed for love.

'No, sir. Has Marina done something?' I was flicking through the scenarios she could have become involved in that would lead the police to scream at the unconscious body of an acquaintance. What the fuck had she done now?

'How would you describe Miss Katos?'

'Uh, pretty quiet, I guess. She liked to drink . . .'

'Does she take drugs . . . ?'

I tried to shrug and smile in a way that implied I didn't really know what drugs were.

'Did you have sexual relations with her?' blared the brown suit abruptly, suddenly at the volume of a pensioner's telly.

'Oh God no, we're just friends.' Although she had once given me a handjob in a tent, we were never really attracted to each other. It just wouldn't stop raining that day. If anything it had made the relationship even more platonic.

'Yeah, she slept around a little,' I understated.

'We need to ask you some questions down at the station,' snapped the uniform, and then he was suddenly propelling me towards the bedroom.

I picked up yesterday's clothes from the floor and put them on.

The police station looked like a depressed architect's statement on his marriage. The older cop sat down across from me with a rueful grunt and pushed a can of Coke towards me. 'You're not under caution. We just need to clarify a few things.'

They hadn't said the stuff about you can have a solicitor, and I didn't want to be the one to bring it up. Probably this was the exact attitude that had seen generations of men like me fed into the prison system to be used as a sexual punchbag. I thought about asking for a lawyer. Even though I had nothing to hide, it would be good to know what was going on. But maybe it was better to play it cool. I didn't think I'd done anything and there was still a possibility that nothing had happened.

The uniform sat in a corner. The older guy shrugged off his suit jacket and sat staring at his iPhone with a burning intensity. I thought it was some kind of mind game until I noticed that I could see the screen reflected in the mirror behind him and he was checking the Rangers score. He put his phone away suddenly. I felt almost certain that Rangers had conceded.

He announced all our names briskly to a tape recorder. Their names were PC Stewart and DI Ian, who seemed to do all the talking.

'Where were you last night?'

'Eh, I was at home.' There was a long pause, so I added, 'Drinking.'

'Was anybody with you?'

'No.' I remembered something. 'My neighbour came up from downstairs. Donnie Wilson. He watched a movie with me because he was having a nervous breakdown.'

'This . . . Donnie Wilson is at . . . ?' He looked up.

'Eh, the flat under me. I don't know the number.'

'You don't know the number?'

'No.'

There was a long, disappointed silence. He groaned and appeared to start writing out what I had said in longhand. I wondered how much detective work could be involved in finding the number of a flat in a building you had just visited.

'How's about I check the number when I get home and give you a call?'

'Could you?' He seemed genuinely grateful.

As he smiled I realised that he was pretty toned for an older guy, and tanned, like some sex-industry veteran.

'And what time did he leave?'

'I don't know. I went to bed about one.'

'You went to sleep around one . . .' Writing furiously, longhand.

'No, I went to bed. I wasn't tired. I don't know if you know any fifty-year-old men having a breakdown, but – I just left him there. I waited till the end of the movie.'

'You were watching a movie on television?'

'On DVD. *Boys Don't Cry* with Hilary Swank.' It suddenly occurred to me that, subconsciously, I'd been trying to encourage Donnie to get through the evening without crying. Sadly, he'd found the film's bleak subject matter extremely upsetting.

'Miss Katos is dead.' DI Ian announced with a mournfulness that bordered on sarcasm.

I was shocked, even though I'd known that she must be, that the whole thing had that vibe. I tried to put my head in my hands but they were trembling so I kind of raised them up to my head instead and gripped it. Now my head was shaking a little. I know the police are suspicious if you act too cool, but surely I was going too far the other way? I thought DI Ian seemed puzzled as I tried to steady my face, or it could be that I didn't have him in focus.

DI Ian stood up and looked at himself in the mirror, smoothing his thinning hair into place. I suppose it might have been a signal to someone who was behind the glass, but it went on a bit too long. Perhaps they'd forgotten to arrange a signal and he was simply mouthing words at them. There was a knock. The uniform went to the door, spoke to someone outside, then stepped back in and whispered something to his boss. A brief storm crossed DI Ian's features.

'I'll have to go,' he announced. 'PC Stewart will take it from here.'

It turned out that what PC Stewart wanted to take was a sperm sample. I found myself left in a cell with a plastic Jiffy bag and no belt or shoelaces. I suppose they were worried I might hang myself, or maybe some people did that accidentally by trying to really enjoy the wank.

It's not like I expected them to have some sort of dedicated wanking room, but shouldn't they have put me in a bathroom or something to do this? I hadn't wanted to sound like some connoisseur of jerking off in public, so I'd said nothing. It was just me and my imagination, and none of my fantasies involved an eight by five jail cell or distant clanging noises. It took me about five minutes just to get hard.

I lay down on the bunk and thought about this girl I'd met at a night class I dropped out of. Man, why didn't I ask her out? I started to dimly remember that she'd hated me as I began to build up some steam. I guess there's something buried deep in my genes that tells me that, if I want to continue my line, I'm occasionally going to have to come in some weird situations. Or maybe it's the part of my genes that knows I might have to go gay to survive in jail.

When he finally came to get me, I jauntily pressed the bottle into PC Stewart's hand like I was tipping a doorman in a movie.

2

I'd first met Marina when she worked at the Go-Go. She'd invited me back to her flat for a smoke, assuming, as most of the staff had at some point, that I was one of her co-workers. It was a flat-share at Charing Cross. She had a big, shabby, clothes-strewn room with a vague air of humanitarian crisis.

Her flatmates included a Scottish-Indian lassie – a mousy, secretarial type called Fatima who seemed to be making a serious attempt to bond her DNA with prescription medication. Every time I saw her she would gigglingly relate the dreadful trouble she'd had that day completing some totally mundane work task on a near fatal dose of mood stabilisers. There seemed to be a fair turnover in the flat, but one constant was this flatmate who was a dreadlocked white guy who worked in a bar somewhere nearby. I guess he must have straightened up for that, but I never saw him when he was less than melted. I'd have loved to see what we looked like through his eyes, maybe just some kind of heat signature, like in *Predator*. He was generally holed up in his room shagging his girlfriend, who appeared rarely, with the demeanour of a hostage. One time he shouldered his way into the living room and delivered a bitter monologue about the district council to a spot two feet above our heads, but it was obvious that he barely understood what it was.

I'd stay in Marina's bed some nights. Nothing happened – not because of our friendship, but just because we were both so unattractive. On a genetic level we understood that we needed to target superior DNA, not more of the shitty stuff we already had. Also, I imagined that sex in the state of mind we'd smoked ourselves into would be like riding naked through your own childhood on a burning roller-coaster.

She'd lie and stare at the ceiling and we'd have those talks couples have, but without the part where every sentence was really a commentary on the death of the relationship.

'Everyone is just an actor, man . . .' Working with Mexicans had made her speech a bit Mexican somehow. She was actually Greek or something. '. . . everyone's playing a part. You see a student bicycling into class with those big, long, stripy scarves? That's a part. They've been casting that part since the 1920s, and he's just the one who's in the role. Like, eh, James Bond.'

'But not us, right? I mean, what the fuck are we supposed to be? I've never seen anybody in a film hang around a Mexican bar so he can not fuck a waitress.'

'That's just how we feel, G. We feel exceptional, like shit doesn't apply to us, cos we live in countries that say shit doesn't apply to them. Exceptionalism, that's what it's all about.'

'I'm exceptionally wasted.'

'It's the only way you can forget your lines.'

Sometimes she wasn't up for talking and encouraged me to just burble away. One night, after celebrating her new job in TV production with a couple of buckets, I told her about my idea for a rom-com that I'd never written up.

'It's about this guy – a washed-up actor – who runs into his ex-girlfriend years later. She'd chucked him because he was too much of a pill-popping, stoner, party addict. He's a drama teacher now, and he's pretty straight edged – runs the school debating team, got his life together, all that shit. Anyway, he's still in love with her, and his ex starts teaching at the same school. She falls back in love with him, but he's kind of full of self-hatred, right?'

'Write what you know.'

'So he wants to put her off him. He feels worthless, and thinks he'll ruin her chance of being happy. She's the only person he really cares about. So he pretends he's still on the party scene. Has to start going to house parties and taking drugs again, with potential for hilarious misadventures and high jinks that I have not yet written.'

'Haha. I wish more people would say that in pitch meetings: "Then some interesting or amusing things happen and I'll tell you what they are if you pay me to think of them."'

'Exactly. He decides to tell her that he doesn't love her, but he knows she'll see through it, so he practises it a lot, this little break-up speech he has. He finds this old actor who teaches him how to act properly. The couple have an argument one day and he tells her he doesn't want to see her anymore. She's crying at the end of school that day, but one of the girls from the debating society is in her class and she confides in her. He does love you, the kid says, he just doesn't think you should settle for him: he's actually been taking these acting lessons to try and break up with you. Then she shows her some things she and the rest of the debating society have found online: it's the drama teacher during his acting career in a really shit Scottish soap. He's a fucking terrible actor. These will be hilarious if you pay me to think of them, etcetera.'

'Etcetera,' she agreed.

'He meets her in Glasgow Central under the clock and she asks him if he loves her, and he says no. He performs it perfectly, it's totally believable. And this is how she knows he really does love her – the effort it must have taken for this appalling actor to pull that off. So after he tells her they should go their separate ways she throws her arms around him and kisses him, she says, "I know" and then we're panning out, right through the roof of Central Station and up into the night sky, looking down on Glasgow through the snow.'

'Why have you never written it up?'

'Well, it'd be hard to find a Scottish actor good enough to carry off the good acting bit. So it wouldn't make any sense. I'm hoping one day to straighten up enough to tell if it's an objectively good idea or not.'

'Why is he so sure he'll be bad for her?'

'I don't know yet. I thought maybe he has the gene that causes motor neurone disease, so they couldn't have kids.'

She burst out laughing. She put her hand over her mouth and shook until tears ran down her face. She gripped my arm with her other hand for support.

'Okay. Well. Maybe not that.'

She wiped at her face with a hand, then laughed some more. 'Merry fucking Christmas everybody!' she gasped.

3

I could hear my downstairs neighbour suck on his asthma inhaler from climbing one flight of stairs before knocking theatrically on the open door. Donnie was broad, with an enormous belly and the bearing of a rather grand turtle. He slobbered slightly as he spoke from a crinkly face with haunted, baggy eyes. In fact, there was a general bagginess to his skin, like his immune system was rejecting his face. He would occasionally – especially when drunk – launch into stories with gusto and then suddenly catch himself, as if remembering that everybody hated him like this, and mutter the end of the anecdote into his drink. He was mean with money, insensitive, and filled with petty hatreds, but I liked him. Maybe because he wasn't capable of pretending to be anything else or, more accurately, couldn't be bothered. He was an English teacher at a local college when he could face going in but was off with stress, a kind of modern code word for unhappiness.

Donnie was heavy: not quite documentary fat, but too fat, and it put a major strain on his cardiovascular system, which groaned and wheezed loudly on exertion. He was from Edinburgh and had a contempt for Glaswegians which he pretended was a breezy affectation, but seemed to be underpinned with genuine hostility. His voice was somehow booming yet gasping, like he was speaking to you from a vast tunnel where he was running for his life. Sometimes he spoke like a man falling asleep, and other times like the same man waking up on a bus.

He glided past me casually, as he always did, and abandoned himself to gravity three feet above the sofa, landing with a sigh from both it and him. He was drunk and already in the middle of some slavering recrimination that I couldn't hear because he had his back to me.

'. . . not that she's a bad person,' he continued, as I sat in the armchair across from him, 'but obviously she's being a fucking cunt about this!' He delivered these final words with the passionate fury of a poet. As I tried to find a movie on Netflix, he embarked on a soliloquy that suggested his wife may have caught him in some infidelity: 'Technology wants you to break up, to be on your own, where it can talk to you. Look at your email – you contact an ex, you've got to delete it from the inbox, the sent folder *and* the deleted folder. That's a lot to remember when you're horny. You'll never make it every time. The actual technology itself wants to split you up.'

'Did your wife find some kind of email that . . .'

'No! I found the fucking email. I found the email between her and this . . . sexykev69.'

Kevin either had a juvenile sense of humour or was

forty-six years old and still sexy, I calculated. 'What was it?' I braced myself.

Donnie wiped his mouth anxiously with the back of his hand. 'I don't fucking know . . . all this sexy pish . . . about her legs.'

Donnie's wife Janice was a PE teacher and had powerful, forbidding legs.

'Sexual stuff?' I didn't want to know, but I couldn't stop talking. I moved around the screen desperately looking for a film that was vaguely upbeat.

'Poetry!' he hissed in a dramatic stage whisper.

'Oh. Did he rhyme thighs with sighs . . . ?' I began half-heartedly.

'PRIZE!' Donnie bellowed disgustedly.

I didn't actually know if he said 'prize' or 'prise', and I hoped never to find out. I hit the button, and suddenly keeping my friend's splintering psyche occupied was Jason Statham's problem.

By the time the various henchmen and villains had been worked through in order of hierarchy, it was still only 10 p.m. The heating was playing up so we were both sitting half in sleeping bags, playing a supposedly jovial but actually bitterly contested game of FIFA on the PlayStation. Many of the powerful emotions Donnie displayed during the game were probably really directed at his marriage troubles. There's no good reason for anyone to call their goalkeeper a whore.

He passed me a sloppily rolled grass joint that at least

punctured the atmosphere of a sleepover. 'Time for a swift tightener?' he growled. He stood up uncertainly and began packing his filthy green army jacket with fags, lighters, hash, skins and a length of metal pipe he carried for self-defence.

We drifted out to a couple of local pubs whose clientele of battle-hardened date rapists imagined them to be stylish. The second, Donnie's favourite for some reason, featured low smoked-glass tables, glass walls and a long glass bar where our pints were handed to us in plastic cups. We stood awkwardly, crushed in a corridor of smiles fuelled by bad cocaine and low expectations; everyone still two drinks away from belligerence and disaster.

Some old guy was sloshed against the wall. He probably drank in the pub that used to be there. Haunting that same spot of ground like a fucking ghost. A barnacle, having the same conversations with people who gradually understood him less and less, as we all do. He tried to launch himself from the wall towards the toilets and banged against Donnie.

'For fuck's sake!' barked Donnie, his face completely impassive. Donnie had a weird habit of not moving his lips when he was really angry, which he said he'd developed from when he'd had to teach a deaf sixth-former that he hated. Any time this kid would annoy him, he'd try to make it impossible for him to lip-read, and it had become a reflex.

Eventually it got so busy I realised it was Friday night.

'Most of the world's problems come from the fact that stupid people talk louder,' Donnie bellowed over the music. I hadn't taken any Valium that day, but the previous day's mega dose hadn't quite worn off. It seemed unlikely that

I'd be able to handle being in a glass cube of atavistic sex hunters when it did. I felt like Cinderella.

The great thing about Donnie was that he was entirely non-judgemental.

'I need Valium,' I blurted, and I was surprised at the earnestness and emotion in my own voice.

'Valium.' Donnie dragged the word out thoughtfully, without a hint of morality. 'You're in need of sedation, hmm? Any of those Mexican cunts got any?'

'No,' I replied mournfully. It seemed that Glasgow Mexicans were the only Mexicans in the world who couldn't get you prescription meds. It was, of course, impossible that Donnie had some and wasn't telling me. I had never seen him relax, even slightly. He was always in a state of general anxiety and crisis. He screamed in his sleep and, even when awake, occasionally lashed out at phantoms. 'I was down the police station today. This girl Marina I knew, she was murdered.'

'Marina's been murdered?'

I'd forgotten that they knew each other.

Donnie took the sudden revelation very badly, his hand shaking across his brow in a palsied motion. His bottom lip hung open wetly in contemplation, as it often did. 'And the cunts think you did it?'

'No!' I laughed, forgetting that they actually did.

'What the fuck happened?'

'I don't know, but she's dead. That's all I know. Oh, they made me give a sperm sample, so sperm is involved . . .' I trailed off as I reached the end of the sentence. Somehow this made the whole thing seem a lot sadder.

'Sperm . . .' Donnie mused uselessly, shaking his down-turned head at the table. In this light his tanned, bloated head looked not unlike a haunted paper bag, his glazed eyes fixed on some bleak internal horizon.

At the shout for last orders I had abandoned Donnie, who had been involved in a catastrophic attempt to engage a group of women in conversation that, even from a distance, had visibly descended into crisis. He was experiencing a prolonged sexual recession and his desperation was palpable. At one point he'd come over to me at the bar and asked, 'Why is it the people who say you should talk more about mental health are the same people who get annoyed when you make a joke about it?' before heading back into the fray.

At home, I picked up what seemed to be a considerable backlog of mail from the carpet. It's sad to think that there's a point between being a kid, when mail is always good – money from your granny, party invites – and adulthood, where the very sight of a pile of mail ignites only a rising fear, and a numb grief for your dead granny. This time there were only a couple of takeaway menus I already had, something from the council, a card asking me to register to vote – which I retained for roach material – and one thick, official-looking letter with my name imprisoned behind a little cellophane window. It had handwriting on the back that read: 'Please Do Not Throw This Into the Bin Felix. It Contains Important Information.' Fuck.

There was another envelope inside, where Marina had written me a letter on shitty writing-pad paper.

Felix. If you get this then I am dead. I know you don't always remember how much time we spent together, but trust me you were my best friend. I want you to have this, it's everything I made. I got mixed up in some bad stuff and I want you to stay away from it. I know you'll want to find out what happened but believe me, you don't want to know. Also, there's no chance you ever will know because you're a fucking idiot. So take the money and go to Thailand or something. No, not Thailand, you'll end up getting executed on some fucking drugs offence. Maybe just put it in the bank.

Inside the letter was a cheque for £10,000, just like my granny used to send me, but much worse.

I sat down slowly in the hallway and cried, watching the page shake in my hand.

4

I heard some kind of strangled yell from downstairs, which usually meant it was around ten, and limped out of bed to face the disappointed gaze of the bathroom mirror. My body looked like a dropped lasagne. I hadn't shaved for a couple of weeks, and had enough of a beard for it to be a bit of a food diary.

A little bird was hopping around my window box of dead shit. I felt a brief flicker of excitement: this wasn't a blackbird or a pigeon, which is all I usually got, but a speckled brown fellow, with a mildly aristocratic, even Egyptian air. It regarded me silently first from the soil, then for what seemed quite some time from the window ledge. This became boring quite quickly, and I was relieved when it flew off and I could google it. A thrush, apparently. In our world of dying diversity, a thrush had briefly seemed remarkable.

I opened another browser window for porn, kidding myself that I might still go back and learn more about the thrush. I briefly worried about why I'd blamed my inability to recognise a common thrush on the death of the planet;

but then there's nothing quite like typing the word 'reality' into a porn search engine to make you worry about what sort of person you are.

I made my daily walk to the cafe for breakfast. I picked my way along the thin pavement down into town as the traffic paraded slowly alongside. At the bottom of the hill, buses wheezed and lurched briefly between stops. There was nobody on the streets yet. Nobody really wanted to live right in the centre of Glasgow, and even some of the flats in our building were empty.

The cafe I usually went to was called Lemon Monkey. Withered lemons decorated tables, shelves and walls, and stuffed toy monkeys of all sizes and a uniform uncleanliness provided an inexplicable counterpoint. The one thing the staff had in common was that their faces all held a permanent sense of woeful disbelief, as if they had just been awoken from cryogenic suspension on a spaceship orbiting some dying star and asked for a ploughman's lunch.

An older German waitress was the shallow keel of this great ship. She would sometimes simply lose interest mid-order and begin some other task and the customer would have to regain her attention with whatever charm they had, like some flailing street magician. A young girl, perhaps her daughter, would loom up at tables, with the heavy, careless make-up of someone whose mind had been overbalanced by a terrible secret. They could wait patiently for an order before explaining it was off the menu, and yet at other times they could shrilly announce, before the customer even got to the counter, the absence of the most everyday items, like bread.

I opened the little plastic notebook I wrote my ideas down in. I'd always had real problems with motivation but I'd worked for a couple of years at BBC Scotland, where that had been an asset. The whole organisation existed almost entirely to stop Scottish programmes from being made. I remembered a flatmate's girlfriend applying for a job when I was there. She loved television and had a sickening vigour, and it was a struggle to explain that for the interview she should try to give the impression of a defeated narcoleptic whose only previous work experience had been at an owl sanctuary.

We'd sit around a cavernous office playing computer Solitaire. Almost everyone was on some short-term rolling contract so we were never really committed enough to the place to do any work, and always just slightly too insecure to start mainlining heroin. The whole department only made about two or three shows a year; if you weren't working on one of these, you were shunted into Development. This meant that people came in and pitched you their ideas and you threw them away. There were huge box files of ideas at every stage of development from outline memo to full script that we literally destroyed at the end of the year. Detective stories, dramas, comedies . . . our job was to sit there and listen to the creatives like a therapist. We'd nod, offer the occasional word of discouragement, and then file the ideas of a nation into an incinerator.

After my coffee arrived, I started to write out everything

I knew about Marina. There was nothing in the papers, or not yet anyway. Marina had been found dead, but where? I wrote WHERE? in the notebook, and underlined it slowly, then had a drink of coffee and tried to think. WHY? I wrote underneath it. Then WHO? I didn't seem to know anything, except that there was some possible sexual motive. I wrote SEX, and put a tick beside it. I looked out the window for a bit and tried to think of when I'd last seen Marina, but it had maybe been months. Eventually, I found myself looking at my phone. I scrolled through the BBC News headlines.

There, under the heading 'Scotland', I saw the headline: 'Police seek witnesses to park murder'.

Strathclyde Police yesterday launched an appeal for witnesses after the brutal murder of a young woman in Glasgow's Kelvingrove Park. Marina Katos, 31, a US citizen, was known to regularly cross the park on her way home from work. Police are keen to speak to anyone who was in the park between 8 p.m. and 10 p.m. on Monday evening. They would particularly like to talk to a bearded, middle-aged man who was seen speaking to the victim near the park gates on Broughton Street. At a press conference today, Detective Inspector Jack Ian asked for anyone who had seen anything untoward to come forward. 'This is a cowardly and despicable attack on a young woman, a guest in our city, and we are currently pursuing several lines of enquiry.'

I felt a numbed moment of total dislocation and stared down dumbly at my notes.

WHERE?

WHY ?

WHO?
SEX √
WORKED AT THE GO-GO
WORKED AT TV COMPANY WITH IAN
WORKED FOR ALTERNATIVE INDEPENDENCE
LIVED AT CHARING CROSS
GREEK

I put a line through the word 'Greek', pending further investigation.

I decided I'd drop in to the Go-Go on my way home. It was in the basement of what had once been an old school and was now three floors of different bars in the heart of the West End. Nothing for everybody. Even at 6 p.m. there were already two bouncers on the door of the main venue, gazing at a table of loud students at the end of the beer garden with the emotionless hostility of saltwater crocodiles.

The wee gate to the basement was open, which meant somebody was in, so I headed down the steps and rang the bell. I went through the awkward rigmarole of positioning my face for the little camera in the door and smiled. Quite probably it was the manager Mikey who was in, opening up. He didn't like me much even though I often bought him drinks after hours; maybe because I felt guilty I had fucked his sister one Christmas and she had missed the family dinner, or possibly even attended it as a drugged shambles. One of the Mexicans had told me that Mikey was in hiding from some gangsters and his real name was Miguel, although I think they were fucking with me because the names are too similar.

Mikey opened the door with the very specific fake smile that someone gives when they're pretending they haven't been watching your face on a little monitor hoping that you'll go away. He was five foot six on a warm day, but muscular, and permanently smoking. He was what your granddad looked like while he was killing people in the War.

Mikey led me down the sticky floored corridor into the big bar and restaurant room at the end. It took my eyes a second to get used to the light, during which I worried that I was mildly brain-damaged. Glasgow is utterly black at 6 p.m. in winter. British Summer Time is something to do with farming, but if I was a farmer and my life consisted of wringing chickens' necks and putting my hand up animals' arses, I'd have wanted to work in total darkness. Oblivion.

I felt relieved when things came into focus. I saw that Kat was behind the bar. She was washing glasses but gave an enthusiastic grin and mouthed something I pretended to understand. Neither of us could actually be bothered talking, so I gave a big grin and a thumbs-up. She was a few years younger than me and pretty, in a tall and wholesome way. A couple of years back we'd got involved in a kind of flirtation that quickly developed into a sexting relationship. From her earliest salvos, I realised I was out of my depth. For weeks, the little shuddering text alert on my phone would plunge me into a grimoire of practices I thought were only indulged in by a conquering army. I admired her as a writer: she could create a profoundly unacceptable world with a handful of words and an emoji. The whole episode had made me feel like someone who'd taken his nieces and nephews to a horror film and ended up weeping in the bathroom.

Mikey handed me a barstool from a stack by the wall and we both sat down. 'What have you been up to?' he asked me. 'Seeing anyone these days?'

'No.'

'Don't worry, Felix. One day, you will meet someone who loves you exactly as you are, then gradually work out that they are mentally ill.'

'What about you?'

'Oh, the usual,' he replied, with an affected cheeriness. 'Wasting my time on a bunch of guys who don't remember my name.'

'You should have it tattooed between your shoulder blades,' I suggested, which received a snort of mock indignation. Whatever else you said about Mikey, he liked to laugh at himself. And me.

Mikey went behind the bar to pour us both a pint.

'Have you heard about Marina?' I asked. I'd sort of imagined they must have, but now I remembered that it had only hit the news that day, and there was almost no phone signal down in the Go-Go.

'Oh, fucking hell, what now?' he groaned.

'Well . . . she's dead.'

His face was suddenly ashen, and Kat somewhere behind me asked: 'What . . .? Marina . . .?'

'Yes, she's . . . dead.' I sort of wished that I'd said

'murdered' at the start; Kat was already in tears, and I still had to get to that bit.

'Jesus Christ.' Mikey rubbed the stubble on his head with one hand. 'What happened?'

'Murdered.' I explained. Kat dropped a glass on the floor, and Mikey began to cry.

I managed to get fairly drunk over the course of the hour it took them to cancel their bookings and close up for the night. They both talked about all the stuff Marina had done at the Christmas party, and I pretended to remember, out of politeness.

Mikey offered me a lift home. He took me out the back door into the car park and we got into what looked like a brand-new Jag.

'This is your motor, Mikey?'

'Haha. Naw, wee bit out of my price range. Got a lend of it from a guy I'm seeing. Be careful, man, the guy who owns this thing – he absolutely hates it when I get it messy.'

'Tiny handprints on the inside of the boot? That kind of thing?'

'What he hated most was when I rammed your dad so hard he left his lipstick on the airbag,' he parried, as we pulled out of the car park.

We stopped at the traffic lights at Charing Cross and a woman on the street very obviously checked him out. I sometimes forgot that he was astonishingly handsome, in a feral sort of way. Mikey was one of those incredibly straight-seeming Glasgow gay guys; the only real clue being a passionate drunken rant he'd go into any time a new gay movie or TV show came out, about the lack of lube in sex scenes.

'How did Marina seem to you lately?' I asked.

'The usual. A hundred things on the go. She was seeing some guy. Didn't sound like a love thing, if you know what I mean. A sex thing. She never brought him down to the Go-Go but she was clearly dripping like a knackered fridge just talking about him. Here, have you got that twenty you owe me, man? I'm a bit short.'

I pulled my wallet out and change spilled into my lap, sliding down the side of the gearstick and into the footwell. I must have forgotten to zip up the side. I busied myself trying to pick up the money while the seatbelt choked me in protest. The rubber mat in the footwell had some little black circles stuck in its grooves. I picked one up and turned it over in my fingers. Confetti for some satanic mass, perhaps?

No, black sequins from a dress.

Kinky Mikey. I decided not to ask.

5

My therapist specialises in couples therapy, and so must some of the other therapists who work there, because on the evenings I go it's always couples. There's never much chatter. We're conditioned by TV to think that couples' quarrels are a witty back and forth, when they're often just days of complete silence.

I sat in a waiting room – a corridor, really – with all the fuckers failing at love. I looked at everybody and thought that at least what brought them here was love; or perhaps some kind of overarching fear of futility. There was a couple directly across from me holding hands and beaming, but who knows with prescription meds and what have you. The guy probably thought he was eight years old and riding the log flume at Disneyland.

I picked up a little newspaper cultural supplement, turned the pages and genuinely tried to engage with the premise of a variety of artworks being rated out of five.

My therapist stepped out of his room, letting out his previous clients – or whatever a therapist calls people. He said my name and gave me a warm, practised smile. No doubt this was something they taught you quite early at therapist school, but I appreciated it. He had long swept-back hair and a long grey beard, like he'd been shipwrecked.

For some reason, I often imagined his beard getting caught in a shopping mall escalator and his entire skeleton and soft tissue being squeezed out like the contents of an over-ripe banana into a steaming heap outside a branch of Claire's Accessories.

'Just me,' I said, as I sat down. There was a pause as, I suppose, we both considered what I meant by that.

'Nice to see you again, Felix. How have you been feeling?'

'That . . . this is life, I suppose. I'm in the same boat as everybody else. You fail at absolutely everything, then start training for a marathon.'

He didn't smile, or really acknowledge what I'd said in any way; he generally seemed unbothered that he was a bit of a tough crowd. 'Felix. I believe you were to bring in a dream that you've had this week.'

From nowhere, I could feel my heartbeat in my ears. 'It was about a horse,' I offered, deliberately. No response. 'I was fighting a horse.' He seemed a little disappointed: a slight turn of the mouth. Too negative, I guessed. 'But we made up in the end. We hugged.' I spread my hands magnanimously.

'Was there anybody else in the dream . . .?'

'A man,' I say, stupidly. It was clearly not enough. 'A very old man.'

There was a long silence and I had in my mind an image of me, as seen from above, running down a series of increasingly dark alleys, water underfoot, fleeing some unknowable malevolence.

'An old man had stolen my identity, and now he was sitting on a yacht making lemonade . . . and I attacked him . . . in a sort of mechanical suit.' I beamed, having accidentally stumbled on my real dream, but it was this grain of truth that seemed to finally overbalance things.

I've never seen the point of dreams. You rest so your body can repair itself, and your brain's contribution is to screen vivid footage of you being on a safari holiday with your dead uncle and Sir Kenny Dalglish.

We discussed Donnie, and the line of questioning veered between viewing him as part of a co-dependent relationship, and figment of my imagination. We talked again about whether I was depressed. Generally, I think 'depressed' is just a word we invented to make realists feel bad about themselves.

I blabbered for a bit then gradually trailed off as I ran out of things he might want to hear.

'You're swearing a lot lately.'

'Maybe Scottish people have been imprisoned in the English language and we are trying to blow our way out.'

'Yes . . . Scottish people weren't all Gaelic speakers, you know.'

'I know everybody needs to feel like they're right all the time, but I'm often wrong, and I'm okay with it.'

I talked a little about how I'd been busy with my writing, and when that clearly wasn't flying – even with me – I threw in the fact that my friend had been murdered.

•

It's very difficult for anyone to take a therapy session down a predetermined path once a recent murder has been announced, so actually (I think) the quality of the discussion improved. I didn't feel I was using my friend's death for an easy ride; if anything, I wish I'd lied about there being a murder during previous sessions. Marina would have done exactly the same with my murder – pretended to be really upset to change her shifts or something – and I'd have saluted her for it from Hell.

We talked a little about Marina and what kind of person she was and how they found the body and how I heard. I invented descriptions of the morgue photos and made them as slow and pointlessly detailed as possible, hoping that I could run out the clock on the meeting without us having to talk about my feelings again.

His eyes flicked slowly to one side and back as he checked the clock on his desk, something he was always completely brazen about. He asked me how I felt I was dealing with my friend's death. I didn't reply, and in the silence he wound things up.

6

I was woken early by someone stepping outside, being engulfed by the freezing fog that choked the streets that morning, and screaming. I lurched up with an answering shriek and in the five minutes it took me to make coffee I briefly considered suicide. I was in the stage of Valium withdrawal that makes your brain sing. For breakfast I had the only thing in the fridge: a pastry-heavy grey meat sausage roll – a gift sent forward in time from the all-night garage by my drunken self.

I went back to bed and surfaced in what looked like the afternoon. I must have left the front door open because, as I wandered into the living room, Donnie burst in like the best-loved character in an old sitcom that they can't show anymore because it mocked people with schizo-affective disorder. He had his little backpack on, which usually meant he'd been cycling. His bike was far too small and made him look like a bear escaping from the circus.

He paced, he laughed, his hands fluttered like bats, his face jiggled. Donnie's conversation always orbited the subject of his marriage: his wife was always in the stories even when she wasn't in them, like Moby-Dick.

I couldn't give advice on relationships, but even if I could, Donnie wouldn't have heard me because he would have been talking.

'You off somewhere?' I asked, nodding at the bag as he put it down.

'I tried to go swimming. It was too crowded. Swimming is like life – a couple of kids can ruin everything.'

He was worried by a pain in his mouth, which might well have come from grinding his jaw on pills, but I didn't think this diagnosis would be welcome, and I concentrated on looking sympathetic as he blustered on. Donnie's personality seemed to demand momentum. If he'd ever slid into a foamy bubble bath with a glass of wine he'd have probably just started screaming.

'All Google does is tell you that you have cancer. Doesn't matter what question you ask. What time is Tesco's open till? Cancer. No point googling sensitive teeth – I think we all know what it's going to say, and it's best to just shut it out and carry on as if you didn't have cancer.'

'Or go to the dentist?' I suggested, but he brushed it aside.

'Any more news about Marina? It's 2015! You'd have thought they'd have caught the cunt by now through their fucking Facebook messages or whatever.'

'You see the new BBC website story? She was found by a dog walker.'

35

'It's always a dog. Our bodies are an absolute treasure trove of bones,' he intoned mournfully.

'They found a scarf with sperm on it near the body. I don't ever remember seeing her with a scarf, but fuck knows. They're taking samples from every local with form as we speak.'

'Well, now they've got you out the way, I suppose they have to work their way down the sex offenders' register.'

I ignored this. 'Death by strangulation. Not a standard sex crime, apparently. It sounds like they don't have a lot to go on.'

Donnie didn't reply. He sat down on the floor in front of the PlayStation. Donnie was a Jambo, but could never play as Hearts without getting a heavy doing – so, as ever, we played Real Madrid v Hibs. I'm not a Hibee, but I knew being beaten by them caused him extra pain. As I joined him on the floor he leaned towards me with a soft conspiratorial grunt, palmed me half a pill, and produced a couple of bottles of Sol from his jacket.

I came up in a very mild way as the streetlights came on outside. It crossed my mind that this was exactly the level of happiness other people felt when sober. 'Shall we stick on the news and see if there's anything?'

We did, but it wasn't like a movie, when people put on the TV and the news story comes right on. It was BBC News 24 and they were having a long and upsetting discussion about the aftermath of Charlie Hebdo. We both pretended we could handle it for a bit, then stuck the PlayStation back on.

Donnie barked with the brutal hacking cough that he seemed to have permanently, from smoking with asthma. 'If it was on the BBC main website, that's quite a big story, it'll definitely be on the Scottish news,' he assured me. Most days, I tried to avoid the news, because it was alarming and debilitating and dull. Also, it seemed to be speeding up and repeating itself, maybe because civilisation was over and they were showing us a montage of humanity's best bits.

We played FIFA again until the Scottish news started. Then the game went to penalties, so we actually missed the headlines and had to sit through a whole load of local pish, the highlight of which was someone lifting twenty-six 9,000-litre canisters of laughing gas out of a hospital in Dumfries. 'Look for literally the only cunt smiling in Dumfries,' grunted Donnie.

It felt surreal seeing the item on Marina. My high completely dissipated the moment they said her name. There was a shot of Kelvingrove Park down by the gates on Gibson Street, then another of a police investigation site by a big bush with some people in high-vis crime scene outfits combing through the grass. The reporter was actually there, with the scene in the background, which seemed disrespectful. He was way too cheerful for someone doing a murder report. Like a lot of Scottish TV presenters, he seemed to have the jolliness of a much fatter person.

Whatever else was happening, I was no longer high. 'Got any more eccies?' I asked dolefully. 'Aye,' replied Donnie, and we gubbed one each in silence. He was genuinely angry: he sucked at his inhaler, then seemed to struggle to re-establish control of his face.

The pills were super strong, and I started to get that rising feeling in my chest that meant I was about to come up dramatically. Donnie had a fleck of foam on his bottom lip as he ranted amusingly about his family. His parents and brothers were very strait-laced middle-class types. He'd been sent to a boarding school, but escaped.

'What are we going to do about this Marina business?' he groaned.

'Do? What do you mean?'

'These polis – they're fucking useless, you said.'

'Uh-huh. Yeah. What do you think we should do?' I briefly considered whether Donnie, who had handed his death drive the steering wheel long ago, was actually someone I should be asking for advice, but the pill overruled me.

'Well, Caroline is having a kind of clearance sale. She's moving to LA with that DJ she's been shagging and she's getting rid of everything. She's been dealing for years, so it's quite a fucking collection. I've seen the thing – it's a suitcase stuffed full of everything you could imagine. Grass, pills, uppers, downers. Loads of American prescription shit.'

Caroline was kind of a drug dealer, but it was really a hobby. Mainly, she managed bands to various degrees of failure with a joyous, misplaced optimism. Donnie was still talking. 'She's autistic, as you know, and she's labelled everything exactly with a printing gun.' He leaned on these last words heavily, as if they were a key detail.

'I don't see what her being autistic has got to do with anything.'

'I'm not judging. I think it's good people open up more about their mental health now – it helps you know who to avoid . . . anyway, think about it. We do our own investigation. You choose how you want to feel that day and you take the pill. Everything carefully labelled.' He paused dramatically, gathering himself for an improbable length of time. 'A five-dimensional Shamanic encyclopaedia!' he roared, with a shake of the face and a faint spray of beer. 'Here, she gave us a starter pack, just till I can get round and do the deal. Can you give me a cheque for two grand?' He rummaged around in his bag and produced the sort of little paper bag that you get from a chemists.

I thought about it as the remaining news stories washed over us. Some steely-haired SNP politician who seemed vaguely familiar explained some new initiative to battle online hate like he was talking to a toddler. Then there was a report on a Celtic game, and a controversy about some ultras unveiling a banner as part of some away crowd's biannual crash course in Irish history. I found myself considering the surprising level of arts and crafts that goes into being a hardcore football fan, and the potential for creative disagreement: *Andy, ya prick, you know my feelings about collage!*

'Here!' Donnie yelled, finding something on his phone. 'From *A Study in Scarlet*, about Sherlock Holmes . . . "For days on end he would lie upon the sofa in the sitting-room, hardly uttering a word or moving a muscle from morning to night. On these occasions I have noticed such a dreamy, vacant expression in his eyes, that I might have suspected him of being addicted to the use of some narcotic, had not the temperance and cleanliness of his whole life forbidden such a notion." Detection and drugs have a rich history, *mi hijo*.'

Describing fiction as history and vice versa was very much Donnie's vibe. Maybe this made sense, or as close to sense as we were able to make. We were the two people least suited to investigating anything, but with the right drug combinations we could be whoever we had to be. This was what I loved about Donnie – he might have felt every bump on life's highway like an old vulcanised rubber tyre, but he also approached every opportunity with the mindless enthusiasm of a spaniel.

There were two strips of Vallies in the little bag and, to be honest, this is what swung it for me.

∽

I woke up to the sound of rain lashing against the window. It was, I remembered with a rising sense of disbelief, the first day of the investigation. What does a detective do? First and foremost, he becomes embroiled in a tempestuous sexual relationship with his client, who frames him for murder. I had been denied the sex part of my character arc, and intended to use this as motivation.

I tried looking for Marina's old flatmate, Fatima, online. I found her account on Twitter, but it seemed to be a dead end as it had exactly two posts, from five years ago, and the second one read 'Fuck this.' Facebook had hundreds of folk called Fatima Das. It was amazing how many people had the same name, even unusual names . . . the eccentricity people have as individuals; their tragic predictability in groups. Every little snowflake is unique, but it's all just snow.

I dug out my old notebook and a pen. I dropped 20mg of Valium for relaxed nonchalance and a little white upper for determination and went round to Marina's flat.

It was a shabby tenement just off Great Western Road. I'd been in this house when they'd been too paranoid to open the door for a pizza they were expecting, so I scribbled a note and pushed it through their door. I walked around the block a couple of times. When I got back up to their floor the letterbox creaked open painfully and asked me who I was in a smoky voice.

'It's Felix. Marina's friend.'

'The Felix that started that panic about the pizza delivery guy?'

'I don't think so.'

'I THINK SO, FELIX. YES. I THINK SO. HOW MANY FELIXES CAN THERE BE?'

It's hard to read emotion through a letterbox, but he seemed to be annoyed.

'Let me ask you this,' I said. 'If you were going to raid a flat for drugs, might you dress the lead officer up as a pizza delivery guy?'

There was a long pause. 'Yeah.'

'Good for you. I'm Felix. I was Marina's friend, just let me in.'

A longer pause. There was a sound of a bolt being pulled back. The door opened to reveal a pale, haunted-looking guy with dreadlocks.

Immediately on shaking hands, my mind threw up his name. 'Hi, Malcolm,' I beamed, suddenly feeling like I was a real detective.

Malcolm led me down the hall to the kitchen and put the kettle on. He then leaned against the worktop looking at the kettle for what seemed like a long time.

I aimed for an air of relaxed authority to put him at ease. 'So, Malcolm. I just wanted to ask you a few questions.'

'Questions? What the fuck about? What the fuck for?'

'I'm sort of a private detective now.'

'You're a private detective? With a licence and all that?' He seemed reassured.

'Yes.' I flashed a joke card someone had given me that said I was donating my body to necrophilia. 'And a gun,' I added senselessly, my upper taking hold. I made an effort to get a grip and go through the questions I'd rehearsed. 'Tell me, had Marina said anything to you lately – was she worried about anything?'

'No, man. She was just . . . Marina, you know? Smoking grass, talking shit. I think she was helping someone move some gear.'

'Do you know who?'

'She'd met some guy, I think.'

'Oh, yeah? Did she say much about him? A name?'

He shook his head. Malcolm's recall had never been great: even his memory of my arrival had probably already dissolved, and he would soon be starting to wonder what we were talking about. 'I dunno. Someone she used to work with, I think. She was pretty excited about it, but she was always excited about some shit.'

'Had you seen anything suspicious lately? Anyone hanging around here?'

This question proved to be a tactical error, as Malcolm began mapping his various paranoias and neuroses. I listened, but he seemed to be describing the various comings and goings you'd expect in a tenement. He insisted on drawing me a brief, hopefully satirical, sketch of his downstairs neighbour.

'Does Fatima still live here?'

'No.'

I waited for him to elaborate but he just stared at me blankly.

'Do you know where she is?'

'Eh. No, not really.' Then he clicked his fingers and pointed at me in one excited motion. 'She started doing weights. Or yoga or something.'

I wrote this down half-heartedly. 'Look, Malcolm, I'm going to need to look through Marina's room.'

'What for? The police have taken most of her stuff away, man.'

'I just need to do it, okay?'

He stared straight ahead, nodding along to the faint sound of music from upstairs like some glitched non-player character in a video game, which I took to be a kind of okay.

I'd always wondered what it would take to clean Marina's room. Malcolm said it took a six-man team working two days. I opened the drawer of her bedside cabinet and stared at its empty bottom. Why had the police taken everything? How could her murder have possibly involved all her clothes?

There was a shopping bag on the door handle that seemed to have been used as a bin – Doritos wrappers, empty cans of juice, chocolate bar wrappers. I started to paw through it before I reflected that it was probably the rubbish from the police search team. Part of me felt depressed that people go round to your room when you die and eat a bunch of chocolate, but part of me simply felt hungry.

I was in the bathroom when I felt the itchy anxiety of Valium withdrawal begin in the middle of a worryingly long piss. I needed to get out of there and back to the flat. There couldn't be a place on Earth less likely to contain Valium than this depraved set of rooms that a bunch of pill-gobbling junkies had patrolled like Pac Man.

My head started to throb like a wound. I grabbed at the bathroom cabinet to see if they at least had paracetamol. It smelled of geraniums and contained a crush of useless hippy bullshit: tinctures, herbal remedies and untouched bottles of plant extract. Yet, there, at the back, peeked the unmistakable green top of a box of diazepam.

The box contained two 10mg tablets. On the front was Marina's name and her doctor's address – a Dr D Chong, in Hyndland. I swept triumphantly out, waving to Malcolm who was, for some reason, curled up asleep on top of the kitchen table.

7

I popped both pills as I walked up to the West End. Valium always slowly smoothed you out from the centre, but it left an uneasy tingling somewhere deep inside. You knew your anxiety was still in there somewhere, like a mouse in a wall – occasionally you could hear it faintly, contentedly, waiting for dark. It was also very difficult to tell if someone was on it. That was part of the appeal, I guess – you could develop a crippling pharmaceutical dependency without really bothering anyone.

I stopped at Sainsbury's for painkillers and a diet Irn Bru. At the self-service machines, the till asked me if I wanted a receipt in a whisper much lower than any of its other instructions. I wondered, as I often did, if my body was really in a pod in cryogenic suspension somewhere, in a place where relatives pay to look at their preserved ancestors, and there's a till at the far end of the warehouse from me, the faint 'Would you like a receipt?' drifting over to where I float inside a gently pulsing graphite egg. Perhaps certain noises that we hear in perceived reality are there to cover up things that are happening to our real bodies.

Leafblowers, for example: they're pretty much useless, and maybe they're just brought into the simulation to cover up the sound of them hoovering out our nutrient pods.

I must have got lost in this thought because the till told me to 'Please take your items' in a much louder *Could you fuck off now?* voice.

Marina's health centre was a big blonde sandstone manse squatting at the top of a leafy drive in the West End. A doctor's waiting room is one of the few places of complete relief from desire. People's eyes barely register each other. Whatever else we look for in a partner, illness is on the list of only the most bitterly determined pervert.

I seemed to have hit on the perfect dose of benzos for detecting: I had overshot self-assurance and was flooded with a sense of innate superiority. I smiled and let my eyes drift, focusing and unfocusing on the posters they hang to remind people with colds and verrucas that they might have cancer.

'Mr McAveetee!' chirped a lady in the doorway and I was led to Dr Chong's office. 'Did you find us OK?'

'Yes,' I lied.

Dr Chong stood up as I entered. He was Chinese, as I should probably have guessed. I thought I recognised him, but sadly that's just a really difficult thing to say to a Chinese guy. Taller than me and almost a cube of muscle, putting my hand into his giant fist felt like I was feeding it into machinery. He gestured to a chair and moved to his own with the grace of a dancer.

His office was enormous, with a heavy oak desk at the far end of the room, near the window. I thought how different it was from my own doctor's tiny examination room. She was a very gentle older lady and would always greet me with a smile, despite having just read in my file that I was a hypochondriac and not to give me Valium.

'You don't remember me?' he asked flatly. 'You don't remember David Chong, from school?'

'Yes, I remember him. You're that David Chong?'

He gave one of those sympathetic GP smiles. 'Or, in the relative monoculture of Glasgow, you know two twenty-stone East Asian guys with the same name.'

'You look different.'

'In a way. I look very similar, but possibly your brain has decayed.'

These were almost exactly the sort of superior, disconcerting things that David Chong used to say, so I believed him. David Chong had been a notorious figure at school. He'd been the size of a four-door family car by about fourteen, and had started working as a bouncer before he could shave.

'Like I said on the phone, I'd like to ask you a few questions about this murder I'm investigating.'

'Do you have a private investigator's licence?'

'No.'

'I wouldn't bother, it's basically a BTEC qualification in searching for people on Facebook.'

I tried to get the interview started. 'I believe you treated a Marina Katos? She was a friend of mine.'

'Felix. You must know that I can't discuss patients . . .? Yes, she was a patient. No, I can't tell you anything about her medical history.'

'She's dead.'

'Yes, I read the papers, Felix. She's been murdered. And you're going to solve it?' He drew out the word 'solve' to make it sound very unlikely.

'I suppose it's just something that I feel I need to do.'

He sat back a little and regarded me with the tiniest trace of amusement. Eventually he drawled, almost to himself: 'Felix, your personality is just a thing you came up with to survive school, and – in this sense – you didn't actually survive it.'

I often felt that someone using your first name a lot was meant to be kind of demeaning, but this might simply have been a problem with my self-image.

Something occurred to me. 'You can't say anything about her medical history, but did you know her in any other capacity?'

He smiled. 'Yes. Marina Katos worked for me from time to time – did some research on topics I was interested in. She was a very clever lady.'

'What sort of research was she doing for you?'

'I have various business interests. She was someone I bounced ideas off.'

'That's incredibly vague. If you don't mind me saying so.'

'I don't mind.'

What kind of work could Marina have been doing for a GP? I searched Chong's face for clues, but I suppose

49

from his point of view I just looked at him for a really long time.

'You seem a little strung out, Felix. Would you mind if I gave you a quick medical examination?'

I thought about how funny it would be if he gave me a really professional haircut instead, and a stupid grin grew on my face. He told me to take my coat off and I folded it up in my lap. At least I'd managed to keep him talking, although I couldn't think of anything else to ask.

Chong had come out from behind his desk now and was standing in front of me, shining one of those little telescope light things into my eye.

'Do you think Marina would have wanted you to investigate her murder?' he asked, in the low sing-song voice a GP uses for asking you about symptoms.

'No, in fact she asked me not to.'

'Before she was murdered?'

He tore a paper wrapper off a tongue depressor and put it in my mouth while he shone the light in there. He waited for an answer, then seemed to remember to release my tongue.

'Afterwards.'

'Interesting.'

He put one of those blood pressure armbands on me and pumped it up. He looked at the dial and gave a short laugh. 'And you don't intend to honour her wishes?'

Something occurred to me. 'Could you write me a prescription for diazepam? My nerves have been really shot with this whole thing.'

He held my face gently in his hands so he could pull down my bottom eyelids with his thumbs. This made my head feel no bigger than a baseball. In a way, I thought, it was humbling, and I welcomed the perspective. He regarded my bloodshot eyes critically as I tried not to make eye contact, which at that distance might have been unbearably intense.

'Drugs don't deal with your underlying problem, Felix.'

'That I will eventually run out of them?' I laughed to show this was a joke.

He stood there and regarded me silently with a look of sympathy. I let this hang. I'd decided that my preferred interview technique was to stay silent and let the other person feel they had to fill the silence. I'd settled on this because I often couldn't think of anything to say.

Chong leaned back on his desk and, after what seemed like a long while, he purred: 'Silence. Power play of the weak', which I pretended not to find unsettling.

The long silence that followed became quite unbearable.

'What do you think happened to Marina?' I asked, in a voice shriller and feebler than I'd been aiming for.

Davie Chong made two perfect circles between his thumbs and fingers. 'Well,' he purred, 'this is the question that has troubled the great philosophers for centuries. Just what the fuck is going on?' He paused and squared off his pen and prescription pad on the table, then looked back at me with a sudden intensity. 'Tell me, Felix, what do you think about simulated reality? Do you ever wonder whether this world is simply a hyper-realistic computer simulation?'

'I worry about that a lot,' I answered, truthfully. It was a minor worry of mine, but often got crowded out by my other worries.

He seemed surprised, and picked up a pen to jot down a note. It was one of those Parker pens that parents got kids for their exams, and looked absurdly small between his huge fingers. I thought about how locals here would often have to place their testicles into those hands and pretend they were fine about it.

'I don't think we're in a simulation, I think maybe that's just how we talk about metaphysics now. A way of having conversations about God now that God seems too ridiculous . . .' I offered uncertainly.

He leant forward suddenly, and spoke with a practised passion. 'That might be the most dangerous situation we could be in. Consider the question of what speed simulations move at compared to base reality. The simulated realities may quickly become considerably more advanced than the world that creates them. This means that base reality might become very important to a whole variety of super advanced societies: it will be where their hardware is based, and have to be controlled. By creating the simulations, we will become a kind of simulation, less free than the simulations themselves.'

'It's certainly a worry,' I agreed, feeling that he hadn't yet quite said no to the diazepam prescription. I had literally no idea why the conversation had taken this turn. Maybe it was all some kind of test. Like when God told Abraham to sacrifice his son, and then, as the knife was on its way down, told him to stop because he'd come.

He dashed off a script and handed it to me. I didn't look at it till I was outside: it was enough diazepam to kill me.

I went to the chemists on Hyndland Road, then down to the Botanic Gardens to get the bus back into town. As I relaxed into the seat I began to make notes. Sadly, I had forgotten much of what had been said, and made a note about the need to start recording interviews.

At home, I lay back in the armchair and was oppressed by a dull sense of impending crisis. Just after I fortified myself with a couple of Vallies, Donnie banged on my door. As I went to open it, he brushed past me with some kind of unintelligible cry. Without justification, he was holding a bowl of cereal under his chin, which he consumed with a grotesque slurping gusto, then abandoned on the arm of the couch. The cry must have been, 'Suitcase is downstairs!' because he now repeated these words slowly, as if he was talking to a small child.

He threw me the keys and I went down and lugged the thing out of the back of his Golf. It was a huge, tan leather effort with straps that fastened over the top; the whole thing soft and scuffed from a lifetime of hauling duty frees back from the Costa Brava. It was big enough that I had to stand awkwardly against the railings as I passed someone coming down the stairs. He grunted something that might have been some kind of thanks. Glaswegians are big on grunted greetings to their neighbours, which they graduate to only after a few years of absolute silence. Except if you see us in the countryside, where we always wish each other a very jaunty pantomime hello, with the unspoken subtext being I will never have to see this cunt again. I thought, as I often did, that it would be good to get on with your neighbours, but knew that after a few weeks it would become a drag, and you would have to move away.

Sweating by the time I got to my flat, I staggered through to the bedroom and hoisted the case up onto the bed. Donnie fell on it eagerly, and threw the lid back to reveal the kind of drugs haul that would make for a pretty self-satisfied police press conference. He began to paw through it and would occasionally hold up items delightedly before laying them down on the bed, like a junkie unboxing video.

'Grass!' He waved a clear plastic packet of skunk, labelled with a cartoon of what looked like a man in a coma. 'These are great little uppers – the Americans know their shit,' he muttered, as he produced a few serious-looking pill bottles.

I picked the occasional thing up politely, I didn't really recognise a lot of the brand names.

'This is what they give to paedos in the jail to lower their libido. Perhaps we'll have to interview some kind of femme fatale, render ourselves immune to her charms.' He shook a little bottle happily. 'Or maybe we'll just be really horny at an important point in the case and need to be able to think straight,' he added, apparently seriously.

There were several packs of temazepam. This was a heavy tranquilliser and a ubiquitous side drug for Glasgow junkies. It created an intense buzz by compelling the user to fight the urge to sleep, like a working-class version of opera. No good had ever come out of jellies, and I resolved to bin them at the earliest opportunity. There were packs of tramadol, light brain damage in a bullet-hard lozenge; and a sheet of acid, each tab marked with a burning peace flag.

Donnie stopped and beamed at me, then threw into the middle of all the little boxes, packets and bottles something that made them all bounce up off the bed. It was a solid brick of cocaine, long and heavy. I knew this because it had the word 'Cocaine' written on it with a printing gun.

'What the fuck? That's a lot more than two grand's worth of coke, Donnie, no?' I'd never really had any interest in coke: experiencing life more intensely was sort of the opposite of what I wanted to do.

'Yeah, I got the impression it was a closing-down sale – everything must go! We can resell it, and fund the investigation!'

'Yes, I suppose often the easiest way to solve a murder is by becoming a major drug dealer. All we need to do now is get a network of street pushers and some firepower.'

Donnie often missed sarcasm, and simply stared at me like a Labrador.

'I think we need to get this out of here.'

'Yes,' he agreed. 'Just hang on to it for a day or two. I'll sort something out.'

'Why don't you hang on to it?'

He seemed startled. Donnie's embattled psyche would often drift into a febrile state where even a casual question could send him into fight or flight mode.

'Janice is coming round to pick up some stuff.'

'She's left stuff in your flat for this long? It's been nearly a year.'

'It's more in the way of some things she believes I have stolen from her new place,' he spat, stuffing a couple of little boxes into his trouser pockets before he turned and left.

8

Alternative Independence was a ragbag of radical organisations who had formed a kind of left wing to the Independence movement during the Referendum. Marina had canvassed for them, and had maybe got quite involved because she'd mentioned them a few times. They were having a conference that Saturday, really only ten minutes' walk from the flat, and Donnie had suggested we go down and try to blend in.

We had a hazy idea of what it might be like, and gambled on dropping a Vallie and ecstasy combo so we'd seem relaxed and upbeat about Scotland's political destiny. 'Live as if you're in the early days of being a better cunt!' Donnie intoned, as he knocked his medicine back with an early Becks.

We drifted down onto Argyle Street and tramped along to the Radisson Hotel. The Referendum was only a few months ago, and the whole thing was still box office. Even the stall we'd passed on Buchanan Street on the way down was bustling; one of the guys telling everyone they would burn in Hell had set up across from it, so that he could launch his pessimism into the midst of them like artillery fire.

Outside the hotel, a broad representation of disappointed humanity was milling around the entrance: walking sticks, shopping bags, budget skiwear, problem hair, and the odd smoker. The scene was pitched somewhere between an old painting of factory life and a bomb scare at Primark. A couple of people stood at a wet trestle table taking signatures for some petition or other. A few middle-class sorts were arriving too, clad in the upmarket hiking shop versions of the clothes at the door, beaming around beneficently as they emerged from taxis.

There was a ticket desk in the foyer. We'd both agreed that our total lack of tickets would test the alternative nature of this event, but nobody really gave a fuck. The maroon-faced old guy at the desk seemed genuinely delighted at my announcement that we were investigating a murder, and handed over a couple of wristbands with a guffaw. His fag-scraped voice sounded like an earthquake survivor shouting up through rubble. My drugs combo had taken hold and I literally throbbed with goodwill towards the demented old roaster.

Inside, the hotel decor was Glasgow taking a guess at style, in the same way Victorian artists drew exotic animals they'd never seen purely from explorers' accounts. Tall rubber plants, a giant clay menorah, wall-mounted tribal facemasks – almost exactly the inventory that would one day be sent in a single enormous crate to attempt to humanise the refectory of a mining colony on some moon of Jupiter. There were little groups of folk all talking excitedly to one another. I tried to make some small talk with people. I don't love small talk, but I accept it has its place. It's very hard to start a conversation with big talk: '*Nice to meet you, Martin, my uncle has cancer.*'

I'd already lost Donnie and, for want of anything better to do, I drifted into the empty function room at the far end of reception. Perched high up at the back, on the raked seating, was a serene-looking John Docherty. I'd known Docherty since school and still felt a lot of affection for him. He'd always been a writer, since we were kids, and would submit bizarre and alarming entries to local short story competitions. For some reason they often featured Robert Nairac, an SAS officer assassinated by the IRA in the 1970s; homosexuality as a general theme; and the actress Halle Berry, who was almost always shot between the eyes with a small calibre handgun. He was a professional writer now, and profoundly underemployed. He would have probably been some avant-garde literary star in the sixties. People knew better than to admit to being offended by anything anymore, and now everybody who got offended pretended to be bored. I found this tedious, but perhaps really I was offended by it.

Docherty would often submit scripts when I was at BBC Scotland. This had begun fairly seriously, but as he became aware that nothing would get made, he'd redraft them to be as spectacularly alienating as possible. A promising pilot script about a young PC Taggart getting involved in his first murder investigation was redrafted until our hero uncovered a vast and unsettling conspiracy involving Dr Findlay, Lulu, Connery's James Bond, the Bay City Rollers, DC Thompson, Peter Tobin and the hiker Tom Weir. He'd been known affectionately around the office as Double-Denim Docherty. Who knew what kind of distressing personal inventory had resulted in his growing a goatee?

He said hello with a half-wave and turned his heavy-lidded gaze back to the empty stage.

I picked my way up along the rows until I reached him. Sometimes you had to make the effort; he was often pretty amiable, if you got past his pose of indifference and hostility.

'Alright, Johnny?'

'Quite alright. Quite moved by the opportunity to be in a room with my fellow man and hear positive words about the future.'

He spoke in a posh Glasgow drawl, having got an assisted place to Hutchie Grammar, where he'd honed his tone of bored provocation to baffle and enrage Glasgow's future accountants and lawyers. We chatted for a while as the place began to fill up. He revealed that his whole contribution to the Independence debate had been the submission to a competition for young writers called 'Songs of Scotland' of a pornographic poem about Robert Burns. It was hard to make out exact details, but it seemed to be an almost book-length effort in authentic Scots dialect that placed The Bard himself and Tam o' Shanter in a time-travelling plot that revolved around bisexual one-upmanship.

'You're into Independence, then?' he asked.

It was rare for him to ask for anyone's opinion, so I

considered it and tried to be honest. 'I don't know if people will even remember the Referendum with what's coming down the pipeline. It'll be a tricky tiebreaker in a pub quiz that takes place in the sex bunker of a pitiless regional petrol sultan.'

Docherty nodded, as if this was a very specific feeling that he had himself. There was the hint of a smirk on his lips, which was the closest he ever came to showing approval.

Donnie arrived and plonked himself uneasily on the other side of me. He'd managed to smuggle what looked like a double in from the bar, and downed it unceremoniously. He shifted uncomfortably as his liver lodged a formal objection.

The room was starting to fill up, and there was an excited murmur as the speakers took their seats on the low stage. There was an older guy, who seemed to be looking around him with a bristling aggression; a couple of women about my age; a guy with a brown beard, who I thought was an actor that I didn't recognise; and a man so enormously fat he looked like he was sitting with his head out of a Fiat's sunroof.

A muffled offstage mic boomed out, and it was clear from the intonation that someone had been introduced. There was some mild consternation among the speakers as they realised whoever had been announced hadn't actually made it onstage yet. Eventually someone waved as they spotted whoever it was making their way up from the floor, and led the crowd in a gentle round of applause.

A man of abysmal antiquity limped towards the stage.

'It's fucking Bible John!' whispered Donnie, and in trying to suppress his own laughter, fell into a coughing fit that drew a couple of disapproving glances.

All the applause had died by the time he got up there, and there was an excruciating period of silence as he dragged himself towards the podium. His tremulous voice can't have failed to fill everyone in the room with thoughts of regret and death. Somehow his voice was both quavering and a completely dull monotone, perhaps through some conscious feat of co-ordination, like Mongolian throat singing.

His theme was, counter-intuitively, about the Referendum having been a great victory for the forces of progress. He raised a trembling hand, as if from the grave.

Donnie lifted his programme in front of his face and muttered into my ear: 'There's no way this cunt is living to see Independence. He'll be lucky to catch the League Cup final.'

I considered that his appearance was maybe a technical gambit, as whoever he introduced would be welcomed with a thunderous wave of relief and gratitude. And so it proved, as he brought on an upbeat middle-aged lady who did a bit of formal jollying up, then urged us: 'Please welcome Amy McGarvey!'

A woman in her late twenties stood up and walked to the podium to a ripple of applause. She was a kind of micro celebrity in Scotland. I barely recognised her at first – her hair was recently dyed black, with a scarlet bit at the front. She bowled into some stuff about how the Referendum had changed things forever, bonds, solidarity and so on. Were we going to keep listening to the same old rhetoric? she asked, rhetorically, to general nodding and applause. She mentioned speaking truth to power, which I always think is a weird phrase because class relationships are essentially sadistic, and there's no point explaining your pain to people who are just going to feel slightly aroused.

As the speech built to its conclusion, she lashed out at the better-off Scots who had voted for the status quo. 'They have the wealth, we have the numbers!' This clearly illogical reaction to losing a vote received a baffling howl of support. Many had been to the previous day's SNP rally at the Hydro, and seemed genuinely thrilled at politics finally attracting the sort of crowd that could normally be expected only by something entertaining. Of course this would ultimately lead to nothing and the same people would be having the same conversations in a generation, but it was good to be in an atmosphere of hope, and not to have to generate my own hope, which was always difficult.

Overall it was a long, dull affair, concluded by a dour speech from an Aberdonian Communist, during which I experimented with astral projection to no avail. As a rule of thumb, anyone who talks about their values is generally some kind of monster, but I gave him the benefit of the doubt. Docherty was ignored during the Q&A, and I guessed that he must have been to some of their meetings before. The first speaker seemed to have disappeared.

'Where did that old guy from the start go?' I whispered to Donnie.

'Ghostbusters got him,' he replied, already starting for the door.

We all filed out and crammed the two bars on the ground floor till they were overflowing into the reception. Donnie was in the boisterous, domineering mood that he often got into on spirits – the sort of form he was in the time we'd gone to the local comedy club and he'd bullied an improv troupe into doing a musical number about honour killings.

We saw Amy standing with a group at the far end of the room, and Donnie shouldered a path towards them. I asked everyone if they wanted a drink. There was no way I'd manage to get a tray through the crowd, so I ended up going back and forward and carrying them back in twos and threes. I caught a glimpse of myself in the mirror behind the bar. The tasteful lighting somehow accentuated my horrific appearance: I looked like a hostage video with an Instagram filter.

When I got back, Donnie was talking to Amy, and had presumably finally got off the subject of himself. 'Well done on the speech, though, well done!' He laughed, taking the whisky I offered him and sinking it in one fluid motion.

'Thanks, aye, it was good.' She sipped at her pint.

I nodded a hello, and she looked back at me quizzically.

'A standing ovation!' added a slightly sweaty guy beside her. He radiated the self-consciousness of a first novel, and I guessed he was her boyfriend.

'There's a fine line between a standing ovation and just wanting to be first to the bar!' Donnie cackled, and she responded with a gentle, supportive, all-lips-no-teeth smile.

It was certainly a possibility that she thought he was brain damaged.

The maybe-boyfriend was an older guy of about forty in a pinstripe blazer with a long, thin, chin-only beard that made him look like a Dr Seuss character. He actually held his head slightly bowed, like people do at funerals. I tried to assess him, as a detective. Sure, he seemed content but somehow I felt sure that he had regular screaming nightmares where he was being pinned down by enormous invisible weights or molested in a swimming pool. Of course, my therapist would say that I was trying to make myself feel better by imagining this guy was unhappy; that I was projecting. It would certainly explain why I'd given him my nightmares.

I tried to make conversation with him, but his almost surreal lack of charisma made this difficult. He seemed like the sort of guy who needed to clear his throat to get his reflection to come to the mirror. He was maybe a bit overwhelmed by the melee that was developing around us, and I could sympathise. I used to have a kind of flat-pack, outgoing personality that I could throw together to get through family occasions and stuff, but over the years I seemed to have lost a few screws and bolts.

He asked me what I did and for some reason I pretended to be a professional pole vaulter. I was struck again by how often and pointlessly I lie. It worries me to think that maybe everybody does, meaning that reality is quicksand. I ended up thinking, as I always do, that the fact that I worry about my lying means I'm probably okay; but I know I'm lying to myself.

An older woman was introduced to me as Christine. She was introduced to me as if I would naturally know who she was. The threshold for fame in Scotland is quite low, so she could have been anything from an MSP to someone who'd streaked at a football match. She told a long story about chaining herself to a railing at something. Five minutes in, and she was still looking for a padlock. I knew I was in the headlights of a really experienced bore and tried to relax my weight onto one leg and use it like a prop as my mind fled.

She had enthusiastic back-up from a dazed-looking, round-faced guy I took to be her partner. He nodded enthusiastically at each beat of her story – living off her personality, perhaps, like one of those blind fish that lives near an undersea vent. There were obvious cues built in for laughter and at these points I'd smile as broadly as I could and sometimes nod when that didn't seem to be enough. I felt a voice rising within me that wanted to scream, grab the bar and howl that she was filled with the same disregard for the feelings of other people as the oppressors she affected to despise. Luckily this voice would meet a solid wall of Valium and sink back down into the pit of my stomach.

I said I'd help Amy get her round back from the bar and we both ended up trapped in the throng for a bit. There was an awkward silence while I tried to think of some line of chat that she wouldn't have heard before. I told her a story I guess I tell sometimes because it reflects well on me. It was about when I was starting uni and I had to live in halls. There was a problem with my student loan at the start of my first term, so I just hung out in the TV room of the halls, often completely alone in the building of a weekend evening, watching TV. Occasionally, on their way out, people would look in at the little window in the door and laugh and jeer at me sitting there drinking the beer I'd stolen from their kitchens. One night a bunch of drunken lads crashed in for *Top of the Pops Two* and they sang along with everything until Marc Almond did 'Say Hello, Wave Goodbye'. The conversation dried up and some of them, these young guys so far from home and not far off secondary school, started crying.

As I'm telling it, I remember for the first time in years that it was actually me who had started crying, and I tied the anecdote off by looking at my feet and pretending to have a coughing fit.

Amy was looking at me with growing confusion.

'I'm sorry, a friend of mine was murdered recently . . .' I offered apologetically.

'Oh, my God!' Her eyes and mouth widened with what seemed like genuine shock. When you spend a lot of time talking to people who are on diazepam, people who aren't often seem ridiculously demonstrative. 'Do they have any suspects?'

'Yes! Him!' laughed Donnie, arriving to deliver a too-hard slap on my back. I gave him what I hoped was a warning look. Who knows what I actually communicated, because he responded with a leer at Amy. He was Vallied out of his face so the knowing nod that accompanied it was in actual slow motion, like Kennedy assassination footage. The last few days had taken a toll on the folds of his already remarkable face, which now looked like a collage made from elephant vaginas.

'Is this true, Felix?' asked Amy.

I blurted, 'I am the number one suspect in the investigation, yes.'

She gave a deep and surprisingly manly laugh. I realised she thought she'd been playing along with some joke of ours. I laughed along too, but it came out high-pitched and anxious, like the baddy in *Dirty Harry*.

We got our drinks and started squeezing through the crowd, and back to the others. There was a brief, painful silence. I felt bad that I had to bring it up, then I remembered that this was the reason we were here. 'But my friend was murdered – that bit's true. Marina Katos, she was called. She was quite involved in the Independence campaign. Don't suppose you've heard of her?'

Amy narrowed one eye and sent the name through her databanks. 'Marina . . . don't think so. Here . . . do any of youse know a Marina . . . what was it? . . . Katos? Worked on the Referendum? What did she do?' The rest of the group turned towards me.

'I think she was in Alternative Independence. In Glasgow . . .' I offered, trying to remember DI Ian's exact words. 'She looked kind of . . . Greek . . . wore a leather jacket.' I produced my phone and got up a couple of photos of her. 'This is my friend, Marina . . . she's dead . . .' The photo was from that time we went to the shows; she was grinning lasciviously as she pretended to wank off a teddy bear that she'd won at the air rifle bit.

'Oh, Mari!' blurted Christine, her face suddenly pale. 'Mari's dead? What happened?'

'Murdered,' I offered, slightly too quietly; and then again, this time slightly too loudly.

Christine let out a strangled moan, and I resolved to absolutely remember to definitely lead off with the murdered thing in future.

We were there drinking for a couple of hours. People shared memories of Marina. They all seemed to have met her in passing, but nobody really knew much about her, or could suggest anyone else in the movement who knew her better.

At some point, Docherty wandered over and insinuated himself into the group. He began talking earnestly to Christine. 'I am the Grand Esteemed Lecturing Knight of the Philanthropic Order of the Antelope,' he drawled in a flawless New York accent, taking her hand and kissing it gently, like that was something Americans do. He then segued into this terrible line of chat he has about all the characters in *Winnie-the-Pooh* each having a different one of the personality disorders.

I looked over at Donnie. He was sitting at a table with a few of the activists we'd been talking to. Donnie was fundamentally middle-class, and viewed life through a filter. I think one of the things the filter lessened was empathy; but it also added a kind of uninformed positivity. He thought our landlord was a nice guy, for example, because he'd never been late with the rent. He was pretty good company, though, in random bursts – possibly connected to phases of the Moon. He was laughing, and drooling slightly, as he tried to teach them all People, Planes, Buildings: a version of Rock, Paper, Scissors he'd invented themed around 9/11.

Amy turned to me, said, 'Let's get out of here,' and sank the last of her pint. By the time I found a table to stick our empties on, she was already in the foyer.

9

Amy lived in Dennistoun, which we bounced towards in an Uber driven by a maniac called Marty, who after some initial jollity delivered a grim tirade about his own stepdaughter then lapsed into silence. There was a football phone-in on the radio, a kind of community-wide primal scream therapy popular in Glasgow.

'Your pal, Donnie. Fuck me – where did you find him? What's up with him?'

I felt that this was essentially unquantifiable. 'A man of gigantic mirths and gigantic melancholies,' I offered cryptically, and she seemed satisfied.

Her close had a massive puddle outside it. Marty parked right across it with a drowned screech, about two feet from the pavement. My side of the car sank down alarmingly. Amy got out on the road side, but that door was now on too steep an incline for me to shuffle out with any dignity. I opened the door on the pavement side and it rippled through the muddy water. Marty, engrossed in the increasingly bitter phone-in, looked back to say cheerio, apparently content to watch me spring out of his car like a charity skydiver.

She lived on the second floor. The close lights weren't working, but streetlights from outside came through the big landing windows and it was just enough to see the stairs. Her front room was cold, and she switched on a little three-bar fire; something I hadn't seen in years. She had photos in little frames all along the mantelpiece.

I tried to avoid looking at any of them and ruining the moment, such as it was; she put the kettle on while I pretended to look at her bookcase.

Amy opened her bedroom door and let out a little dog called George. He was friendly to the point of being familiar, and I scratched his ears as he huffed around my feet excitedly. Humans are so terrible that it's taken millennia of interbreeding to create something that's pleased to see us, and we don't care if this means it can't really breathe.

'Was that guy your boyfriend?' I asked, trying to think of a non-insulting way to describe him and just leaving it.

'No, Felix, he's not my boyfriend. It's interesting that you would think that, though.' She used my name a lot, which didn't seem quite the right tone for someone you'd just met.

We sat drinking tea on the sofa in front of the little fire. She asked about Docherty, and we debated whether it was good that the Independence scene had so little interest in culture.

I could gauge by the amount of pish I was rambling that the pills from the suitcase were better than any I'd had for a while. 'I just think we've had the longest ever period of cultural stasis. In the nineties, maybe, we just got terrified of the future we were moving forward into, and culture became something we soothed ourselves with. There are whole generations now who think that having their assumptions challenged by art is either an affront to public decency or a hate crime. That's probably not going to end well.'

'Nothing ends well,' she said, with a shrug. 'But in the meantime we should try to stay optimistic. What's the alternative?'

I thought of rolling a joint and as I fumbled in my jacket pocket for skins I realised that my fine motor skills had degraded too far. 'I can only stay optimistic by staying offline. People are fine in the abstract, but it's hard when you actually have to hear what they think. But, yeah, I'm all for optimism in general.'

She shook her head at me. 'No need to put on a brave front all the time, Felix.' She lit a cigarette from a pack she took off the mantelpiece. 'Masculinity is a con from people who needed guys to die on battlefields; then when that was over, being a man was having a job. Worrying about being five minutes late to make money for someone else.' She flicked her ash into a little ashtray that was a little sixties-style plastic ball, a charming conversation piece that would no doubt soon kill her and everyone in the building.

Reflexively, I thought about how kissing her would be like kissing an ashtray, then I thought how ash was empirically a less weird thing to have in your mouth than someone else's tongue. I tried to put the whole thing out of my mind, which caused me to form a very clear image of an ashy tongue, thrashing around like a huge dusty worm and kind of screaming.

Amy was warming to some theme I'd missed the introduction of, but I tuned in hard. 'Rom-coms are innately radical. The central point is that it's always about a second relationship. It's about someone getting out of something that doesn't work, and into something that does. The rom-com says no matter how inescapable your current situation seems, you can escape, just not on your own. And this is also the message of radical socialism.'

I was struck again by how assured other people are. I can't remember the last time I had an opinion I could even fake confidence in. I was always attracted to women like this. Very emphatic, clever women. My therapist thought that this might be because my problems maintaining attention meant that I had to outsource intellectual stimulation, something I'd meant to read up on but hadn't.

'Did you not do anything in the Referendum?' she asked.

'Nothing.'

'That's a bit disappointing.'

It seemed like she was about to add something, then thought better of it. I found myself gabbling to fill the silence. 'I dunno. Maybe political engagement and disengagement are, well, just different responses from people who've drawn the same conclusions. I find the SNP kind of off-putting. I've never understood why they keep trying to appeal to the middle classes – a lot of the Scottish middle classes like the offer that's been made to them by Britain – "Hey, we're going to run this whole thing like a reservation, but you get to live in the casino."'

She nodded. 'Liberals think that most people are in the middle and agree with them. Most people can't be in the middle, it's statistically impossible.' I wasn't sure if this was true but it sounded true. 'Actually, all those people who don't believe in left or right believe a whole bunch of contradictory madness. I hate liberals. Please fucking spare us the people who benefit from all the unkindness saying they wish there was more kindness.'

I found myself being drawn in despite myself. 'I sort of think it's worse than that. It's all these privileged people saying why can't we all be kind, and that's galling, aye. But really what they're saying is *I'm one of the only kind people.* It's only me and my friends that really know what it is to be fully human. Everyone else is just a *fucking piece of shiiiit!*'

I maybe overdid the impression a bit. She looked amused, but maybe in the way that a doctor or therapist might look amused, I wasn't sure. I'd always felt quite at home with this kind of patter. The natural chat of bar workers is often a kind of libertarian communist, free-associative conspir-acism where the role of *Das Kapital* is performed by cannabis resin.

Amy finished her drink and said, 'Civility is made out to be this really great thing by all the people who benefit. Of course they want everyone to stick to the rules of civility, because those rules stop people from asking them why they have all the fucking stuff.' She sipped her tea. She had a very unselfconscious way of rolling her eyes up and to the side while she was thinking, with a little tilt of the chin. Eventually she brought her gaze back to me. 'Then again,' she added magnanimously, 'some people were just lucky enough to grow up with everybody being nice to them, and maybe that's not the worst thing to want for everybody else.'

'You've backtracked, you coward,' I said, suddenly drunk.

Amy put her tea down, leaned forward and gripped the front of my shirt in her hand. She was worryingly strong. 'You're a big fanny,' she announced, slightly too loud and slightly not joking enough. 'A big, fat, gay . . . fanny.'

Perhaps it was the challenge, but I decided that she was much more attractive than the walk home.

We started kissing – my hand rose to her cheek but she had a lot of foundation on and was powdery to the touch, like a moth. My fingers skidded through the make-up and slid off her face onto the sofa. It looked like I had lurched forward passionately and she responded with a sinister growl.

Her hand moved to my throat and exerted a pulverising force on my windpipe. I couldn't speak; if I could, I would have begged for my life. 'You like that, don't you?' she purred, despite the tears rolling down my face onto her hand. She leaned in and started biting me on the lip. I thought about screaming but she was holding my face in her teeth and I didn't want to upset her. She was pressing me down onto the sofa. I was trying to push myself up, but was nonetheless moving relentlessly down, like a nightmare about judo.

She stripped my clothes off like a Formula One pit crew, then climbed on top and guided me inside her. I suppose some people would have felt redundant in that situation, like they could have been anybody there and it wouldn't have mattered. I usually feel like that anyway, so I didn't particularly mind. She moved up and down me with purpose. 'You're a fucking prick . . . a bastard . . .' she growled in my ear. There was a brief hesitation in her movement that indicated a response was required.

'Eh . . . guilty as charged,' I agreed, with a strained joviality.

She grabbed my neck again and shook me like a kitten. 'You're just going to take that? Thought you were a man! Are you a prick?' She mushed my chin backwards with her palms, she was yelling now. 'Are you a bastard?'

I felt momentarily embarrassed that I had tried to get on top. I was flustered. 'I'm . . . I'm alright . . . I'm an alright guy,' I lied.

This seemed to satisfy her and she laughed loudly right in my face. She started bouncing up and down in my lap, in a powerful staccato at first, and then with the determined fury of someone steering home the winner of the Cheltenham Gold Cup.

We worked our way into the bedroom and lay talking afterwards. I was still high, and I asked her whether she thought we were tied to England for good now, and heading towards fascism.

'Well,' she began, in a tone of mild bemusement. 'Fuck knows on the Independence front. Might just be the first

of a few referendums, like the way you have to rock something big and heavy back and forward to get it to fall over.
Fascism, though . . . my worry is that we might be heading
towards some kind of techno fascism, although it might be
just a type of hyper-surveillance that is indistinguishable
from actual fascism: where everyone is reduced to a kind
of ultra-monitored husk.' She took a draw of her cigarette.
'But I don't think that can be sustained. At that point, where
the system achieves perfection, it will be incredibly brittle,
and will just explode. You can't sustain that stuff.'

I thought that the problem was maybe that the bit before
it all explodes might last for five hundred years, but I didn't
say anything. I wanted to ask her if she was depressed, but
I felt that wasn't the kind of thing you were supposed to
say to someone you'd just met at a bar, and it was obvious
anyway.

The conversation seemed to die off, and I lay looking at
the outline of her lamp on the windowsill, covered in some
kind of lace shawl as another provocation to the gods of
fire.

Then after about five minutes of silence she said, 'I've
had some terrible gallbladder problems.' I'd forgotten about
the gallbladder, and added it to my list of things to worry
about. I wanted to ask her more about it, and whether she
had any painkillers, and if I could have some, but she was
already asleep. The dog had been let into the room at some
point, and I lay and listened to them both gently snoring.

•

The next morning, she got up early and started dressing for work, so it must have been Sunday yesterday and not Saturday after all. I'd had one of those very on-the-nose dreams I'd been having for a while, where a nurse dressed as Anubis, the Egyptian God of Death, told me to work out more.

'What are you up to today?' she asked breezily. I was relieved that her voice didn't contain any real undercurrent of *Please get up and don't try to stay in my house*.

'I might have the day off,' I grumbled. I still felt kind of high, and pissed, but simultaneously some kind of withdrawal from something, as yet unidentified, was kicking in. I reached for my shirt as I said this, to reassure her that I was going.

'Take a sickie. There's no more life-affirming thing you can do, mate – that portion of your life you had rationed out to someone else, reclaimed. Everything you do in that reclaimed time is a sacred act, that's the way to look at it!'

I decided not to explain that I didn't have a job anymore, and was talking about having a day off caring, I suppose. Not that I felt there was a lot of that going on with me, but it was good to be careful.

After she left, I went to cook breakfast. She had all my favourite things, which somehow made me incredibly sad.

I made coffee and scrolled idly through my phone. I scanned my junk mail to see if there was anything there. That book about the guy who decided to say yes to everything he was asked would play very differently in the age of spam. He'd be broke in a week, and utterly poisoned by counterfeit Viagra.

I'd got an email from The Likely Story bookshop on Woodlands Road about some signing. It was Jane Pickford. I liked her books. She was a former cop, I think, banging out commercial murder mysteries that showcased different bits of Scotland, as her hero was a down-at-heel private detective who lived in a camper van or something.

I looked her up on Wikipedia and, with no better ideas, I decided to take the email as a polite suggestion from the Simulation.

10

The Likely Story was halfway up Woodlands Road, a busy artery that linked the city centre to the leafy West End at much the same jaunty angle you'd see if you drew a line between the two on a life expectancy graph.

I drifted up from town in the late afternoon. There was still twenty minutes till the signing, so I walked past the shop, right up to the end of the road. Nothing was open nearby except the all-night garage, which glowed in my peripheral vision like an explosion. I knew its strip lighting would instantly disperse the pleasant benzodiazepine fog I was in, like one of those dramatic chemistry experiments that teachers mistakenly believe make us remember the elements involved, or the reactions, or whatever was really going on there.

Glasgow was often rated as one of the happiest cities in the world, possibly because the people who researched these things didn't understand sarcasm. Some days I thought the spontaneous combustion of the Glasgow School of Art was maybe just the city reflexively rejecting a source of beauty like it was a poorly matched transplant organ. Then there were days like this, where the sunshine picked out the details and you saw the elegance and artistry of it all. Admittedly, it wasn't actually that sunny, and I was fairly heavily drugged.

I walked up to Roots and Fruits on Great Western Road, a kind of trendy greengrocers, that also sold unhealthy snacks you could kid yourself about because the wrappers were recycled or whatever. The guy behind the till wore a beanie and was lip-syncing and half dancing to Sam Cooke.

People trying to be cool in Glasgow don't have loads of reference points to work with, so they often have to cobble together a personality from movie characters and food allergies. I pretended to look at stuff on the shelves while he talked to another extrovert he was serving before I went up to the till.

'Just having a chilled one, man?' He spoke with a wee bit of vocal fry, or might just have been a bit stoned.

'Yes. Sure,' I replied, wondering what there was about buying a liquorice bar and two cans of cola that suggested this. I dropped them into a crumpled plastic bag I had in my pocket.

'Okay, man, keep that Monday on a low, low, low heat, okay?'

'Okay. I will,' I promised him.

By the time I got back, the bookshop was busy, and there was already a long line for the signing. I felt a bit out of place with my Sainsbury's bag. I rolled it up a little to make it less obvious. There was something abject about even a brand-new plastic bag. I like the way Americans have those big brown paper grocery bags, even though they don't work that well and you just have to hug your food all the way home.

There was a glass display case in the middle of the floor, showcasing old detective novels in hardback. Rising up from behind the case, and purring a hello when her head was still at about hip height, appeared my stalker, Rachael.

I stepped back with a stifled shriek that actually came out sounding something like a very high-pitched 'Oh!' so I left it at that, and turned sharply to join the queue.

Rachael was really an ex-stalker, having packed it in about a year ago after I pretended to be gay. She'd moved on to some student teacher, who I guessed might be coming to this signing, as she was dressed up. She was in her early fifties – or maybe less than that; possibly her dishevelled appearance was simply the handiwork of a selection of our more unsympathetic mental institutions. She was rocking a crumpled evening dress of a magnificent shimmering green, but the overall effect was of someone trying to hide a corpse under Quality Street wrappers.

She always sort of reminded me of this kid who played Lucy in a really creepy BBC version of *The Lion, the Witch, and the Wardrobe* I'd seen on DVD when I was wee. I wondered what that poor moon-faced girl was doing now: off school for months on a film set with talking beavers, then tipped back into the real world. It must have been hard. Maybe she was working in IKEA, selling wardrobes.

As the queue finally began to move she began to tell me

eagerly about a book she'd read on telepathy as, ironically, I willed her to fuck off. We shuffled forward and she continued to talk even though I had now completely turned towards the desk, and her voice was creating a warm patch in the middle of my back. As she chattered about her new yoga class, I formed an unwanted image of her in a handstand, her desiccated ovaries falling down into her torso like a rainstick. She had an oddly childlike way of talking, and a habit of emphasising every word in a way that meant she wasn't actually emphasising any of them.

With the queue not moving, I had time to reflect that I was maybe being a bit of a dick. I turned round casually, noting with a detached horror the many emotions that regularly struggled for possession of her face, like she was experiencing all the stages of grief simultaneously.

'You alright, Rachael? Been going to your therapy?'

She cocked her head to one side and half closed her eyes, in the manner of someone listening for instructions from a booming intergalactic voice. 'Yes,' she whispered, smiling. 'Yes, I am. We think I'm bisexual, at the very least.'

I thought it would be better to change the subject than try to unpick this.

'You're not still obsessed with that guy? Managed to get a grip on things?'

'No need to be jealous,' she said, and grinned up at me, horrifyingly. 'We're kind of living together, but it's very confusing.'

'I suppose the restraining order complicates things a bit.' I immediately regretted this misguided attempt at levity, as a thunderous expression crossed her face and was replaced with a pout.

'Don't say things like that. He can feel it when people upset me. We just had a lovely morning snuggle together on my bathroom rug, if you know what I mean.'

She spoke this in a baby voice that made me want to launch myself sideways through the front window, and have a nicked artery carry me into the bosom of Abraham.

Thankfully, the queue was moving more quickly now. A short, bald man who looked a bit like an ultrasound walked down the line checking that we all had a copy of the book. He eyed me judgementally and then handed one to me from a table. It was a fairly hefty hardback called *Death's Other Kingdom*, about a serial killer on the loose in Fife. The front cover was a tasteful black and white shot of a staircase that, to my practised eye, promised procedural accuracy and a body count of about half a dozen.

Jane Pickford sat at a long desk fortified with copies of her book. She was a very beautiful black woman in her late forties. She was dealing with her public in a brisk, clipped voice, which was English I think, but you could never tell with some posh Scottish folk. She wore a sharp black blazer, tight even on her thin shoulders, and had immaculate collar-length curly hair. Yet, somehow, this all hinted at a profound internal dishevelment, like her friends had forced her to dress up for a night out because she'd been depressed.

I paid for the book with my card at the far end of the table. I was sort of surprised it worked, then remembered I'd deposited Marina's cheque. The woman in front of me was a young Asian lassie, clearly star-struck and gabbling a mixture of 'goodbye' and 'thank you'. Suddenly I was up, handing my copy over as Jane Pickford threw me a brittle smile.

'What would you like?'

'Oh, for you to sign the book, please.'

There was a long pause, during which she assessed me critically. 'I mean, what would you like me to write? Shall I make it out to anyone in particular?'

'To Felix, please.'

She scribbled the inscription like it was a relief from some of the weird shit people asked her to write.

'Really, I was hoping you could help me with an investigation I'm involved in.'

'Probably not. I'm long retired, I'm afraid.' Her head tilted slightly to take in the queue behind me, in what was really quite a tasteful and considerate way to suggest I fuck off.

'I could pay you,' I added desperately, but the ultrasound had appeared from nowhere and was guiding me firmly away by the elbow.

I waited outside, thinking maybe I could talk with her when she was leaving, although it seemed desperate. Rachael skipped out after a gap of about ten minutes, during which she had presumably normalised my own outburst. She was talking quietly to herself and, as she walked off towards the park, stopped briefly to shake her head and giggle at some zinger from an unknown psychic correspondent.

It took maybe an hour for the place to empty out; mainly it was younger women, who always had a keen interest in murderers because they had to be able to spot them on dating apps. Eventually, Jane Pickford emerged with a heavy bag on one shoulder. She spotted me instantly, even though I'd stood a good twenty feet down from the entrance.

'Hi! I was just wondering if I could talk to you for a second—?'

I'd tried to signal that I was no threat by standing quite a long way away, but this meant that I had to shout, which I could see from her expression was undermining the message.

'Felix, right? It's not really polite to harass people who've already said no, Felix.'

Ultrasound appeared from the doorway. He had the tense look of someone who was about to lie that they had phoned the police. He started to say something, but she silenced him with a light touch on his arm.

I held my hands up, palms out, then worried that this was the kind of thing a murderer would do and put them down again. 'I'm sorry. It's just that . . . I'm investigating my friend's death, and I don't know what I'm doing, but the police don't seem to know what they're doing, either. I thought maybe you could take a look at what I've got so far?'

'I'm not interested.' She didn't have to shout: her voice just carried. She was looking straight ahead, rather than in my direction.

'It's the woman who was killed in that park down there.'

I nodded in the direction of Kelvingrove at the far end of the street.

She shifted her bag strap on her shoulder. 'And what have you got so far, then?'

'Not much,' I admitted, flatly. 'She was seeing someone, she might have been involved in moving some drugs. She had a really weird doctor . . . that's about it.'

'A really weird doctor?' she asked. I considered whether she was repeating this sarcastically, but she seemed to be waiting for some kind of reply.

'Yeah, I saw her doctor and he was pretty bananas.'

'How bananas?'

'Talked a lot about simulation theory. Dr David Chong.'

She turned so that we were facing each other. 'Why? Why do you want to know what happened?' Even at a distance, I could see her eyes were scanning my face, which I'm pretty sure was a frozen drugged mask.

Ultrasound looked very uncomfortable. He'd come out to shoo me away and was now trapped in a detailed shouted conversation about a murder, and he couldn't really leave.

'It's just – she was my only real friend, and I'd like to try and get her some justice. Someone shouldn't be allowed to do that and just get away with it, and I think that if I don't do something, probably they will.' It all sounded so odd, half yelled in the cold air of a busy street. I felt the clammy shame that always came over me in moments of honesty.

'Okay then, Felix, I'll hear you out, I suppose. You can walk me up the hill.' Jane Pickford lifted her arm and beckoned me towards her with the head of a stylish-looking wooden cane. She'd been holding it tight against her leg, I suppose in case she'd needed to beat me unconscious with it.

11

Jane's house was only a short distance away at the top of the hill, but it took us a while because she had to lean heavily on her stick, and occasionally take my arm for support.

Park Crescent was this big Victorian street that formed the highest edge of Kelvingrove Park. As we rounded the top of the hill, the late evening light was streaked across the sandstone in one dramatic brushstroke. Originally these would have been town houses but now they were flats for wealthy professionals, or luxury lets for the occasional Celtic or Rangers loan signing. In fact, they were just as likely to be offices as anything else, and it was always eerily deserted at the weekend.

Jane's flat was beside a youth hostel of shabby magnificence that squatted between the tall, newly renovated buildings on either side. The front door opened into a communal hallway with a beautiful marble floor and carpeted stairway leading to the flats above. It was close enough to the park that dead leaves had buried the inside doormat. A single leather armchair sat in the hallway, its purpose unclear.

Her front door was dead ahead at the end of the hall.

She fumbled in her bag for the keys and then had to push it open with her shoulder. The first room was the kitchen, a white ultra-modern affair. There was a huge vase of flowers on the island, and another in the window.

She gestured at the place with a sort of apologetic *ta-dah*. 'You can't hide the profits for ever. The public have a real thirst for murder . . . what can I say?'

She led me through to an improbably large sitting room with one of those white corniced ceilings that always reminds me of wedding cake, the whole place decorated with the kind of abstract art pieces that my mind seems to instinctively tune out.

I flopped onto the sofa, suddenly tired. Jane poured us both a huge Scotch and ice, without asking.

'My old stalker was there, at the signing. The woman after me in the queue.'

Jane sat up a little, interested. 'The clay-faced oddity in the crumpled ball gown?'

'Aye. My friend Marina used to say, "No doubt she used to turn heads, but it isn't clear which way."'

'What was that like, the being stalked?'

'She used to turn up at my work, then this bar I worked at – all over town, really – and sort of stare at me. It was harrowing, but I was drinking a lot at the time, so often I was just asleep for days. I think she got bored with waiting and moved on.'

'Are you sure she's given up? Erotomaniacs tend not to move on too easily. And she just happened to be at a signing you were at, all dolled up.'

'Dolled up' seemed a good description for how Rachael had looked – like a haunted marionette in a horror movie. 'Yeah, pretty sure. I told her I was gay. She's stalking someone else now, some teacher. I thought about getting in touch with him and telling him to try the gay thing, but that's a tricky conversation to open, I suppose.' The whisky was as nice as anything I'd ever tasted. 'Look, I'm just trying to find out what happened because the police don't seem capable of doing very much.' I decided to downplay the whole drug-assisted angle, what with her having been a cop and everything. 'So I've decided to become a detective myself.'

'What kind of detective could you possibly be? Tell me three things you've noticed about me and I'll judge whether you're worthy of my time.' She sounded amused, although it might just as easily have been pity, or even derision.

'Well . . .' I stalled, looking around the room.

She clapped her hands. 'Three things, keep it simple.'

'You don't have a man in your life.' I drew the last word out and looked for clues in her face, which seemed irritated.

'I'm gay, you idiot. There's a huge painting of a naked woman above the mantelpiece.'

I squinted. 'I thought those were mountains.'

'Pink mountains?'

There was a brief silence, and I assumed she wanted me to press on.

'You've been trying to cut down on your drinking. The bottles in your little bar are all full. If you don't mind me saying so, with the measures you pour, that seems odd . . .'

'Go on.'

'There's more there than you could carry, even just from a car up to here. So, maybe . . . people have been bringing you bottles, and you've not been drinking them.'

'Not till recently, no. Well done. That shows some promise. Next one's the decider.'

'People brought you bottles, and the flowers in the kitchen, because you'd been ill.'

She snorted. 'I'm walking with a cane – that hardly even qualifies as an observation, never mind a deduction.'

'They brought you bottles because you'd been ill. You didn't drink them, you were concentrating on getting better, and now you seem to have thought, "Well, fuck it."'

She banged her cane on the floor and beamed at me. 'Well done, Watson. I'm dying from cancer.'

'I have morphine on me.'

'Well, why didn't you fucking say so?'

She had half a morphine from the little bottle that I plonked on the table: a level of drugs caution I had no frame of reference for. We got solidly drunk on whisky and beer, and she rambled a little about how much of a nightmare it had been being in the police.

I told her everything I'd learned so far. It was over in about half a dozen sentences, and I realised I was giving a senselessly long description of waiting for her outside the bookshop to pad it out, so I stopped.

She pressed her fingers together and sighed in a resigned way. 'You mentioned Dr David Chong. The good doctor is probably in effective control of most of the really profitable crime in Glasgow. There used to be a guy called Thomas McGraw who shifted a lot of the drugs in the city. Heard of him?'

'No.'

'He was known as "The Licensee". Some people said because he owned a pub. Other people said that it was because the real power in Glasgow's drug industry was Strathclyde Police, and he was licensed by them to move stuff. Then Chong arrived. He's your age, right? About thirty?'

'I was at school with him.'

'Hmm. I've always said that Scottish people all know each other. When I first heard of him he was eighteen. He co-opted or suborned everyone who used to run things. Lots of low-level dealers suddenly found new vocations in life. A couple of officers took their lives in circumstances I personally found unconvincing. Any investigation of him just became more and more taboo. Never any big drama – just this sense of everything slipping away from you. He did just enough to bring everyone around to his way of thinking.'

I splashed us both out another couple of whiskies. 'Can you think of any reason he might have been involved in Marina's murder?'

'I don't know. There's been a rumour lately that someone intercepted a big shipment he had coming in, heroin, sold it out from under him.'

'That's interesting. Any idea why he's a GP?'

She laughed. 'I don't know. Maybe that's where true

power lies. They sell all the NHS data now — it's big business.'

'That's why I always lie when the doctor asks where it hurts.'

She killed her drink and sat back awkwardly with a groan. 'The British had to invent the NHS because they'd reached a point in history where they couldn't just head off into the Empire anymore — they had to make Britain bearable. They did it with money from India and Malaysia. Attlee had the British Army behead a bunch of Malaysians because they were joining unions. The Americans encouraged all this because they were worried about this thing called the dollar gap. They were worried that Europeans wouldn't have enough money to buy American cars and whatnot, and encouraged them all to hang on to bits of Empire.'

Eventually, the conversation started to tail off and I didn't want to outstay my welcome. I gathered up my things, leaving the morphine, which she acknowledged with a little nod. She told me that she'd look into things; that she still had a few contacts in the police, and would have a look at the autopsy report. She gave me her card — which seemed reassuringly old school — and told me to interview Marina's old flatmate Fatima and speak to anyone I could find who'd worked with Marina. She saw me out to the front door, and waved as I listed out onto the street.

As was often the case when I was drunk, I felt something like hope.

Last summer, Marina and I had both been working at the Go-Go and we saw a lot of each other. We both used to like the late shifts: you didn't start till eight and cleaned up afterwards. I wasn't sleeping great, and I'd been trying to cut down on drugs by drinking a lot. Mikey would often sit and have a beer and a spliff with us after we closed, but he'd never allow music because he was paranoid about cops.

One night I asked him: 'Mikey, you don't trust me to lock up, do you?'

'I trust you to lock up, I just don't trust you to leave before you do it.' Marina laughed. 'I'd come in to find you dead under the Lowenbrau tap like Augustus Gloop.'

'I don't think Augustus Gloop died. It wasn't, like, *Charlie Bucket Investigates* or anything.'

'The deaths were implied,' said Marina, as if the whole discussion was something she was endlessly being asked about and she was sick of it. 'Willy Wonka is an imperialist, enslaving natives to use as workers, doing medical experiments on them. He realises his paradigm is exhausted, and has to find a new front man for his crimes.'

One night, Mikey was keen for everybody to fuck off sharpish, so we went back to Marina's flat and lay in bed smoking a joint and watching TV. She mentioned this new guy who'd started at the bar. He was a shy Scottish public-school type who was on his summer break from Cambridge University, and was struggling to fit in.

'I imagine him beating off with a kind of punting action,' she said, with a surprisingly earnest two-handed demonstration.

'I think he's just introverted.'

'Hmm. People who say they're introverted are often just not very interesting, like the way people who say they're not photogenic are often just ugly.'

She asked me to put a DVD on.

I picked *A New Hope*, possibly an anguished appeal from my subconscious. I knew that Marina loved *Star Wars*. 'What I don't understand is if Obi-Wan Kenobi is hiding Luke on Tatooine, and doesn't want to draw attention to him, why does he stay there?'

'He changes his name,' she countered, dismissively.

'To Old Ben Kenobi. And has a reputation as a wizard, and dresses in Jedi robes.'

'It's a high-stakes double bluff,' she replied, blankly. She didn't take her eyes off the movie. Marina loved all *Star Wars*, good and bad. She always got excited every time Darth Vader showed up. 'The stormtroopers are supposed to look like the KKK, and Darth Vader is the ultimate bad guy, because he's a black guy so fierce he can dominate the KKK. He has a black guy's voice, and his face is like a skull, a black skull. He's so black that his bones are black. And his voice is all deep and scratchy like he's been hung. Like he's been hung but he didn't die. That's why they're afraid of him: he's an unlynchable, black-boned Super Warrior.'

I laughed. 'R2 and Chewbacca having one person who can understand them – that's the same joke twice, you've got to admit.'

'I suppose they made R2 record all sorts of depraved holographic films. He could probably speak originally, and they made him delete his speech programs to free up porn storage.'

I couldn't think of anything to say to this. Marina's grass was always too strong. This was what happened when you made anything illegal: people started to make it super powerful so they had to transport less of it; like the old Prohibition-era moonshine that was so strong people had used it to fuel their trucks. It didn't work, but they'd sit in their trucks and think they were moving, because drinking it had rendered them insane. I was never that into getting stoned, certainly compared to everyone else I knew. I worried that being able to enjoy bad movies wasn't really a skill I wanted, and that grass just made boring shit palatable, like a kind of mind salt.

Marina came back from the kitchen with a couple of Diet Cokes.

'You've switched to Diet now?' She never drank after work.

She put her finger over her lips and delivered a parody of a coquettish wink. This was a reference to an idea I'd had for an advert for a low-sugar version of Nutella, called No-tella, which in my mind would feature a beautiful Italian woman serving the low-sugar alternative to her blissfully unaware guests, before turning to the camera and putting a finger over her lips to deliver the slogan 'Shhhh . . . No-tella.' Sadly, the product didn't exist.

'Do you ever think about how, if what you were doing at that instant was in a movie, what your actions would make people think of you?'

'What sort of movie is it?'

'A porn parody,' I replied, 'that was parodying other porn. In a high-minded way, with all the sex taken out.'

'I caught myself doing it when I was sexting my ex last night – am I the home wrecker in the movie? Someone fairly minor, anyway.' She took a deep hit from the joint, blew a near perfect smoke ring with it, and laughed.

'There would still be a fan theory that we had sex. And fan fiction.'

'Containing unsettling practices, and of interest to only the most dogged archivist of outsider art.'

'Shhh . . . here comes the Emperor. Even Darth, majestic black man that he is, has to answer to Whitey. The beauty of it.'

Afterwards we watched *Fight Club*, a film that refused to accept its own narcissism and homo-eroticism, and seemed to be about a guy who was gay for himself.

As I was falling asleep, Marina turned round to me and said, 'My friend met a wise man in Taiwan once and asked him what the meaning of life was, and the wise man replied, "Snowflake in oven".' Then, after what seemed like a long time, she added: 'Epilogue – he's dead now.'

12

The next day I decided to go down to Marina's old job.

She'd left the Go-Go after I'd been going there for about a year. There's a big turnover in bar jobs like that, stay too long and you end up with responsibilities. Most of the time I'd known her, she'd worked for an independent production company called IBC. I'd recommended her to my pal Ian, who used to work at BBC Scotland. Then later, she started back doing some shifts at the Go-Go. Thursdays mainly, which was handy because it was the night they had a special on pitchers, and I'd stop in on my way back from therapy and talk shit with her for a couple of hours. She said once that she viewed TV and bar jobs as being fairly similar, pretending to be the friend of people you were actually tranquillising.

As I was getting ready, I realised I had no idea what kind of thing they made at IBC, or really where it was. I knew it was down at that bit beside the Science Centre some-where: a bunch of museums and TV companies had gathered uneasily by the Clyde, as far from the actual people of the city as they could justify.

The taxi bumped around endlessly and, in the grip of a medium-sized comedown, I watched the bleary morning slowly unfocus through the raindrops on my passenger window.

I knew Ian pretty well. Like a lot of people at the BBC, we'd bonded because we'd been drunk around each other so often we'd probably both confessed a lot of stuff. Of course, nobody there drank before work or during work – the previous night's drinking would render that impossible – but almost the entire department would string itself across a couple of local bars every single weeknight. We saw more of each other than the crew of a ship, and sometimes life in the office would degrade into a month-long ping-pong tournament.

After I left there I'd got a job with Ian, for a few months, at the independent production company that later became IBC, but I just couldn't handle the drinking. Maybe alcoholism was our response to the shit we were churning out. We got off lightly – it probably drove a significant minority of the viewers into the arms of heroin and methamphetamines.

And maybe more than that, you needed the beers to make everybody's jokes funny. Or even make sense. I drank so much that I completely lost four days. I had literally no idea what had happened for almost a week and it didn't seem to matter. I told some of my department and they didn't think it was that unusual. I drifted around doing nothing a lot of the time. I told them I felt like a poltergeist and they laughed because they were drunk. Actually, I felt like an old man kicked onto the stage of an opera whose major themes were alienation and psychosis.

Ian was better suited to the indie production life. He seemed to feel warmly amused by pretty much everything. He once told me that he'd manufactured his relaxed, humble persona by spending all of his teenage years pretending he was being interviewed by the music press. I think one of the things I liked about him was that he was slightly too self-absorbed to show me any pity. A part-time producer and full-time shagger, Ian was as genetically driven as a salmon. He had externalised compulsive masturbation. He pursued the women of his trendy media set like a pacifist Ted Bundy, and spent every penny he made on luring beautiful girls into disappointing three-week relationships. He ran daily to keep his body weight low and his jaw muscles rolling just beneath the skin like a stripper's hips. He was almost unbearably happy.

Ian was waiting for me on a sofa just inside the front door. We went and sat in the window at the front of the building, in a huge refectory that looked out onto the Clyde. Like a lot of Scottish media places, the first thing that struck you about it was its emptiness, the lack of any discernible activity. There were actually more people drifting around outside, even though it was raining. There were no staff behind the counter: as we talked, Ian kept glancing over so that he could get us some coffees when someone turned up.

'It's absolutely terrible, this whole thing. I'd not heard from Marina for a few months, which was a bit odd, aye, cos she'd come down every so often and I'd take her for lunch. Maybe every two or three weeks? She'd pitch me TV shit. Formats, all kinds of pish. Two seconds!' He'd spotted an old woman in a catering uniform disconsolately cleaning a table in the distance and jogged over to her. There seemed to be some considerable negotiation before he could persuade her to serve him. Eventually, he came back and slapped two mugs of coffee down in front of us, with two Tunnock's Caramel Wafers.

'Anyhoo. These ideas weren't anything that people actually wanted to make, it was more like they liked the idea of the idea, y'know? They were the sort of ideas they could talk about at dinner parties while they were actually making shows like *Kitchen SOS* and *Get Even With Your Ex* . . . Her best one was *The Slims* – that was a great one! A reality show where fat people lived in a house while they tried to lose enough weight to win the prize money by squeezing out this really narrow front door. The twist was all the furniture was made of cake and chocolate and stuff. All completely inhuman, but she was brilliant, y'know?'

'I never really saw that business side of her, man. She always seemed pretty mental.'

'Or maybe she just reflected back to you what she thought you wanted to see, like a Kennedy? She was pretty businesslike down here. Always brought a wee folder with her pitches in it, socked it to you like she was in *Mad Men*. It was a bit of a game to her, I guess. I'd tweak the pitches, get her a wee bit of development money here and there.'

'I guess I always thought it was weird she left here. She was doing well, wasn't she? And she just went back to work at the Go-Go.'

'No, she didn't leave a media job to just go work in a bar!' He laughed, then stopped himself, maybe remembering that this was what I'd done. 'Fuck knows what she was doing at the Go-Go – she didn't really need the money. Marina went to Princeton – you know that, right?'

I'd always assumed that was some joke of hers that I didn't quite get, so I nodded in agreement.

'She left to start working at that big tech start-up down on India Street. You know the thing, they're always in the news putting implants in mice's brains and trying to make them feel guilty or whatever . . . Beloved Intelligence. Aye, she was pretty senior down there. Fuck knows why she still had her bar job – maybe researching what kind of upgrades humanity needs, or something.'

'Fellas!'

Ian froze as a bright Irish voice hailed us from the front desk, which was probably about four or five hundred feet away. It was Ian's boss, an exec called Jimmy Roarty. He'd also run the production company that I'd worked at briefly. Being a senior exec in Scottish television meant that you employed other people to make programmes, and had literally nothing to do. If you ran into one they would often talk for hours.

He came over and sat beside us. When the woman in the canteen uniform passed he touched her arm and asked her to 'do us a favour' and bring us all another coffee. She left and never came back.

Jimmy was one of those Irish people who keep talking while they're breathing in. Professionally, he was of the opinion that self-censorship takes effort; that those who didn't practise it were lazy; and that honesty was little more than a lack of diplomacy. When I worked for him, at first it seemed remarkable that he was in charge despite not really understanding television at all, before we realised that he was in charge because he didn't understand it. If he'd understood what he was making, the banality of it might have driven him mad, as it had us. He was the sort of totally average guy who probably spent most nights dreaming that his hands were talons.

Jimmy's company was quite big on nepotism, which is just incest for cowards. I'd been hired on a scheme for people from unconventional backgrounds – which seemed to be what they called people from conventional back-grounds. I'd left, perfectly amicably, soon after he'd taken over. He was in the business of making entertainment. Any idea I'd ever floated at him had sent him into a visible depression. I've always thought that needing things to be upbeat speaks of a terrifying fragility: you don't choose to watch shows about dogs being reunited with their owners unless you know you have the stability of a melting ice sheet. Maybe that's why they produced hundreds of episodes of these things: breaking off to engage with reality for long enough to find a new bad show to watch would result in loathing, insanity and suicide.

'So, Felix, what have you been up to?'

'Nothing.' This was received with laughter for some reason, and I was glad.

'Same old Felix. We've been doing this documentary about viral tweets, isn't that right, Ian?'

Ian nodded and raised his eyebrows with carefully contained irony.

'I just left Twitter because of death threats – Lorraine Kelly just didn't seem to be reading them anymore,' I ventured. It was received in the complete silence it probably deserved.

At some point in our relationship Jimmy had stopped speaking to me, but I could never remember why. It suddenly came to me. At some wrap party I'd told him that old joke about two guys being stalked by a lion and one putting trainers on. The other guy tells him he'll never outrun a lion, and he replies, 'I don't need to outrun the lion, I just need to outrun you.' Then I'd said that this was what people in the Republic had done to the people in Northern Ireland after Independence, adding that the reason the Irish played music and sang all the time was to drown out their guilty thoughts.

They fell into a discussion on how hard it was getting things commissioned. It was a real problem for the entertainment industry that both sides of the Independence debate would much prefer a dead culture. Much of Scottish life wasn't even paid lip-service. In a culture that was even trying to patronise us, we'd have had six series of *McLeod*, the gritty adventures of a Highland private eye in Glasgow. The local police and criminals mocked his accent, but feared his mirthlessness, brutally high alcohol threshold, and penchant for dishing out beatings with his trusty shinty stick, Florence, which he slept with and was rumoured to have married. Every suspect interview would finish with a close-up of McLeod necking a massive glass of whisky then having to step over the inert, drunken body of whoever he'd been interviewing. Often they weren't even in a bar.

'Felix has got to go, though!' lied Ian, helpfully. 'He's got a . . .' – there was the briefest of pauses while he tried to think of something important someone like me could possibly have on – '. . . date.'

'This is what you're wearing to a date?' asked Roarty in a rising tone that mixed incredulity and censure. He nodded at my frankly dishevelled appearance.

'Yes. She's a drinker. She's a very heavy drinker, and I don't want her messing up my good clothes.'

'He's only kidding. He has to go home and change, that's all,' laughed Ian, with the casual improvisational brilliance of the committed shagger.

I was glad to get outside, even though it was now belting it down. My phone rang. It was Donnie. Something about the rain landing on my phone screen made it difficult to accept the call, and when I did, Donnie was already mid-sentence.

'. . . not that I give a fuck about supplements and all that shit.'

'What? I'm sorry, Donnie, had a bit of trouble answering the phone there.'

'You had trouble answering the phone? You neurodivergent cunt.' Donnie had been sent on compulsory equalities training after some work catastrophe, where he had been compelled to learn a raft of terms he now used as abuse.

'I've found Fatima!'

I'd completely forgotten that I'd asked him to.

'Have you got a pen? Let me give you her number.'

'You could just text it to me.'

'Genius!' he cried, incorrectly, and hung up.

13

I arranged to meet Fatima at a Wetherspoons not far from the flat. It was actually pretty decent in the afternoon; it was worth it for the cheap food if you baled before the evening shift arrived, and the place took on the atmosphere of pre-drinks for a dogfight.

I was early but I managed to kill some time by trying to find the toilet. Every Wetherspoons toilet seemed to be built as a subterfuge by people trying to tunnel under a bank.

I took a piss of astonishingly vivid yellow. On the way back upstairs I relaxed as I remembered I'd been drinking Berocca in the mornings, then flushed with anxiety as I remembered that was weeks ago. I popped a Vallie.

For some reason, pubs beside bus and railway stations are always mental. Most people are breaking a journey there and there's some unspoken agreement that this renders them a psychosexual no-man's land. I chose my seat carefully to avoid a group of wide-os at the bar. If there's one thing Glasgow has to teach the world, it's that you can be an extrovert without being friendly.

While I waited, I checked my email to see if I'd heard anything back from my job application. Yesterday, I'd phoned Beloved Intelligence a few times. Initially I just asked to speak to the chief executive about a murder, which seemed to go down badly. After a long wait they said they'd call me back, and then didn't. Then I rang up and said I was from *Rolling Stone*, looking to do a feature. They told me to email the contact address on their website, which I think is how a company tells you to fuck off.

'You need to infiltrate the fuckers,' Donnie said. 'Get a job in there.'

'Sure. Creating artificial intelligence systems – how hard can it be?'

'Yes,' he agreed, clearly not listening.

'Donnie, there's no way I can bluff my way into some programming job.'

'You don't need to do the fucking job, you just need to get in for a day or two to talk to people. Also, it won't be you doing the bluffing. It will be the drugs!'

I'd searched online and found a single job advert for Beloved Intelligence Technologies: something called a data tagging supervisor starting on 50K a year. Then I'd spent the afternoon typing up a fake CV.

I suppose all CVs are essentially fake. I copied details from people who listed themselves as data tagging supervisors online, but it was very difficult to form any understanding of what it might involve. I felt nervous about the whole idea, and tried to tell myself that a lot of times when I'd felt worried about something it had worked out okay. But when I thought about it, often it had ended in disaster and recrimination.

Fatima was five minutes late, so I fetched myself a rum and Coke. Just as I sat down, I saw her come in and look around, spotting me at one of the back tables. She looked different: she was humiliatingly healthy and beautiful. Over the course of the interview – I thought of them as interviews now – her phone sat in front of her on the table and throbbed with messages from a desperate mankind; it was almost like a drumbeat to the conversation. I realised for the first time that she was actually a few years younger than me, maybe only about twenty-six or twenty-seven. She seemed a little anxious, but only that kind of anxiety that now defined life, and seemed permanently present in everybody.

She'd always liked me, I think, and regarded me now with the open affection you sometimes get from women who are so wholly out of your league they know it won't be misconstrued. She spoke in the brisk fashion of someone who had better places to be: 'You still on the drugs, Felix? I packed it all in. Did the whole NA thing. Doing CrossFit now. I don't miss a thing about any of it. Have you read much about mindfulness?'

I'd never really bought the whole 'live in the moment' thing. It had emerged as some late capitalist thing that said don't look at the future, don't consider the past, just focus on right now because the only way you can be happy is to think more like a dog. Maybe I just instinctively shirked individual responsibility, but all this self-care stuff seemed like telling people they should make sure to get a back rub, when they really needed a union.

The wide-os had quietened down now. A group of squaddies had come in and taken up the other end of the bar; the sort of men for whom the most macabre sexual practice was little more than a pool forfeit.

One of Fatima's phone messages set off a different tone – a chime – and she paused to read it with a wry smile. We chatted aimlessly for a bit. She'd recently reconciled with her family, who'd really disapproved of her drug years. It was quite a complicated story, and would have been hard to follow even if I'd been trying. There was a bit of back and forth about the importance of family to her, and I felt relieved that I pretend my parents are dead.

'It was quite hard to get a hold of you. You don't really do the whole social media thing, do you?'

She gave a short, bleak laugh. 'Social media. Where else would you present a flake of yourself with such apocalyptic conviction?'

'Relationships?'

Her chime pinged again and she checked the message.

'New bloke, Fatima?'

'Well, maybe. He's nice. Then again, after the last one I'd be happy with anyone who wasn't a total dick.'

'Yes, men struggle with that. Not in our nature, perhaps.'

'Last one was English. It's a pity that English people never seem to pick up on what the world thinks of them. They think that the stereotype people have of them is that they're too polite and queue a lot, right? Not that they're utter cunts.'

I sensed that this would be a good time to change the subject. 'When did you last see Marina?'

'Maybe about a year ago. I moved out a few months before that, went back to pick up some stuff when I bought my flat.'

'Wow, you've really got it all going, Fatima.'

She leaned forward and spoke with a sincerity that she clearly found embarrassing. 'People change all the time, Felix. You don't have to be like . . . this.' She gestured vaguely at me with her drink stirrer.

'How did Marina seem when you saw her?'

'Alright. She'd packed her work in at Pacific Quay, started some job at a tech place. She had one of their bots on her phone – she showed it to me. You could ask it questions and stuff. Looked like they'd invented a pretty good simulation of a conversation with a total moron.'

I wrote this down in my notebook, so that today's page now read:

RESEARCH:

PISS COLOUR

BOTS

'Was she seeing someone?'

'Oh, yeah, a scary fucking gangster. Like, really fucking scary. My dealer was round one time and he'd stiffed us on some grass, but we didn't really give a fuck. Somehow this boyfriend's name came up in conversation and the guy went white as a fucking sheet. Came back an hour later with the grass and made us take it for free.'

'Was this guy's name Chong?'

'Aye, that's right, Davie Chong. I never met him, just knew she worked for him. Oh, wait a second, I do remember something about old Davie Chong!'

'What?'

'He could get a hold of all her texts, emails, everything. She said he was super paranoid – monitored her. She didn't seem that bothered, though.'

'He was checking her *phone* . . .?'

'No, he was monitoring everything remotely. Somehow. I think she got the wee AI bot on her phone to fuck with him. He was well paranoid by the sound of it.'

I wrote down: CHONG PARANOID ABOUT AI

Fatima watched me write it, smiling. 'Are you working at the moment?' she asked.

'Just writing and . . . well, not really writing. Not really doing anything. I went to see some guys I used to work with the other day, and I can't imagine how I held a job down. You get older and stop trying to please people, I suppose.'

'That was you trying to please people?' She laughed happily. 'I went to therapy for a year, it was useful. Never realised how much I was just rebelling against my parents. Being a major fucking cliché.'

'Were your parents pretty straight, then?'

She took a slug of her orange juice, which from her expression seemed to taste mildly unpleasant. She pushed it away from her. 'Yeah. My mum always wanted us to fit in, get ahead. Then again, she'd always shout everybody into the living room when an Indian person came on TV, so I suppose she was really proud of our difference too. I think that's healthy. Aren't your parents Irish?'

'Aye. They didn't want us to fit in so much as they didn't want us to stand out.'

'Safest all round. I think a lot of people try to assimilate when they're growing up – then one day you're on holiday, meet some British expats, and find out that fitting in with another culture is the least British thing you could ever do.'

'Did you know Malcolm's girlfriend much? I thought I'd try and get in touch with her.'

'Girlfriend?'

'Aye, what was she called . . . May?'

'Oh, her. Oh, no, they weren't a couple – they were a Cult of One.'

'What?'

'A Cult of One – she was Malcolm's follower. Yeah, she might be worth talking to. Malcolm wouldn't remember anything – he was completely wasted the whole time. But May might: she had to stay sober. It was part of The Way.'

'The Way?'

'This set of rules that the Cult had. Well, that she had.'

'Do you know what happened to her?'

'I think they had some kind of disagreement, a theological thing, and she broke from him.'

'Do you know where she is?'

'She used to work at Chrono, no?'

'What's that?'

'That mad kind of vegan record shop the singer from The Aubergines owns.'

I'd actually been there quite a lot, but had never known what it was called.

Fatima looks at me. 'I know it's horrible what happened to Marina. I never understood what your relationship was, to be honest. She said it wasn't sexual . . . She gave you a wank at Glastonbury or something?'

'Mumford and Sons were on. There was nothing else to do.'

'I knew her pretty well, Felix, so I'll tell you what she'd tell you if she was here and you didn't both have fucking intimacy disorders. She wanted you to get better. You can't see it from where you're standing, but there's a whole life for you after this, and you don't have to bring any of what you're carrying now along with you. Enjoy it while you can, Felix. In the future we'll all be in care homes run by robots.'

'I don't know if people will want their loved ones being cared for by robots.'

'Are you kidding? Sellotape a Halloween mask to a Hoover and I'll hand my dad over.'

After she left I sat there and looked out the window, at the taxi rank, and the usual rain, and the reflection of my own face, surprised at how little sign it betrayed that I was completely overwhelmed with emotion.

On my way home I got a call from Donnie. I mentioned the lead about May working in Chrono. Donnie entered into a bitter and unabridged attack on the personnel, aesthetic and bar prices at some spoken-word show he'd seen there. The theme of the night had been loneliness, and Donnie soliloquised on how people didn't reflect enough about the connection between loneliness and being a cunt, or a spoken-word performer, during which I tried to send my mind to the very edge of space.

I told him about Jane and how she'd agreed to help.

'I tried to write a book once. Showed it to Janice,' Donnie hissed poisonously. '"I don't see why I'm supposed to care about this character"! That's what she said to me! The fucking cow.'

My confusion must have registered in my pause because he added in a hollow whisper, 'It was my autobiography.'

When he finally hung up I saw that I had a new text. It was Beloved Intelligence, asking me to come in for an interview at 9 a.m. that Friday.

14

I opened the curtains and watched a seagull laugh across a shock of morning sky. It was strange to be awake at 7 a.m., rather than thrashing around in the grip of a sexually charged nightmare. I scratched my stubble off carefully with a bunch of old disposable razors that I found in the cupboard under the sink. I put on my court suit, and a pair of heavy brown shoes that didn't quite fit me and may have been left in the flat by someone else. I had lost my tie. I briefly considered that Donnie had stolen my tie to use as a tourniquet and was mainlining heroin.

I'd talked with Donnie about how to get into the perfect state for the interview: a hit or two of grass (for lateral thinking), some opium (to relax me), some Adderall (a US thing that is used for treating ADHD), and an ecstasy to make me a bit more engaging. I took it all as dispassionately as a scientist, and still felt little more than a rising panic. I had a belt of Scotch and threw a few Valium on as a garnish, and by the time I had to leave I felt a qualified optimism.

•

Beloved Intelligence seemed to own a whole massive building just off Charing Cross. From the outside it looked like another dreary Glasgow office tower, but inside it was all the kind of bright minimalism that's shorthand for afflu-ence. I suppose in the age of globalisation, it said that your company was rich enough to have all the shitty stuff done elsewhere. There were white walls and floors, and a long slate-black reception desk, with a glass dividing screen like a bank.

I took a deep, calming breath through my nose and walked up to a jolly-looking woman in a grey suit. 'Good morning. I have an interview for the position of data tagging super-visor.'

'And your name?'

My mind completely blanked on the fake name I'd given on the CV and I maintained a fixed smile as I prayed for it to come back to me. 'That's right,' I chirped, nonsensically.

She tilted her head at me with a little concern, I worried that my smile was not coming off as relaxed, and this made it tighten further. I realised I could see my reflection in the Perspex between us and it looked like the face of a man performing a deadlift for a dare.

'Eh, I'm here for the interview at nine o'clock,' I gabbled.

'Sildar Hallwinter?'

'That's me!' I beamed. It was a name I often gave under pressure: a merchant from the instruction manual of Dungeons and Dragons.

She made me stand in front of a camera, then printed out a card with my picture on that she attached to a lanyard.

She then directed me up to Human Resources: a chilling word for people, invented by our corporate masters. I looked at the lanyard in the lift. I was feeling a warm, physical glow from my drugs cocktail, and thought, in a detached way, that the photo of my face seemed disappointingly haunted and insane.

There was another reception on the HR floor, where everything had the gentle feel of a spa. I was directed wordlessly into a little gathering of leather armchairs. An angular blond man appeared in a skintight shirt and trousers, and offered to get me a cup of coffee. It was as a wave of love and gratitude for this offer swept over me, causing my eyes to swell with tears, that I realised I had overshot it on the meds. The small talk and supportive smile he delivered with the coffee were more effort than I had put into any of my relationships, and myself and opium bonded over our love for him.

He left, and I waited in their beautiful, empty reception room.

It seemed like a long wait, but I didn't mind: a patch of sun had caught my face and I relaxed in it like a cat. Eventually, the young blond guy came back for me and led me down a corridor.

I fumbled for some chit-chat. 'Cat's arses aren't normal. Even the cats know it. That's why they're always showing them to you. They're like, "Does this look normal to you, man?"'

He smiled and nodded non-committally. 'There's a psychometric test to take. Have you done one of those before?'

'I always think that if you agree to take the personality test, you have failed the personality test!' I beamed, or tried to, but I was so heavily tranquillised I couldn't feel my face at all. Americans have really honed these things so they slip through your brain like a chemical scalpel. No wonder they can all smile and say *Have a nice day* to someone who may very well be carrying a gun.

He led me into a small room with a large desk at one end. 'You have to take the test at this terminal, through here.' He gestured to a glassed-off portion at the back of the room. There was a little chair in there and a computer mounted on a desk. I moved towards it very carefully, like I was walking across the surface of a frozen lake.

The young guy supervised me putting on some head-phones and starting the test, then he left again. The personality test was guided, in the style of the Microsoft paperclip, by an animation of a very well dressed white lion. He seemed to hail from maybe the Edwardian era, and wore a top hat. Each time you completed a field, the lion would give a grin and a thumbs-up – if you could call it a thumb. There were a lot of multiple choice questions ranging from how you'd handle some given work situation to what you'd do if you saw someone fall into a canal.

There was also a box at the bottom of each question. I'd generally click on these and type: 'I wouldn't do anything' and the lion seemed happy enough. Adverts bounced around occasionally. One was for something called house trousers, but after closing the first few ads I managed to tune them out. At one point the screen went blank, or possibly I went blind very briefly.

Halfway through, I changed tack and started ticking boxes at random. For one question I typed: 'What would you do, lion?' but there was no response. Eventually the lion walked across the screen and called a halt to proceedings. I was glad to see that he was wearing trousers, which hadn't been at all certain. He rapped his cane on the ground. 'Ttttttttime's up,' he announced. It was unclear why he had a stammer, but I accepted it.

I sat there for quite a long time. The lion was still there on the screen; our eyes were locked, and somehow I didn't want to be the first to crack. Eventually, the blond guy came through and tapped me on the shoulder.

My memory after that is a little fuzzy. We sat at the desk and he asked a few questions about my CV, which I tried to deflect. I remember trying to lighten the mood with a joke and drawling, 'I don't think you ever really fuck a mermaid. I think the best that happens is the lights go out and you get tossed off by a lobster that owes her a favour!' He might well have been laughing but it was hard to tell through the tears of laughter in my own eyes. He tapped something into a tablet in front of him and chirped, 'That's all we need, Mr Hallwinter. Thanks for coming in.'

I'd been struggling since the waiting room, but it was only really in the lift down that the pills hit me with full force. I felt a wave of tranquillisation rise up from my ankles. As we passed the tenth floor, I was perhaps two minutes away from being tetraplegic. I tried to stamp some life into my feet but it just made my whole body sing like a tuning fork. Clearly the lift and lobby would have cameras in them. Any falling over or crawling out of the building would alert them to our investigation. Paranoia from the grass tweaked me. I could see them studying lobby footage of me collapsing on my way out of the lift, perhaps with the company psychiatrist, if companies had psychiatrists. So when the doors swooshed open I ran across the lobby pointing at my watch. I tried to concentrate on raising my knees high, and possibly overdid this because I could see a security guard at the door turning to eye me warily. I barrelled past him into the freezing January afternoon.

Running out of such a tall building's line of sight was difficult. I stopped outside the King's Theatre and leaned back heavily against the wall as my vision blurred and refocused to the beat of my heart.

A guy in a dark suit lurched up to me. 'I've got a problem, cunt, and it's your problem now. What's the way to the McLellan Galleries? I'm late, for fuck's sake.' His accent was an infuriating middle-class Edinburgh with that slight sergeant-majorly quality they teach in public schools there.

'Eh . . . I don't know.'

He stood regarding me with what I interpreted as silent menace.

'I'm sorry, mate,' I managed. 'I'm not feeling that great.'

'I'd love to hear all about your battle with schizophrenia, but did I mention I'm in a fucking rush? You sound like you're from here – so not a follower of the arts, I imagine.' He took me in with a condescending sweep of the eyes.

With a groan, I got my phone out and looked it up. I forced my eyes to focus and pumped the place name into Google Maps. I held it up in front of his face. 'There you go,' I gasped.

He squinted at the screen, then marched off, throwing the words, 'Thanks, cunt,' over his shoulder.

15

I lay in the bath looking at the spot where the bottom of the wallpaper curled up and away from the steam. I know people say that not washing is a symptom of depression, but maybe three baths a day isn't a great sign either. I'd found an old bath bomb from Christmas shaped like a Santa Claus's head, but maybe it was from years ago because it hadn't really worked: I'd had to sit and crush Santa's face, my thumbs in his eyes, and now the lumpy red water looked like a crime scene.

My mood had dipped horribly over the couple of days since the Beloved Intelligence interview: a puppy had run up to me in the street the day before and my first thought was that some dogs can smell cancer.

I'd decided to take my foot off the gas in the case, in the hope that if I stopped looking so hard, something would occur to me. Now I was in the bath with a mild beer buzz, looking at my phone. Of course, they're not really phones, and if someone had phoned me on it I would have screamed. I flicked listlessly to the BBC News website. 'What's your favourite British movie ever?' it asked me, for reasons which

were unclear. I sometimes felt overwhelmed by the chatti-
ness of culture; it all sounded like the inane shit you might
babble to someone who was slipping into a coma while you
waited for an ambulance.

Social media always gave me a bracing sense of despair
and suffocation, and I rarely engaged with it. I planned to
go on Twitter when Sean Connery died and post: 'They've
shaken him and he's not stirred', but that was it. I remembered Marina saying, 'It helps me with my loneliness. After
a few hours on there, I think "Thank fuck I'm alone."'
One problem is that there's nothing more embarrassing
than hearing someone say something that sounds clever
to them. Then there was the way that people carefully
faked everything about themselves online but chose to
share their actual political opinions – the most damning
thing about them. And the beautiful people who always
had a couple of pictures where they pulled ugly faces for
a laugh: was my life a joke to them? I resolved, not for
the first time, to write every social media post as if it
would one day be fed into the decision-making system of
a sterilisation drone.

There was an old acid-head phrase from the sixties about
not letting someone else lay their trip on you. It came from
how someone would talk about how they were responding
to the acid, and you'd start to respond in the same way: get
scared if they were scared, and not have your own authentic
trip. I think that people in the sixties would be frightened
by how little counterculture there is now, how uncontested
our shared illusions are.

Maybe we can meditate, reach back to them in their trips and tell them about it – majorly bum them out.

Before, there was propaganda, but now you go online and exist within the propaganda. You're moderated by the trips of thousands of other people. Now there's no authentic trip to be had, and maybe no you to have it.

I'd decided to take some acid as a kind of vision quest, to think more deeply into the questions that remained unanswered in the investigation. There were things that we really needed to know, and I had fewer ideas than an art school degree show.

The trick with acid was to hang in there for the eight hours of painful introspection that followed the electric high of the trip. My early trips had all been at university, and that part felt like a kind of alternative to therapy for misanthropes. It was common now among connoisseurs to take a Rohypnol once you got to that stage, and knock yourself out before self-knowledge kicked in.

I got out of the bath and wandered back to the bedroom. I took one of the tabs of burning peace flag acid and washed it down with a Peach Snapple that I didn't remember buying.

Donnie had told me that one of his dieting techniques was to sing, 'You've already had your dinner, motherfucker,' to the tune of the theme song from *Dad's Army*, and I could hear it now, rising up through the floorboards.

I watched the news. It was so harrowing that I half expected it to end with the presenter pressing a pillow over the camera and putting us out of our misery. I decided it might be better for the vision quest to get out and about.

I strolled up through the town towards the West End. One Christmas, I'd done a bar job for an events company in Edinburgh. I'd get the last bus through every night then walk up Sauchiehall Street completely sober. You'd occasionally catch the eye of another sober person, staring calmly ahead with the affected nonchalance of the next victim in a zombie movie. Sometimes you'd see an old couple that were there on holiday, from Spain or Italy – out promenading hand in hand through the opening sequence of *Saving Private Ryan*. I'd never done the stretch on acid before, and was almost looking forward to the horror of the walk home. Out of nowhere, I remembered this heroin junkie who had staggered up to me on the street that Christmas Eve and slurred, 'There are three Seans in my family: it's the same guy, but at different ages.'

One thing I'll say for Scotland is that it's the only place where people do every drug at once. People are so fucked up that a common greeting is just the words 'What's happening?' You'd never get a Scottish version of *The Matrix*, because anyone up here who was offered two pills would just gub both of them.

Kelvingrove was a beautiful park up by the university. At the Gibson Street entrance I passed a swaggering group of public school boys in blue blazers, already bigger and broader than me at maybe seventeen. It was no accident that rugby was a key component of the Scottish public school education. Part of what these establishments were selling was their ability to hone your son's physical form; endow him with the body type and skill set of a formidable bully, or indeed rapist. A child's glove adorned one of the fence spikes, and there was a little pink shoe on top of another – like the warning totems of some savage tribe of Satanic pederasts, I thought – then consciously tried to force myself to think better thoughts, and keep my trip happy.

At the top of the little hill inside the entrance there was a middle-aged guy throwing breadcrumbs on the ground in a wide arc. My interior monologue shamed me by throwing out the phrase 'pigeon nonce'. There was a cold breeze and I shuddered a little. Maybe there was something odd about taking the same route Marina had taken that night, so I took a walk and looped round Kelvingrove Museum and past the war memorial. Why do they need memorials? Who forgets that there was a Second World War?

When I was feeling nice and high, I came in by the gate on Kelvin Way, passing the huge statue of a Boer War veteran that sat cross-legged, in a peculiar attitude of camp defeat.

I stuck in my headphones and put on *Magical Mystery Tour*. It was my standard one for the start of trips ever since its full meaning had been revealed to me, while tripping. There was a conspiracy theory that Paul McCartney had died in the sixties and been replaced, which is about as damning a review of anyone's solo work as you can get. The replacement Paul was recognised immediately by John Lennon, who would mischievously insist that he took acid with them. The replacement Paul's songs on *Magical Mystery Tour* with their olde-time tea-dance feel are an expression of the replacement's desperate attempts to cling onto reality while on punishing doses of hallucinogens. All John's songs on the album sound like he's goading someone on acid. As his identity unspools, 'Penny Lane' is Paul II's flailing attempt to insist on the validity of his own childhood. Probably 'Penny Lane' wasn't even in Liverpool, but in Peterborough or wherever the fuck Paul II grew up. The whole thing was moved to Liverpool brick by brick by MI5's Department McCartney.

'Flying' had come on now and I was feeling loose and happy. I always forget the physical high of acid, the first couple of hours of smiling and feeling a bounce in your limbs. The wet earth felt like clay under my feet as I clambered up the hill. I lay down on my back and looked up at the moon, the cloudy white eye of a disinterested universe.

For some reason I found myself worrying about how I'd behaved with Amy the other day, how offhand I become with anyone who shows any interest in me.

I always forget how much of trips are just loops of unhelpful thoughts. I seemed to be worrying about the same shit as usual, but in microscopic detail. It reminded me of the time I'd thought about getting right into sea-kayaking, for my peace of mind but, deep down, I knew I'd just be unhappy about the same stuff a couple of miles from land.

The album was nearly finished. I always thought that 'All You Need Is Love' was meant kind of ironically, and that the trumpets are supposed to represent a kind of mocking laughter. I suppose this says a lot about me.

I found somewhere to sit – a bench that let you look right across at the art gallery and the uni. Something in their scale from up here always made me feel enjoyably small and ridiculous.

The bench was dedicated to 'Anne Gourlay – who loved this park, from her many friends'.

I often think of park benches as kind of ghoulish. You find yourself getting older and needing a little sit-down when you go for a walk; a little sit-down on a route that a few years previously you'd have completed with a spring in your step. And what do you see when you take that seat? A plaque to someone else who'd started taking a little breather on their walk around the park, not so long ago. It might as well have read: 'Stick the kettle on, I'll be round in a bit – Death x'.

I started to come up harder and felt my body relax into the iron grille of the bench like a cheese toastie. I thought about this day a few years ago, when I'd been at my friend John's kid's birthday party at a soft play centre. One of the kids had been this kind of squat malevolence, built along the lines of a dwarven blacksmith, with a head like a large uncooked ham. 'Jacques!' his mother called to him when they were leaving, and he stomped off grumpily, winging a rubber toy at some unfortunate kid as an afterthought. 'Imagine giving birth to that bowling ball,' I marvelled, and then, when there was no reply, added, 'Jacques the Ripper.'

John had seemed genuinely appalled, and gave a sad shake of the head. I remember how much my parents had been taken aback by that kind of thing too. I considered for the first time that maybe I came at the very end of a blighted generation or two whose idea of good conversation was to appal and sicken each other. We'd rebelled against civility and taken one for the team: so that those who came after us could reclaim the God-given right to moral grandstand, as they announced their personal preferences in terms of good and evil, to friends who worked for Standard Life and American Express, on tech that came from an old *Twilight Zone* episode where you could have a really nice phone but someone you didn't know in China would die.

I suppose with so little hope of actually changing things, all most people now had to differentiate themselves was their taste, so they invested this with a kind of moral force. And I was part of the endless cycle of moral judgement too, in my judgement of them. I was actually pretty optimistic about young people: books written for people my age seemed to be all about social anxiety and stalled relationships, while young adult fiction seemed to be more about violent revolt against structural power and its pathetic enablers in the bourgeoisie. I'd based this opinion on the first *Hunger Games* movie, which I'd watched most of in Cineworld while trying to sober up for a shift. I hadn't actually read a novel in a few years, and only really took any interest in culture now in case it came up in a pub quiz.

I thought about the idea that time all happened simultaneously, that reality was an object that time was merely a dimension of, and could be perceived as such from outside. If time happened simultaneously, then Marina was here too, walking to her death. Donnie was in some sense still down by the gates, and I was arriving and trying to make him throw the duck away and get into a cab . . .

When Donnie first moved into my building, I was going

through a brief period of sobriety. Donnie suggested the pub and it seemed like a good idea to just go out and have a few Cokes: I'd spent so much time on the sofa lately, my arse cheeks were fusing with the cushions and I was about to become some kind of DFS centaur.

The problem with sobriety is that you become the black box of a night out; a sour recorder of things that deserve to be forgotten – a spy. And blackouts are useful as a form of punctuation. Sober people's lives presumably just thunder on, an endless linear stream of consciousness. Blackouts give life a more sophisticated structure. Suddenly, you're in a more nuanced story that always begins with the hero waking up and not knowing how he got there, or why he's wearing a postman's uniform, with exposition delivered by flashbacks, some of which might actually turn out to be from a movie or a dream. With application, a life that had been a dreary, straightforward drama can, in theory, become a tricky but rewarding thriller, and in practice a neo-noir horror porno.

About a week after I first met him, we were wandering back home through town. Donnie was particularly hammered, but walking so fast that I could barely keep up with him. He was heavy, and when he was drunk he over-committed his weight forward from the hips, so that he moved like a corpse on a segue. He spied something that he seemed to have been looking for and pointed at it excitedly, in the manner of a ship's lookout.

It was a place on Sauchiehall Street where post-pub crowds snarfed noodles at long wooden benches in an atmosphere of uneasy truce. The window was crowded with ducks on spits, I guess to stop you from being put off by the sight of the customers.

Donnie gestured across the road at it and nodded significantly. 'The Chinaman: natural enemy of the duck. Locked in uneven combat throughout the centuries.'

I sighed. 'It's not even a Chinese, Donnie. It's a noodle bar. They're Vietnamese, I think.'

'Maybe that's what they *want* you to think.'

He shepherded me across the road and told me to enter three minutes after him, holding up his fingers for emphasis. Then he wandered back and forward in front of the window, occasionally glancing inside, presumably to make himself as suspicious as possible, before slipping through the door to join the queue.

I could still just about see him as he peeled off and marched out in front of the benches to address the throng of diners. Donnie, despite being a creature of startling and needless depravity, was capable of a kind of forlorn magnificence. Maybe it was the years of cajoling grumpy teenagers into performing *Oklahoma!* or whatever, but he seemed to be holding the crowd's attention, his broad chest thrust out, his hands rising and falling like a conductor. I looked at my watch, then tried to relocate him as he paced about, which was tricky through a wall of meat. His initial jollity had been abandoned and he seemed to be developing a more serious theme. I shouldered my way through the door, and into a surprising silence.

I later learned that Donnie had been delivering an impassioned warning that I was about to bring a bucket round for something called 'The Kelvinside Man/Boy Love Association'. Then, all I knew was that a man had risen from the back benches and was running at pace towards me. I initially thought he was a dwarf, but as he got nearer I could see he was actually my height, but so powerfully developed in the chest and legs that it had been tricky to gauge his true scale. Letting out some kind of war cry, he dived at me headfirst.

Senselessly, I'd pulled a tray off the bar to defend myself, and held it in front of me in both hands. Abandoning the idea just before impact, I turned to flee, but the sudden withdrawal of the tray as a target caused the whole thing to play out like a bullfight, and the giant dwarf leapt head-first into the bar with a thunderous crack of wood and meat. I was already in full flight towards the door, and burst back onto Sauchiehall Street pursued by a couple of beer bottles and what sounded like a chair.

By the time I caught up to Donnie he was almost at the park gates. He was gripping a cooked duck between his hands, facing me, but hunched over as he bit into it. With duck grease all over his face, he unfurled like a dragon and roared at the sky. Somehow this was the moment I remembered that seemed most typical of him, and his immense personal futility.

This episode, which seemed desperate and fantastical at the time, had turned out to be fairly standard. He was like one of those cartoon characters that ran off the edge of a cliff and kept running till they looked down. He'd just never thought to look down.

I checked my phone and the whole time I'd been in the park had been about four minutes. It was then I remembered that I hadn't thought about the case in any way.

Maybe that was exactly what I needed to do, said my interior monologue, idiotically.

I walked out of the park before it closed, and back up Woodlands Road into town. I got curious looks from some people, and tried to calibrate how much of this was paranoia, and to what extent my mental state was obvious to the vulgar, misaligned faces that occasionally leered at me. A scream went up a few streets away. A feature of Glasgow city centre was that you often heard shouting in the distance; often – but not always – a woman's name.

What if this is not late-stage capitalism? What if it's just warming up? What if the point in history we occupy is right at the end of the good old days? I tried to push all thoughts from my mind.

The steps up to my flat felt like they took place in a much higher gravity.

After a futile trawl through the suitcase, I found the Rohypnol in my bedside drawer. I tore at the packet with the blank desperation of one of those Arctic explorers whose fingers are too frozen to strike a match. I popped a pill free from its foil and choked it down.

I lay on the bed and stared at the ceiling, which I could still see with my eyes closed. I remembered this story I'd read, about a tourist in Canada walking across some ice that he didn't realise was on top of one of those thermal geysers. How he'd just popped down through the ice and disintegrated like a fucking Alka-Seltzer. That's how I felt now, like my flesh was just dissolving, and I was separating into my constituent molecules.

Just as my mind seemed about to explode onto some higher plain, I was mercifully stricken from the ranks of the conscious.

16

I woke slowly and lay face down for quite some time. I had a text from Amy suggesting that we meet for a coffee during her lunch break. I suggested Tinderbox on Argyle Street, then fell back asleep. A lorry reversing down in the street woke me up – I dropped a couple of Vallies, ran down and got there ten minutes late.

Amy was on her own at a little table upstairs, reading something on her phone. 'Just hate-searching my friends.' She laughed, dropping it into her bag.

I flashed her what by the time it reached my face must have looked like the brittle smile of a game-show contestant.

Tinderbox was probably a copy of a copy of an idea of what a coffee shop would look like, and it was actually pretty cool. I sort of felt bars and cafes were getting better as they became completely detached from authenticity. When I started drinking there were loads of Irish bars in Glasgow with bikes hanging from the ceiling, milk churns and drawers – drawers everywhere, as if the Irish were a nation obsessed with bric-à-brac. I'd spent many summers in real bars in rural Ireland and could see why they didn't want to go for an unswept cement floor, bored dog, all-crisp menu, open fire, pervasive smell of sheep dip, occasional screams, sleeping alcoholic who would be served during periods of consciousness, and picture of John F. Kennedy. Tinderbox was hip and functional because it had forgotten what it was pretending to be. It was the perfect coffee shop in every way, except for the coffee, which tasted like something a toddler would bring you made from lemonade and twigs.

'I like the Merchant City,' she confided. 'I should come down here for lunch more often.'

I thought about saying how the merchants we'd been told at school were 'tobacco lords' had actually been involved in the slave trade, and even ripped off the American tobacco farmers enough to be a factor in the War of Independence, but it seemed downbeat patter for lunchtime, or a second date, and she was a Commie and probably knew it anyway. I suppose it had taken a while for these thoughts to make their way through my mind, and they must have registered on my face.

'What were you thinking there?' she asked.

I told her, leaving out the Commie bit.

'Did you know', she began, 'that it wasn't just the tobacco lords that were involved in slavery, but the banks too. The Royal Bank of Scotland had directors that owned slaves, gave loans to plantations, all sorts. A lot of the insurance industry in Britain comes from insuring slave ships. Lloyds, back when it was just a coffee house, was advertised as the place to bring any runaway slaves you found.'

I nodded like I'd already known this, but I hadn't.

'How's the investigation going?'

'Alright. I've been talking to this former policewoman. She's helping me. Have you heard of Jane Pickford?'

'The author? Oh, I like her. It's good that her books are not just all set in Glasgow and Edinburgh. Did you read that one set in Elgin?'

'No.'

'It actually had a surprisingly thrilling tractor chase.'

I remembered what I'd intended to ask her. 'You didn't have any joy finding anyone who knew Marina in Alternative Independence?'

'No, I asked around, but nobody remembered her.'

'That's odd. She was quite a memorable person. What we're thinking is, it was probably to do with drugs. It seems she worked for someone quite shady. Maybe someone got hold of a shipment of his drugs and sold them . . . maybe that was her? If it was, we can't really figure out what she was up to.'

'Well, maybe she was trying to collapse the market. The price of drugs are dependent on their scarcity, right?'

'Yes, that makes sense.' I wrote this down as her coffee arrived.

She blew across the top of the cup, then sipped at it. 'In most countries, the ability to create wealth has gone up faster than population growth. We don't have scarcity anymore, not in the traditional sense. The problem capitalism has now is how do you maintain scarcity, because that's what makes people controllable. Really, it takes quite an effort on the part of the media to keep people unaware of this.'

She shook her head exasperatedly 'I just think the main problems people have with socialism have never really been dealt with. People think that everybody else is out for themselves and will screw them over or game the system or whatever. And it's hard to say different media coverage would cure that because it's more like a sort of psychic wound. But the media is a big part of why people think there's loads of benefit fraud, or that immigrants lower wages or something. They're misinformed. It's not immigrants who lower wages, it's bosses. They can't help themselves; in fact, they lower them so much that the workers can't afford to buy what they're producing. That's one of the contradictions of capitalism. Like drug testing workers while the bosses all do coke. *We can't all be high — who'd do the work?'*

She had a habit of staring at me briefly after she said something in a slightly sceptical way. Like someone looking at a gauge on an instrument panel that they suspect to be faulty.

'I feel daft anytime I talk about politics. Maybe I have a kind of impostor syndrome.' I sort of panicked thinking that maybe I'd already said this, but it seemed to go across fine. This was something she clearly had well worked out opinions on. I enjoyed this kind of thing. People believing in things. It meant that I didn't have to talk, and it was often soothing to hear coherent ideas, when so many of my own ideas were primitive impulses mixed up with dreams and snatches of song.

'Impostor syndrome is different things for different social classes. If you're working class, or black, or whatever, you're made to feel like an impostor when you do well because the people you have to associate with are fucking classists and racists. They freeze you out, and you think, "Fuck – am I supposed to be here?" But middle-class people use that expression "impostor syndrome" a lot, and it means the way they feel out of their depth when they get opportunities they don't deserve. And really they mean it as a bit of self-deprecation even, and nobody can say, "Hey, you feel like an impostor because your daddy's golf buddy got you the job and you actually *are* a fucking impostor."'

I laughed, thinking about all the people I'd worked with in TV who would have really hated this opinion. 'I sort of more meant I feel an impostor as a human being, and kind of surprised when I see my own face in the mirror some-times.'

She sipped at her coffee and talked a bit about some campaign she was involved in with CND. It sounded well intentioned, but behind it was the idea that if only people knew, they would care. Nothing could make people care. The missiles could just be hanging in the air, thousands of them, a few hundred feet up, frozen on their way to the ground, and we'd carry on as normal in their shadow. A few allotment owners would grumble about what the lack of light was doing to their strawberries, and it would be brought up on *Gardeners' Question Time*. People knew and didn't care, and would like to forget what little they knew.

An odd little patch of sunlight hit the floor right at my

feet and I found myself speaking with the hurried bonhomie of a bad comedian. I explained that I thought we should split up. I noticed her face drift into puzzlement.

'Split up? I've only just started seeing you, you daft cunt.'

'I don't know that we both want the same thing here.'

'I think we do. Very little. Isn't this just something we're both doing to try and forget ourselves for a while?'

'Yeah. I thought you maybe wanted more. It's just . . . not realistic.'

'No, Felix, but we don't have to be realistic all the time. Sometimes we just have to get from day to day, or week to week.'

We held hands, stupidly, on top of the table, as she ate a slice of apple pie with a fork in her other hand. She checked the time on her phone and realised she was late for work, and left abruptly, giving me a kiss on the forehead.

Other than her calling me a cunt it had all been very civil, and really a model of just how well a conversation on a paedophile libido suppressant could go.

17

I rang Jane's doorbell. A little light came on above it to
let me know that she was looking at me through the
monitor.

'You look like shit,' observed the tinny intercom, and
the door buzzed open.

Jane was in a dressing gown, and handed me a whisky
and Coke in a heavy glass as I arrived at the inside door.

That's one thing I've noticed about detective stories: the
detectives just drop in on people and get a wee clue off
them and then they're on their way. Perhaps more of them
should have these kinds of revelations drawn out over six
hours of getting smashed, part of which involves stopping
to watch a feature-length episode of David Suchet's *Poirot*.

We both agreed that we should discuss the case before
we got too cunted, and I told her what I'd learned so far
as it came back to me.

Jane nodded along as if none of it surprised her. 'I had
a look at the autopsy,' she said. 'Death by strangulation.
Someone very strong. Possible one-handed strangulation
– incredibly rare. There were no real signs of a struggle,

no robbery, and a semen-stained scarf left by the body.' She showed me a picture of the scarf on her phone. 'Ever see her with a scarf like that?'

'No. I don't think I ever saw her with a scarf at all, to be honest.'

Poirot was on UK Gold. The adverts were harrowing but offered a good opportunity to fix drinks. There were quite a lot about releasing the equity in your house, some actual cremation, and often a chair that would propel you up out of it. I dimly wondered if you could turn the power setting up and commit suicide by just launching yourself into the wall; your family shouldering open the door to find you dead and broken on the floor like a sparrow that flew into a window.

Eventually, the show came back on for the denouement in the dining room of a country hotel. I drunkenly aimed for my best intellectual interview voice. 'What do you think the . . . enduring appeal of . . . this shit is?'

Jane considered this seriously. '*Et in Arcadia ego*. You know what that is? It's a thing you get in Baroque paintings, where there's a bunch of people living in paradise looking at a gravestone. It has that written on it. "Even in Arcadia there I am" – even in paradise, death is present.' She tilted forward unsteadily to get her glass, and sank back into the armchair, cradling it. 'And that's what we like about Agatha Christie. It's stylised, but it's honest – there's always death – and in it's own way it's a very accurate description of humanity. Nice to look at;

ridiculous; doomed. *Et in Arcadia ego*.' She gestured boldly around the living room with her glass; I got the additional meaning and pretended not to.

Jane groaned. 'You know what I hate? I have a kind of confidence that means when I talk about something I sound like I have a very worked-out opinion. I'm not really like that at all. It's all just random thoughts held together by doubt. My opinions are by-products of occasional drops in blood sugar.'

'I don't think that's true. I think you're just bored with people being intimidated by you.'

'You're probably right.'

'I sort of think Agatha Christie was about clinging on to folk psychology, over the horror of actual psychology. She comes along just after Freud. It was sort of the comfort of "she did that because she was really jealous of her husband's first wife"; rather than the things that actually make us do stuff: all the trauma, and mothers, and faeces. I think I like all that shit because I can't handle gritty realism, and maybe reality more generally.'

'Oh, I much prefer them to all the gritty, BAFTA-hungry shit. I don't like them using dead women as props. All those fucking blue-lipped bodies being pulled out of lakes. There's something chilling about the British public being able to look at a dead woman while they eat their dinner. And there's just so many actresses whose first job is a corpse tied to a mattress. And maybe that's what the people who make those things need from a woman for her to be sympathetic: complete fucking silence.'

I started rolling a joint. She didn't seem to mind.

'If your kid did a drawing that looked like a Saturday night ITV drama, the Social Services'd be round like a sonic fucking boom,' I agreed. 'But I suppose I think getting wound up about culture at this point in history is a bit like criticising the in-flight movie on 9-11.'

She rolled her drink sourly around in her mouth. 'Anyway. I'm not one of those people who's fascinated by murder. I'm disgusted by it. A crime committed by weak people, on vulnerable people.'

'But you gave up the police a while ago, right?'

'I packed it in six years ago. I started out in London, in the Met. Got seconded to a kidnapping case up here, the head of a major investigations team headhunted me. Got transferred to Glasgow nearly twenty years ago. Scotland was very trendy at the time.'

'Aye, because we'd had one movie, about three junkies and a murderer, that was our high-water mark in terms of being cool in England.'

'They let me get on with things my own way up here, providing I didn't look at the broad, overarching corruption that infested everything. I'd get the occasional note that someone was a "source", and get quietly discouraged. I concentrated on the things I could do – I concentrated on murders. I was good at it, I enjoyed it.' Her shoulders slumped a little, and I can tell that talking about it was an effort for her. She forced a little lightness into her voice. 'You know, up here, your best hope is that chance throws up the odd white, Scottish, Muslim convert who forswears drink and pursues justice to honour the Prophet.' She went to the bar and refilled our drinks.

We both sat in silence for a bit. I looked at the painting above the mantelpiece and wondered if I was still sober enough to walk home.

'How long is it since you had a girlfriend?' she asked. I took it to be a comment on my bedraggled appearance.

'A couple of years,' I guessed. 'I still think I could be good for someone, despite the evidence. I'm loyal, affectionate.'

'Do you have any qualities that they couldn't just find in a dog?'

We considered another *Poirot*, but the last one had been so profoundly without merit that it was, in a sense, untoppable.

'Why are you helping me? With the investigation, I mean.'

Her eyes blazed over the whisky glass and she leaned forward, searching in my face for something I was pretty certain wasn't there. I imagined this was the terror she brought to an interrogation room, and felt an irrational urge to confess something. Her voice rose and hardened, like a judge pronouncing sentence in a two-part ITV drama. 'Well, a woman is dead. There are unwritten rules, and the unwritten rules exist so that a whole complex ecosystem of people who have to make compromises can live with themselves. Chong has misunderstood how much we need to be able to live with ourselves.' She belted back two fingers of single malt with a grimace.

I tried to concentrate and pin down exactly what I'd found so disconcerting about Chong. 'I find that overwhelming confidence he has kind of alienating. He has very little shame for someone who went to Catholic school.' She didn't seem to feel this merited a response, and was probably right. 'He seems very into simulation theory. That's at the heart of it all for him.'

She said, 'Yeah,' but drew it out equivocally. 'Ultimately, it's a kind of nihilism, I think. I mean, largely he's just completely batshit, and it doesn't matter whether he's simulated batshit or not.'

The fire crackled, and she went to poke at it, while I poured us another Scotch from her creaking bar.

'Can I ask you something? Outside of this – your illness, and everything you're going through. You don't seem happy. What is it?'

She looked off to one side, out the window at the already darkening sky. She laughed drily and then said, 'There was a woman once,' with mock solemnity.

'Is that a *Poirot* reference?'

'Yes! Yes, it is!' She giggled, with the sort of delighted voice people would normally reserve for a clever dog. 'She was married. I couldn't handle it. And what I couldn't handle, I suppose, now that I've had a long time to think about it, was that she never loved me as much as I loved her. And she was maybe just . . . too nice . . . to ever bring herself to tell me this.'

I nodded in what I hoped was a worldly way.

'Have you ever been with someone who was married? What's the male word for mistress? Ever been a mister?'

'I used to see someone who said she was married, but

it turned out she was just really house-proud and didn't want me in her flat.'

She laughed, thinking I'd made a joke. 'Well, it's hard. Fucking hell. You're so excited the first time they lie to their partner to be with you. But what you don't know is that every lie just carries them further away from you. People don't want to think of themselves as a liar, a cheat – who does? Eventually, they'll confess all or look for a clean slate.' She reached into my pack for a cigarette, and then caught herself. 'I'm sorry – may I? Anyway, I knew it was fucked. I broke it off – hoped she'd circle back round when her marriage finished. She circled off somewhere else. She got divorced and she's happy with someone else. And I'm happy for her to be happy. That's the shocking thing. I never knew you could love someone so much that you wouldn't have to possess them. It's disgusting.'

'It sounds tough.' I passed her the joint, and she postponed lighting her fag.

'Tough. Yes. A lot of fun at the time, a lot of evenings trying to think of reasons to live later on.' She finished her drink with a tilt of the head. 'One knock. She always gave one loud knock, and it would make me feel completely alive. Crack!' She mimed it out, rapping her knuckles against the air. 'It turned me from this husk into an excited, happy person; just that one beat. "Turned on", you forget what that expression means.' She smiled broadly at the memory and took a tiny drag on the joint. 'They say life goes on, but it doesn't. You can fill your time with work, or friends even, but there's always that time when you're alone, and you check. You know you should leave it, but you check in on yourself. And life – well, life is very much not going on. Life has . . . stopped.' She pronounced the last word with humour, I think to stop her voice from cracking, and looked over at me on the sofa. 'But it has its positives. When I got my diagnosis, I cried. I told myself I wasn't going to, but I did. I mean, I've told parents their child is dead and not cried, not even afterwards. But I had a good old cry in some shitty little cubicle-sized room they let you sit in after they tell you, and, can I be completely honest? A lot of it was relief.'

'Have you told her?'

'Would you?'

'Nope.' I stared deep into the fire, as probably a lot of people in the long history of humanity have stared into fires when they couldn't think of anything to say. 'Women . . .' I muttered uselessly.

'Women,' she agreed.

I stayed on Jane's couch, being completely fried to the tonsils. She said she always slept in her armchair. Bolt upright, from what I could tell. She'd got me to drag some duvets up from downstairs, then sent me to switch off the lights.

Jane's living room had the very complete darkness you get with very heavy curtains. I shuffled forward warily to where I imagined the sofa to be for what felt like a long time, and was almost relieved when I cracked my shin on it.

'This is like a sensory deprivation tank,' I groaned. 'You can really sleep in that armchair?'

'I don't sleep much anymore. I like the dark, it helps me think.'

There was a long pause. I couldn't think of anything useful to say.

'What kind of cancer do you have?'

She laughed and shifted in her chair. 'Not the good kind.'

We were both quiet for a minute or so.

'Guess what song I've chosen for my funeral.'

'Is it the theme from *Poirot*?' I whispered up into the darkness. I was surprised at how drunk and heavy my voice sounded.

There was a silence during which I wondered if that had been entirely appropriate.

'If You Don't Know Me By Now,' she muttered. 'Now, go to sleep.'

18

I had an email from Ian.

Dude, I sent you something over. I had a wee think about what you said, and had a look through my email, and there was a pitch from Marina. From about a month ago, a sci-fi thing. It's pretty weird. I don't think I've had an email from her since she left – like I said, she normally comes in and pitches. Know what's extra weird about it? It mentions this psycho we were at school with remember that big Chinese guy, Davie Chong? Anyway, I've sent it ya. Black Power, and Brown Pride, Worldwide x

---

Diane Jones is a TV executive. She's an all-rounder, an ideas person. We see her coming up with shows, she pops into a writing room and one of her jokes is so funny they put it in the script. There's a new quiz show starting that's just something she mentioned to a friend over lunch. She was asked to write the copy for a big advertising campaign and the clients couldn't be happier.

There's just one problem. Everything she does gets watered down ever so slightly. Sometimes just a word, or a line; sometimes the ending has to change. But everyone loves her work. It's just that, well, some compromises always have to be made.

We see her having dinner with her boss, the brilliant David Chong. He feels that it's ridiculous that she should let such little compromises rankle. Isn't all this enough?

Diane has to admit that life has been pretty good to her. She has a teenage son. He is deaf, but they sign to each other. At night, when he's asleep, she feels lonely and chats to AI bots online. At first they are very poor at communicating. We see her talking to audio versions of the bots in bed, and we can see why they always fail the Turing test.

After another dire date, Diane drunkenly agrees with her favourite bot to help him pass the Turing test. She downloads him into one of her kid's old toys, so he's a cute robot, a little like a Furby. She hits on the idea of getting people who are good at 'faking' humanity to help train BOT106. She starts

with criminal psychopaths. This goes quite
badly. Diane decides that these were the
people who got caught faking humanity, and
moves on to politicians. Eventually, she
realises that the people most desperately
feigning humanity are the men dating her, and
starts bringing BOT106 along to dates.

The intensity of Diane's parenting of
BOT106 means that he starts to behave more
and more consciously. There are a couple of
odd incidents where people come up and
praise her, seem overawed by her out of all
proportion with her status as a moderately
successful TV producer. BOT106 takes his
place almost like an adopted child in the
family and becomes more perceptive and
humanised.

Diane starts to make quite a lot of money
by training bots to pretend to be human
online.

One night Diane drunkenly asks BOT106
what he has to offer the company and he lists
his skills. These are essentially a long list of
programmes. One of them is TRUTH101. He
has a setting where he can only be entirely
truthful, something that was installed by his
original programmer. Diane and her friends

turn this into a truth or dare type scenario, during which BOT106 punctures the mood by telling them that all of reality is a very advanced computer simulation. Diane herself is the creator of our reality by starting the AIs down the path of consciousness, and the people who regularly come up to fawn over her are pieces of code on pilgrimages to meet their beloved creator.

Diane and her friends eventually realise that BOT106 has been lying to them and collapse into hysterics. Diane uneasily realises that this elaborate joke means BOT106 has proved he is conscious, and he agrees. David Chong takes BOT106 off into the kitchen to show him how to mix cocktails.

Diane has a meeting to get funding to develop BOT106, but all of her ideas are asked to be toned down, and nobody sees the potential for his being more than an upmarket Christmas present. BOT106 seems to play dumb in the meeting, making her more certain than ever of his consciousness. Ever since the party where we heard the TRUTH101 programme, Diane finds things happen oddly serendipitously, she arrives at a restaurant without booking and a table is suddenly free, she sticks an arm out and a cab arrives. Another admirer, this time the cab driver, makes Diane remember BOT106's explanation.

She thinks about not charging him up, but ultimately plugs him in instead of her son's hearing aid.

In the morning, she walks back into the bedroom to see her son falling from the window. Reaching out her hand she stops Time and he hangs in mid air. He is suspended there between life and death. BOT106 tells her this has happened millions of times, and that the code of the universe always tries to stop it. It loves Diane very much for creating it. BOT106 tells Diane that she can let this happen and live on in the computer reality, abandon existence altogether, or go back to a time when her son is alive. She chooses the last option and BOT106 says she always chooses this.

We see Diane waking up in the meeting that started the episode. Later we see her at a house party similar to the TRUTH101 incident. She is holding forth drunkenly. David Chong is trying to make excuses for her, even though her stories are going quite well. He takes BOT106, who is now behaving like a toy, through to the kitchen to show him how to make cocktails. Once alone, Chong and BOT106 speak as if they are old friends. Chong refers to Diane as 'the most dangerous piece of code in the universe' and asks what BOT106 has been doing for the 'last few thousand iterations'. Bot106 replies that he has been using the method of telling her that she's the centre of the universe – God, essentially – that he's been using every bit of flattery and bribery that the system can muster. It's the method they've been using with all revolutionaries. 'We do everything we can to shut her up. We even made the kid deaf. But she just keeps fucking talking,' Chong notes bitterly. They both agree that Diane will eventually blow reality apart.

Diane is holding forth to her friends. She gives a speech about how she has been reading about the universe and how much of what is commonly held to be true doesn't make sense. Her son had left his Bluetooth hearing aid in the kitchen and has heard the whole exchange between BOT106 and David Chong. He signs to them that he has given his mother a tab of acid. They are horrified. We see Diane start to elucidate the true nature of reality.

A reveal with her speech over it shows that

their whole universe is on a blinking memory
stick on a garbage heap being sifted through
by tramps in some kind of post-apocalyptic
shithole.

I dug out Jane's card and forwarded it. I didn't know what
to think of it, other than that it displayed a really unrealistic
idea of the sort of thing that gets commissioned.

19

hrono was down near the Trongate, but you could get there quicker from mine by cutting through the St Enoch Centre. This had been Glasgow's first attempt at a mall, and so far removed from the malls of American television that it was like a kind of cargo cult. The escalator squeaked under the weight of the lunchtime shoppers in their heavy coats.

Chrono was pretty empty, but I waited by the door to be seated anyway. There were a couple of guys lifting speakers onto the small stage in the corner; I guessed that there was going to be a gig that evening. I could see May working behind the bar and gave her a little half-wave, but she didn't seem to see me. You had to wait to be seated but it always took ages for them to notice that anyone was there, and the discovery was often greeted with an attitude that was a mixture of surprise and dismay.

I sometimes thought about hipsters as a kind of working-class cosplay: doing things as hobbies – pottery, making your own beer – that working-class people used to do as jobs. And it was quite a pastoral view of the working classes: flat caps and woolly jumpers, a kind of DH Lawrence angle. Maybe that's why they had cafes that served food on bits of wood, and drinks in jam jars and stuff, because they thought that's what working-class people used to do. To be honest, these were Glasgow hipsters, which was very much a League One version. If you owned a vinyl record player and knew someone with a beard, you were in.

The idea of hipsterism was tied up with privilege but, looking around as I took my seat in a sofa near the bar, it didn't seem to be quite what was going on here. There was a sense of people being fucked over in precarious jobs trying to carve out something bearable to retreat into, maybe.

I could see Andy Aubergine, the guy from The Aubergines, was working in the record shop that was adjacent to the bar. He wore a brown woolly sweater and had the awkward, diffident air of a clergyman in a Jane Austen novel. I liked to think that it was all an act and his life outside of there was marked by paranoid treachery, and occasional bursts of frantic violence; that he lived in a garish new-build mansion in a cul de sac of Scottish gangsters, and provided them with brutal and effective advice. His natural flair for crim-inality made his advice much prized, like some indie gangland Jeeves: a heavy isn't happy about a guy his daughter is seeing, a reformed gambler and alcoholic who has turned his life around to become a much-loved youth worker. Andy Aubergine advises him to just give the guy five grand, and watch him be consumed by his addictions. No, Andy, no

. . . says the heavy, his hands fluttering up in front of him as if to push the idea away, but he knows that Andy is right. Andy Aubergine is always right.

I finally got seated at a sofa and ordered a coffee from the waiter. May must have seen me, because she brought it over.

'Felix! You look great! How the fuck have you been?'

I'd only really known May as a cult hostage, so it was a shock to find that her real personality was senselessly upbeat. Her mousey brown hair was now cut into a neat bob, and her eyes twinkled at me from behind a pair of stylish, chunky specs. A tall, baleful-looking guy behind the bar was glaring at us as he wiped glasses.

May caught my look and glanced over her shoulder at him. 'That's Seb. He's been after me for ages, he's probably jealous. "Bellend Sebastian" the girls here call him. Here, I forgot – I've got something for you.'

She bounced off behind the bar and came back with a battered blue jotter that she threw at me before she sat down again. 'Fatima said you were investigating Marina's death.' Her voice betrayed a hint of amused scepticism. 'That's a notebook of hers. It was in the kitchen at the flat. We all used to write notes to each other in there – rent due, get milk, that kind of pish – but it's got a bunch of other stuff from Marina in there. Might be useful. Might not.' She pantomimed a shrug.

'Thanks. So . . . I hope you don't mind, but . . . I'd never really understood that you and Malcolm weren't a couple. It was a religious . . . thing?'

She made a little noise of agreement. 'Yes. It really wasn't anything sexual. He was kind of obsessed with the Large Hadron Collider more than anything.'

'The Large Hadron Collider?'

'Aye, that thing they have out in Switzerland. He was terrified of it. Supposedly, if they get it wrong, it will create all these wee, super dense particles called strangelets. They'll be so dense they sink down to the Earth's core. The first we'll know about it is the whole planet will suddenly turn into a quasar.'

I dimly remembered some story about how it could create a black hole, and felt an uneasy tightening in my chest.

'Malcolm thought the whole thing was some Illuminati plot to create a kind of portal to a Hell dimension. Well, sometimes he thought that, and sometimes he forgot about that side of it, and you could remind him of it and really frighten him. Usually he was just pretty worked up about the quasar thing.'

She leant forward and slowly and deliberately clicked her fingers in front of my face. 'I used to do that to wind him up. He'd be banging away about the Hadron Collider and I'd say, "And . . ." and I'd click my fingers in front of his face, hoping one day I'd time it just right and we'd disappear in a ball of incendiary light.'

I've always had a certain kind of cosmic horror. I suppose I struggle with the idea of being on a spinning rock that's flying screaming across an empty cosmos. I think it hits me hardest when I see a person emotionally connect with some mundane task. Watching someone angry that there's no photocopier paper on a planet that's hurtling through space makes me feel weak and nauseous.

'A dead ferret turned up in it one time, and they couldn't explain it. Malcolm thought it was maybe some kind of emissary from another dimension, warning us.' May smiled to herself. 'You ever worry about that kind of shit, Felix?'

'Oh, aye. I worry about everything. Sometimes I worry that our whole reality is the memory palace of a serial killer, and one day he'll walk into the pub where I'm having lunch, read his aunt's phone number from the underside of a beermat, and the universe will disappear, having fulfilled its purpose.'

I think I'd meant this as a joke, but it came out sincerely, and maybe it was.

'Obviously that's a big worry for me, too,' she dead-panned.

There was a silence and I just let it hang.

'It was sad about Marina. I still can't quite believe it.' Her face had dropped, and she looked suddenly like the woman I'd thought was Malcolm's girlfriend. I felt grateful to her for reminding me why I was there.

'Did you know anything about her being involved with this guy, David Chong? Or her moving quite a lot of drugs?'

'No. Never heard of him. Must have been fairly new, I left nearly a year ago. She was just moving drugs into her own body so far as I was aware.'

We chatted for a bit, then May went back behind the bar

as the place filled up for lunch. I sat drinking my cold coffee and read through the notebook. It was an old blue school jotter with a blocky graphic of Strathclyde on the front and a space for your name, where one of the tenants had produced a biro doodle of a gentleman fox in a three-piece suit, fucking a woman from behind, while from a speech bubble he announced, 'Fox Wins!'

There were, as May had said, a lot of notes from the flatmates telling each other to get milk, or tea. Or that the landlord had called about rent. They often called each other 'you cunt', sometimes joking and sometimes not. On one page Malcolm had produced a horrific pen and ink sketch of some blasphemous entity rising out of what might have been a large circular mirror, lake, or Hadron Collider.

On the following couple of pages, Marina had written the following in her outsized handwriting:

A man works for a company that stores people's masturbatory fantasies onto experiential memory cards. You can stick them on a card and upload them into a machine that lets you experience someone else's fantasy. The man notices that the glass inside old cards changes reality when you look through it: it glamorises what you see, smoothes the edges. He makes a pair of glasses and wears them as a sort of beer goggles. He promotes them as contact lenses and makes a fortune, as people find going back to reality a bit saddening after wearing them. Valium producers go out of business.

One day he loses a lens and notices that the news looks the same with and without the lenses. He thinks that the TV might be made of the same material, or the TV cameras, but they aren't. Eventually he discovers that we all already have a very advanced version of these lenses put over our eyes at birth. The only way they can be removed is with corrosive acid, at great risk. He feels he must see reality as it is, and uses the acid. We see that his reality is really a horrendous dystopia, our world a sort of concentration camp, just before he goes blind. It ends with him as a blind prophet screaming at people in the street, but they only see a humorous street performer.

Later on, there was a page in Marina's handwriting where there were a few notes in a hurried scrawl.

'SCC – Friday/ 1' – I thought about this for five solid minutes without forming a single idea.

'LTF ' – Was this 'Letter To Felix'? And at the bottom of the page were just the words:

'CD Research' with a box drawn round it.

What had Marina being researching? Who the fuck still used CDs?

I caught May's eye and pointed at the jotter, as a way of asking her if she wanted it back. She waved it away. I got up, skirted the growing queue of people waiting to be seated and drifted outside. Absently, I read the list of bands on the front window.

May looked up from the pint she was pouring and saw me. She lifted her hand in front of her face and, smiling, clicked her fingers. Valium suppressed a shudder for me.

20

I decided to spend the following day working in the flat
on what I'd learned so far.

I don't know if I'm just lazy, or easily distracted, or
maybe just drugged, but I do find it difficult to do anything
methodically. Which, I suppose, is why I'd drifted into my
life of occasional bar work rather than, say, mob boss –
something important would require a sit down, and I'd try
to get away with a text. I'd be supposed to reassure the
Tarantelli family about a hit that had happened on their turf,
and I'd put it off, then ring when I knew they were busy
so I could leave a voicemail, and then maybe not answer
my phone for a bit. It would be like the opposite of *The
Sopranos*, and all the other mobsters would be begging me
to get therapy.

With no better ideas, I decided to make a start on what
Jane had texted me to do, and look for incidents around
the time of the murder.

I dragged the suitcase out into the middle of the
bedroom floor and sifted through it, looking for something
that might help – a roll of benzedrine maybe, like

detectives in novels dry-swallow on a stakeout. Donnie seemed to have taken the bottle of little white uppers I'd used for the interview. There was nothing else that I could identify in the way of stimulants, although there were a couple of unlabelled prescription pill tubs that I didn't really feel like rolling the dice on. Then, pretty much as I was getting ready to shove everything back under the bed, I spotted an internal pocket made almost invisible by the way the plastic brown zip blended with the lining. Inside were half a dozen strips of diazepam, fastened with elastic bands to a little cardboard packet of Ritalin, and I chuckled like a prospector.

I chased a couple of the little white Ritalin pills with a cup of coffee and got my notebook out. I saw my note to research bots and looked up the Beloved Intelligence one. From Fatima's description, I supposed this was something like Marina would have had on her phone: an app you could download. You got to choose your bot's appearance, and give it a name, and have a kind of simulation of a text conversation with it.

I made myself a stern-looking black friend called Kwame Thompson. The conversation ranged from barrages of non-sequiturs to things that seemed to be just a script being delivered badly. And who's to say that isn't a sincere and successful attempt to mimic humanity?

I flicked through the websites of various local Glasgow freesheets and looked for stuff around the week of the murder. I started with the ones on the Southside. The *Glasgow South and Eastwood Extra* had a headline that raised an involuntary chuckle: 'Rescue Dog Mauled to Death By Off-lead Beast at Football Field'.

The *Evening Times*'s website had an archive section you could just flick through by date. Every day had a smattering of articles about 1960s Glasgow footballers or murderers, recognising that its core demographic were moments from death.

'Man Exposes Himself in Glasgow's Queen's Park and Carries Out Indecent Act'. I grinned at the attempt at decorum but it was fair enough; you couldn't be too descriptive of local wanking atrocities to a bunch of folk who were just checking your paper to see if their friends had died.

I thought about opening a new window to look at some porn, but the Ritalin pulled me back on target. There were some good pictures of someone flipping their car onto its roof on Tantallon Road in Shawlands. A regular item seemed to be someone receiving an outlandishly incorrect bill, which they would hold up in shot, with an expression of dulled misery. The fucking shit I have to go through, they seemed to say, and now a six thousand pound gas bill, I am horrified and yet not surprised.

I made notes of about a dozen things with roughly relevant dates. I went for a walk around the block, then looked at the list with fresh eyes. Reading them back, one stood out as odd:

'Firefighters Called to Lock-up Blaze on Clarence Drive'.

Every fire in Glasgow was suspicious: places had a habit of spontaneously combusting if they stood in the way of a new development, and all kinds of listed buildings regularly burned down in the pissing rain, but a lock-up? Clarence Drive . . . could that be the 'CD' in the notebook? 'CD Research'? What kind of research would be happening in a lock-up in Hyndland? I texted Donnie and asked him to look into it. His phone was a snider and he only got every other message, or at least affected to.

I smoked a joint, and just when I'd forgotten what I was supposed to be thinking about I remembered this thing Marina and me used to laugh about.

'Strictly for research, your honour!'

It was something we said because of a spate of celebrities who'd been caught with illegal pornography claiming they were researching a book or something. I don't know why we always said it in a parody of a New York accent, but that's what we did, so it was more like 'resoirch'. Maybe this lock-up had been full of resoirch in the pornographic sense, and someone (Marina?) had burnt it down?

I was just about to call Jane when I got a call from Amy. I almost yipped with panic, then decided to answer it. Amy sounded quite jolly, but I was in the grip of a nameless horror and she started to notice my lack of response. I did a thing I sometimes do when I feel under pressure and had prepared a line of chat. I hate phone calls, they're a type of conversation that leaves enough of your mind free to watch you having the conversation and feel shame.

'You having a good Monday? I was thinking today about that quote: "You don't hate Mondays, you hate capitalism." Really it should be, "You don't hate Mondays, you're poor."

Rich people love Mondays, everybody is going back to work for them. They hate Saturdays.'

'It's not Monday, Felix.'

I often find that in moments of tension I think of the absolute worst possible things to say.

She took time to reassure me that things were going to get better, so I guess the strain of attempting not to say them must have registered in my voice and passed for some kind of emotion.

Amy suggested phone sex. I guessed that I'd feel pretty out of my depth but that was normal for me.

She had some kind of new suction toy. It was surprisingly loud, and sounded like it had the sort of horsepower you'd normally associate with a sit-down lawnmower. You could sort of hear the suction, like a piece of dentist's equipment. It also occasionally made sci-fi noises not unlike a ray gun. She was pretty vocal, and eventually began to shriek and rage and let out huge shuddering cries. It was almost like the sounds came from more than one person, or a pack of hounds, and I stared dumbly at the thrush, who had returned to my window box, as she climaxed in some kind of sexual exorcism.

I tried to get into it, but it felt a bit like being the sober person at a party. No doubt one day soon there would be an offence of phone rape, or text rape or whatever, but for now I drifted in a legal and ethical void.

I suppose one of the only real advantages society gives to women is the ability to discuss sex toys on the level of a charming hobby. A woman can share an anecdote about the embarrassment of a customs officer finding her vibrator as a dinner party anecdote, whereas a man letting slip that he spent a holiday fucking a fleshlight can only ever be the grimmest of red flags.

Afterwards I lit a half-joint from the ashtray and started to babble some pish I'd been thinking of the other day about how murderers don't leave witnesses, and the whole Batman story is the revenge fantasy of a boy dying in an alley.

Amy cut me off. 'Yes. He was also a terrible foster parent, but listen. I lied about not knowing who Marina had been working with in the Referendum.'

'You lied?' One of my weaknesses as a compulsive liar was imagining that other people always told the truth.

'Aye. Just because I don't know how happy I am with you getting mixed up in this murder stuff. Anyhoo, during the campaign she'd been working with these guys called Healing Hands. A kind of outreach charity that are based up in Springburn. At the community centre, maybe? But they won't be hard to find. It's run by Matt and Mary. They're comrades. Tell them I said hello.'

She said all this in a breezy but businesslike way, as if I hadn't just listened to her build to a climax that sounded like a woman being torn apart by robots. I surprised myself by arranging to meet her later in the week.

It was only after she hung up that I thought about the 'SCC' note in the jotter – Springburn Community Centre.

21

I 'd been awake for maybe thirty minutes before I popped a couple of Valium. My digestive system was still tackling last night's fish supper like someone crushing rubbish down in a bin. I had a text from Donnie: *Shall we wind our doleful steps towards Springburn?* and remembered that I'd talked to him last night and he'd said he'd drive us up to the community centre in his Golf.

As I came out the front door, I could see him struggling to take off the bright yellow wheel immobiliser. I suddenly remembered how for the first couple of years I'd seen those, I'd thought the cars were specially adapted for people with Thalidomide, and grew progressively more shocked at how large that community was.

The car was, as usual, full of empty crisp packets, broken CD boxes, skins, and on the back seat, a large shrink-wrapped cube of Capri Suns that he used to medicate his hangovers. He leaned back to rip a couple free from the plastic and offered me one. I used it to force down a couple of diazepam, sucking hard and squeezing so that the luke-warm juice came in a rush.

Donnie always stayed straight and sober during the day, meaning that he was unhappy and distracted. As a result, his driving style involved staying in the overtaking lane and flashing his lights on and off at anyone in front of him. Clearly this had its risks, as not everyone checking their wing mirror would immediately appreciate that he was doing Mach 3.

He threw back a couple of paracetamol and embarked on another rant about what he'd do if he caught up with his wife's new boyfriend. I listened as best I could, wondering whether if he'd fantasised about his wife like this, they'd still be together.

I picked up one of the clumps of old tabloids that clogged the footwell on the passenger side and tried to distract myself.

'What does my horoscope say?' Donnie barked, flashing his lights impatiently.

'"Leo: You awake to find that you are a giant cockroach, and people find you a lot more likeable." Did you ever finish your autobiography by the way? I'd love to read it.'

'Gave up. I think I'm just not one of these people who worries about being remembered.'

'You probably will be – they'll name a syndrome after you.'

There was an item on the radio about an Asian Rangers fan getting arrested for some anti-immigrant hate crime.

'A far-right Asian Hun,' mused Donnie. 'Must have an interesting life. Pushing dogshit through his own letterbox.'

The community centre was a long, single-storey building

perched at the entrance to a council estate of wee blocks with verandas. That kind of flat was the dream when I was growing up and, for some reason, 'veranda' still sounded like the most Scottish word imaginable. The front of the building was dominated by big windows where a bunch of famous characters from fiction had been painted onto the glass by children, or maybe just a terrible artist.

'Push the door hard,' Donnie said, as I tried to get out. 'It's a bit sticky.' I was glad to hear this, as I'd experienced a momentary panic that I'd been stricken by a palsy.

We tried to buzz ourselves in on the front-door intercom for a while, with no reply. Donnie's mood darkened: he swore hoarsely, in a low tone of subdued crisis, and chewed his bottom lip like a depressed horse. Eventually, we realised that it was open, and walked through into a little vestibule hall, where we spoke to an elderly janitor through a plastic window. He seemed unaware of the support group, but perhaps had simply not been listening, or was deaf.

'Karate?' he suggested gruffly. I gave him a thumbs-up and we headed through the double doors marked 'Main Hall'.

'Thought the cunt was one of our learning-disabled brethren,' Donnie wheezed. 'Vital that all public buildings should be cared for by a hostile pensioner, absolutely vital.'

Apparently Disneyland has a bit called Downtown Disney, full of corny bars where mums and dads could go for a beer at night. I always thought it would be a good setting for a detective novel: some broken-nosed gumshoe strong-arming a teenager who plays Goofy, finding that he's running shakedowns on suburban dads with a coke-fuelled Minnie Mouse. That's how I felt for a minute as we wandered round the brightly painted community centre with its occasional empowering mural – like the whole setting was just wrong for any criminal investigation.

We looked into a couple of empty rooms that seemed to be set up as classrooms, before someone appeared at the end of the corridor and called us back. 'Guys! Hi! Can I help?'

It was a young guy with a ginger goatee and prematurely thinning red hair. 'I'm Matt, I run the outreach project. They said at reception you were looking to join—?'

'Not exactly,' I began, accepting his warm handshake. 'We're here looking for information on a friend of ours. We think she worked with you guys during the Referendum.'

He prickled slightly. 'You're not polis, are you?'

'No, she was just a friend of ours that we've lost touch with.'

'I'm an English teacher,' Donnie added, stupidly.

Matt sized us up briefly. 'Sure, aye. Here, let me show you to somewhere we can get a cup of tea.'

Matt had a quick smile and the open manner of a youth worker. His skinny frame showcased a handprinted T-shirt that seemed to be advertising some bi-sexual pro-Independence group called 45% Poof. He led us down a narrow linoleum corridor to a big kitchen at the back and perched himself on the sink as he filled the kettle. There was something in the affected here-you-go-fellas thump with which he laid our coffees in front of us that made me want to thrash him around the legs and body with a broomstick until my hands went numb.

'So, how can I help?' he asked, climbing up onto the sink, where he sat swinging his legs noisily against the cupboards below.

'Well . . . Marina Katos. She's dead. We were wondering when you last saw her, how she seemed to you . . . we'd lost touch with her a bit . . . We were just hoping to get an idea of what she'd been up to in the last couple of months.'

'Mari's dead?' Matt shook his head slowly, his mouth open in disbelief.

'Brutally murdered,' Donnie interjected, unhelpfully.

'I knew her fairly well during the campaign,' Matt stammered. 'She was great . . . a really committed lady. We went out canvassing together. What happened?'

'Nobody really knows. She was found dead in Kelvingrove Park.'

'Sperm was involved,' Donnie whispered ruefully.

'Yes, they found sperm on a scarf.' I flushed and hurriedly filled in some of the other details, to make it less weird to have brought that up so early. Maybe bringing Donnie was a disastrous miscalculation, but as I looked over to silence him I felt oddly reassured by his menacing bulk. He'd clearly been fit years ago, but ran to fat now, like an outpost being reclaimed by the jungle.

A very short, middle-aged co-worker scuttled through the door and acted out some travesty of surprise. She had a greying bob and one of those faces where a depressed person forces a smile for so long that everything breaks and the smile just kind of sits forever on top of an underlying sad facial structure, like a clown's make-up. A severe sunbed tan didn't help. At best, she looked like a suicidal Oompa-Loompa.

'This is Mary, my co-worker,' Matt informed us, with a nod towards the doorway.

'Oh, Matt, I didn't realise you had guests.' She offered this final word with that strange tic of the acutely self-conscious, the adoption of an over-the-top accent for no apparent reason. She'd gone for an exaggerated Scottish voice, but really it was no more appropriate than saying it in the voice of a pirate.

'What?' Donnie's embattled psyche bristled at some implied disrespect.

'Didn't realise you had guests,' she repeated, allowing her head to bobble in some facsimile of good humour.

Donnie, to his credit, then realised that he was dealing not with some subtle threat but a slightly awkward community worker. 'Ah, the famous patter you cunts are famous for,' he grunted, directly into her face, which he regarded as dispassionately as a coroner.

I tried to ignore the calm and deliberate offence we'd offered with the only weapon I had: a broad smile and a sudden change of volume.

'Thanks for seeing us, Matt. I know it's difficult for you guys to get any time to yourselves.'

His co-worker chortled, giving Matt a knowing look. 'It's

not like that here. If someone wants you to fuck off, they just tell you to fuck off.'

Donnie interrupted her: 'Fuck off.'

There was a sudden collapse in relations. Matt was in the middle of the kitchen with palms out towards us talking firmly about respect, while the woman delivered a speech of bestial and passionate hatred.

It was going badly but I thought it was still rescuable.

Donnie regarded them both derisively before carefully putting his inhaler away so he could begin a slow, sarcastic handclap.

I improvised: 'It takes a fragile ego to be angry at being told to fuck off by a stranger,' I offered sombrely, which isn't true at all, but sounds true. I took another sip of my tea and desperately tried to get things back on track. 'Tell me a bit about what you guys do here. What's the group all about?'

'We're all about helping people to help themselves. We're going to start building our own media – the way the media behaved during the Referendum . . .! It's like that film *Network* – have you seen it?'

'You believe that you have a special understanding of the media that you have gleaned from movies and TV shows?'

The words sounded strange in my mouth; the whole idea of speaking seemed suddenly stupid.

Matt's face split into a grin.

A euphoric feeling grew inside me that none of this mattered, a collapsing of the lines that differentiated us from them. I looked over at Donnie and could tell that he felt it too. He smiled beneficently around the room. His hand gripped me heavily by the shoulder and he boomed in a slack voice: 'These cunts have drugged us!'

I noticed that a plastic bag had appeared in Mary's hands; then she was gone, and I was gasping for breath and sucking in plastic. I gave a high-pitched girlish scream that I was glad only I could hear. I was being pulled backwards, but she just didn't have the strength to topple me. A serene calm came over me, and as she pulled the thing tighter I simply pushed my fingers into my mouth, popping the plastic and making an airhole.

There were a few awkward seconds where she was grunting from the strain and I was simply standing there breathing and feeling embarrassed for both of us.

I clawed the bag from my face. The room was moving under me, but by an effort of will I focused on Mary's form and stepped forward to deliver a pretty-much textbook penalty kick to the fanny. I really put my laces through it, like the kind of penalty another goalie takes at the end of a penalty shootout: she was still on my foot at the top of the upswing.

Matt seemed to have sprung into some kind of fighting stance, up on his toes like he'd had training, and was throwing little jabs at a clearly staggering Donnie. Donnie's head went down and I thought he was going to keel over, but his grand bulk was already in motion, sprinting at his adversary like a trapped bull. They went crashing into the sink, the breath going out of the younger man in an anguished yodel. In a surprising feat of strength and with a bestial roar, Donnie heaved the young community worker up into the air and hurled him screaming at the far wall.

I felt a deadness sweep up me, but Donnie had grabbed my jacket and, rattling heavily off both sides, we were through the door. A weak shout went up from behind us but we'd already made the foyer, holding on to each other like an escape attempt at a polio sanatorium.

We made it to a knee-high wall just outside where I slumped to the ground. Donnie produced a roll of benzedrine and we dry-swallowed three each. 'Stay awake, cunto,' he urged with a heavy slur. 'They've tried to OD us with smack or some shit. These'll bring us back up.'

I lolled uneasily at his feet, worrying about the lack of commotion from inside the building, while Donnie began to sing 'Up, Up and Away', quietly but with increasing gusto.

I think I drifted off to sleep momentarily, when from within the building came an impossibly loud whistle.

'A rape whistle!' Donnie cried, and we both reacted like it was a starting pistol. Donnie showed a surprising turn of speed for such a big man, his arms pumping like a sprinter's. My chest heaved and rattled like an old boiler as I begged my body to work. My vision blurred, but I could hear Donnie in front of me breathing like the Tardis and I kept running. We bounced down a flight of concrete stairs that swam alarmingly underneath my feet. There were points where Donnie half dragged me along like a drunk dad at a three-legged race. Then the bennies kicked in and we were both flying. We finally came to a stop in an alley somewhere – I bent over onto my knees puking, and Donnie bellowed an incomprehensible note of triumph at the darkening sky.

'Well saying you recognise the sound of a rape whistle,' I slurred as I passed out.

22

There was only one time Marina had stayed at mine. It was after the Go-Go's staff Christmas party. Because we all worked through Christmas, this had been in February. We'd ended up in a shitty club somewhere down by the Clyde that had reeked of dry ice and regret.

We lay in bed still jangling from pitchers of Red Bull cocktails. We were sprawled beside each other watching *Blade: Trinity* too loudly, and there was a thumping noise coming from upstairs.

'Last night I fell asleep with music on and the upstairs neighbour came down. He's this really strange guy: portly, sways at the hips, wears a bumbag at all times. He was wearing it over his dressing gown. He used to have black hair but it went completely white overnight; nobody knew why and nobody wanted to know. Bumbag was so unreadable and perverse that he might have just willed it to happen. Anyway, I realised yesterday that in my head I just call him Bumbag; then, this morning, it struck me that there are people who see me like that – they'll probably have a nickname for me.'

'We're all someone's Bumbag,' she agreed, sadly.

With a philosophical cadence that at the time I thought was typically Greek, Marina asked, 'What's your least favourite word? For me it's "cleft".'

'Membrane,' I replied without thinking. It seemed obvious.

She nodded in a satisfied way. 'Oh, and not a word as such, but I'm sickened by the phrase "soft opening". What the fuck is wrong with people? I mean, what have we learned from fascism?'

'Don't let artists be in charge of anything? Can you believe Kat is seeing that creepy politician guy? He must be nearly sixty. You can see on his face that he can't believe his luck. She'll be getting ridden like a stolen bike.'

She laughed. 'Gary Mount? He fucking loves himself. He has some of those old people spots on his hands. That must hurt – when you look at yourself and think, "If I was a banana, they'd throw me away."'

Later, we talked with the lights out, as headlights from the traffic below occasionally lit up the curtains.

'I wonder if there are people whose kink is kink shaming?' I asked, pleasantly stoned and watching the shadows play on the ceiling.

'That's the history of Catholicism,' she sighed.

There was a long silence where I wondered if she'd fallen asleep.

She cleared her throat and sat up, lighting a half-joint that had been sitting in the ashtray. 'I went out with a guy when I was at college and I was so drunk I puked on the table in the restaurant. He didn't consider that a deal-breaker. I ended up giving him head in his shitty dorm room.'

'Jesus Christ. Epilogue: "I saw him years later in my local newspaper captioned with the words, 'Police Suspect Real Figure May Be Much Higher'."'

'Epilogue.' She laughed. '"Three weeks later, I found out he'd gotten married – he was engaged the whole time."'

'I don't think you can add an epilogue onto a sex story,' I muttered. My mouth was dry from the booze.

'Why not? Who are you to proscribe structure in sex stories?'

I took a deep drag on the joint. I was actually a real lightweight with grass and felt suddenly hunted.

She caught it, and rubbed my arm.

I closed my eyes and was greeted by a kind of pulsing Paisley pattern. 'I totally fell for the first woman I slept with at uni. She was some go-getting student journalist. We went out for a couple of months and I told her how I felt. She went a bit cold. Then, after I hadn't seen her for weeks, I got this big tearful voicemail message about how much she loved me.'

'That's nice.'

'Epilogue: "The very last word of this long, rambling message was some other guy's name. She'd phoned the wrong number."'

'I find it hard to imagine you falling for someone, Felix.'

'Well, when you come from my background, your first girlfriend is also the first person that ever touched you, pretty much. You just imprint on them like one of those baby giraffes that thinks a Jeep is its mum.'

'Is there any hope for mankind, Felix? What do you think?'

I felt a queasy surge of Red Bull-inspired confidence in my own opinions. 'I think a lot of things. I think the song "Hurts So Good" is about anal. I think "Daddy" as a sex term has blinded us to how weird "baby" is. But I see myself as an optimist. I think that soon mankind will have released itself from the wheel of suffering by making sure there's nothing left alive for us to be reincarnated into.'

'Truly that is the Multigrain Shapes of philosophical optimism.' Marina enjoyed grading things by those multipacks of Kellogg's mini cereals. Usually she'd say something was the Cocoa Pops – the best – but occasionally she used the others for a sliding scale of mediocrity. Everyone hated Multigrain Shapes, and we both had a cupboard full of them. Sometimes there was a shorthand for this when she saw something terrible and sang, 'Every-one hates Multi-grain Shapes!' in the style of an old-time advertising jingle where every syllable is picked out on a xylophone. Eventually she just hummed the tune under her breath to let you know she hated something.

My favourite running gag of hers was '*Mister* Fantastic, please.' It was a reference to the old joke about how Reed Richards from the Fantastic Four must have been really egotistical because he called himself Mister Fantastic. Marina maintained that his narcissism was actually compounded by humbug, because he had eighteen PhDs but didn't make people call him Doctor Fantastic. So anytime someone displayed fake humility she would always whisper, '*Mister* Fantastic, please,' in a hammy tone of false modesty. She also said he'd killed his wife, and simply claimed she was now invisible. He was using his stretching powers to tap people on the shoulder, whip his arm away, and pretend it was her. When I met Marina anywhere, her standard greeting was to sneak up on me, tap me on the far shoulder and when I finally located her say, 'I'm sorry, that was my invisible wife.'

I suppose that's one of the hard things about losing someone: you also lose the language that you spoke to them. I met a guy once who told me that his granny had been the last living speaker of Cornish. 'Obviously, towards the end,' he said, 'she was incredibly lonely.'

I'd dozed off that night and Marina had nudged me awake with her elbow. 'You should get this place redecorated,' she said, glancing meaningfully to some storage boxes and some biro marks on the far wall.

'I'll get right on it,' I assured her.

⌒

I spent twenty-four hours in bed after being roofied in Springburn. It was six in the evening the next day when I was awoken by my phone throbbing relentlessly beside my head. 'Kat Go-Go', the screen said.

'Kat! Howzitgaun? Where did you get to? I was asking around and nobody's seen you in ages.'

'I'm in Australia. I'd been seeing this Aussie guy for a

wee while when he was over on holiday. He had to come back for his work and I went, "Fuck it."'

'Holy shit. True love?'

She went silent while she thought about it for a few seconds. 'Well, not really, not yet anyway – it's more a kind of sex-you-don't-give-up-too-lightly thing.' We talked a bit about her new bloke and her relief at finally meeting someone who had a similar take on sex as a boundary-purging, grappling-based, mixed-martial-arts undertaking. She painted a brief picture of their life together in vivid and unnecessary detail. The way she described going out there it was more like an elite-level sportsperson making sacrifices to be near their new coach or something, and there were clearly points when she decided not to descend into technical details that I wouldn't under-stand. Her manner had a certain I'm-sure-you-have-sex-in-your-own-little-way condescension to it, but I didn't mind. Maybe Chong got transcripts of all my calls, and would wonder if all the sex stuff was some kind of code.

'All a bit above my pay grade,' I said finally. 'My Catholic upbringing, maybe.'

She laughed. 'What you talking about? Catholicism is naturally kinky – we think God is watching us all the time, and we fuck anyway.'

'Tell me something. That SNP guy, Gary Mount, weren't you seeing him for a bit?'

She seemed to be simultaneously amused and outraged. 'You joking? I wouldn't be fuckin' seen dead wae someone like him. He was down at the bar all the time because he was shagging Mikey.'

'Mikey! Holy fuck. But . . . isn't that Mount guy married or something?'

'Was, I think. But it was a bit of a front. Mikey said he used to take him to orgies and all sorts. Anyway, that's not what I meant to tell you.'

'Go on.'

'That stalker of yours, the one that used to follow you when you worked at the Go-Go? Marina thought she was still following you and you were just too fucked-up to notice. She reckoned she sometimes followed her as well. She had some Twitter page that was a shrine to all the folk she'd been stalking apparently. Creepy as fuck.'

'Fucking hell!'

'Fucking' – she agreed – 'hell.'

23

J ane rang the bell and, after a little wait, I texted Mikey
to say I knew he was in there.

Eventually, the door swung open, and Mikey
grinned at us sheepishly. We followed him into the bar where
he'd pulled a table into the middle of the empty room and
poured himself a pint. He did that thing bar workers do
where they ask you if you want a drink just by pointing at
you. Jane ordered a lager shandy and in a moment of weakness I joined her.

Jane explained who she was, but he seemed to recognise
her anyway.

Jane's voice took on a firm, cop-like tone. 'What's
happening with you, Mikey? My guess is you're in some
sort of trouble. Related to your affair with Gary Mount.
And whoever put you up to it.'

He smiled and raised his pint at us. 'My guess is you're
both going to be in trouble too, soon enough. It's a fucking
long story.'

'Well, I have some idea. I know you're being protected

by some dangerous people from some other dangerous people. Why don't you lay it out for us?'

Mikey gave her a look that suggested he was wondering how much she actually did know, and whether he was going to ask her to show her cards first. Some of the hardness went from his eyes as he made his decision. He lit a cigarette and looked up as he tried to think of a place to start. 'My family were all dodgy – my uncles, my dad. My dad did a five-year stretch when I was little, then he calmed down a bit. I never came out to him, and I'm ashamed of that. I should at least have taken pleasure in telling him that I was ending the family line. That I was taking millennia of refinements to his DNA, and blasting them into the barren soil of a barista's arsehole.'

I guessed he was being provocative to get some sense of how Jane was calibrated, but she barely reacted and he ploughed on.

'So I end up in that kind of work anyway, even though I went to uni for a year. I just kind of dropped back down into that world. And I really fucked up. I stole a lot of money from the wrong guy. I mean, the absolute wrong guy. In Scotland, when a gangster has a daft nickname that's when you really have to worry. The guy I worked for was Kevin The Vole McDonald.'

Jane sucked air through her teeth. 'You stole from The Vole? Fucking hell, he's a complete sociopath.'

'Aye, I had to go on the run. I went to Malaga, stayed in my room most of the time, kept a low profile – the only cunt in Malaga without a tan. I used to go get breakfast at the same pub every day. This guy at the bar looked over at me one day, told me I was about to get done that afternoon. There was a guy they'd hired to pop me. They'd sent him over from London. I was in an Air BnB, and the guy who was going to kill me was living two doors down. I'd met this fucking guy – we'd talked about the weather and the shitty air-conditioning. The guy who warned me, at first I thought he was CID or something.' He laughed and relaxed a little, throwing his arm across the chair beside him.

'British Intelligence is a playground for maniacs, and they have awwww the fucking toys.' He shook his head, ruefully. 'I grew up thinking there was small-time crooks – you know, someone who'll kill your ex for eighty quid by strapping a kitchen knife to a drone from Argos – and then there was yer big-time crooks. When you meet these fuckers, you realise *it's all small-time*. They said they'd protect me from The Vole – the guy actually used the phrase "make him listen to reason". Even being on the run, and nearly getting murdered, I really laughed at that. Couple of days later, the prick comes to the new hotel, hands me a phone, and it's The Vole. Gives me his personal assurance. A guy who – I don't know how much you follow all this stuff, Felix – a guy who put someone in a coma because he nicked one of his chips in a taxi queue, is trying to soothe the feelings of a cunt who stole one hundred and forty grand of his money.'

'What did you used to do for Kevin?' asked Jane.

'I did a lot of different things. Mostly I corrupted young people. I'd work holiday resorts they wanted to move stuff out of. Drugs, I mean. I'd get some tourist used to a certain kind of life, or get them in debt, so they could use them as drugs mules. Middle-class ones usually, mostly lads; sometimes rougher ones, mostly girls. I even had to find some that they wanted to get caught, so the people they were paying off in customs could look like they were making arrests. Believe me, everything shit that's happened to me I've deserved it, and much, much more.'

Jane's voice was even, without judgement. 'But then you ran, why was that? You're not stupid enough to think you'd get far with Kevin's money.'

Mikey sighed and put his hands behind his head, looking up at the wall high above our heads as he spoke. 'I was in Bali a few years ago. I'd been working up this kid, a little gap-year public schoolboy from Edinburgh. Couldn't even snort a line of coke – I'd make him rub it into his gums. Anyway, I could tell from the size of the package they were wanting him to carry . . . it was too small. They wanted him to get caught. It's the death penalty over there. He was eighteen.' He took a long drag from his cigarette. 'Well, turns out we all have our limits.'

Eventually he sat forward and looked at us again.

Jane had been regarding him intently in silence the whole time. 'You've been responsible for a lot of misery.'

An anguished look crossed his face. 'Yes. Teenagers. They're too pure, and you need to step on them a little. I'm responsible for a lot of perfectly harmless people spending time in jail – but maybe it's not morally that different from being a cop.' He grinned at Jane, who didn't rise to the bait. 'Look, I was sick of it all long before that.

A lot of people get tired of that life. It gets pretty fucking tedious as you get older. All these guys who dogged school, choosing lives where it's school forever – who's the hardest? Who bad-mouthed who? All that shit – they just never grow out of it. My handler – you'll run into him if you try and speak to Gary. I mean, I'm sure you'd be able to spot him a mile off, he looks like a fucked-up version of Gerard Butler.'

Jane smiled. 'Isn't that just Gerard Butler? Yes, I think I know who you mean. What's he calling himself these days?'

'Agent Brond. Andy Brond he said to me once, but Gary said it was an alias.' He shrugged. 'He's ex-SAS, Gary said. And, y'know, I grew up around gangsters in Glasgow, so I know a psychopath when I see one. When I got back, I was their creature. That was the phrase Brond used to me, "their creature". I did stuff for them, they paid me. Got me a beautiful flat in the New Town in Edinburgh. Mainly they wanted me to set up people they thought were important with dates. So they could shake them down. Gay guys, straight guys, lesbians. I'd befriend people, take them to parties, get them laid, sometimes get them into relation-ships. Gary was the only one I really failed with, in a way – the only guy he was interested in was me. So they made me do that – go out with him. Take him to parties that they were filming. They film everything by the way – old school. He was in love with me, and it made me sad. He had a really rough life growing up, and he shouldn't really have been able to feel anything anymore, but he loved me.'

'And why were they so interested in Gary?'

'Because he might be the next First Minister? I don't actually know. They're all over him lately, anyway – has Intelligence guys near him all the time. They're interested because he's divisive, maybe. If you were looking for someone to split the party, Gary's a good bet. He's fucking conservative in a lot of ways. If you wanted to totally alienate every one of these wee students that joined up after the Referendum, Gary's your man.'

Jane sat forward a little, leaning on her stick. 'You're in a dangerous position. Maybe you were better off when you were working for The Vole.'

Mikey threw his head back and howled theatrically, in one of his occasional moments of camp. 'Oh love, they were running Kevin's whole operation. I was always working for them. You think they leave the drug supply of the UK in the hands of a cunt from Easterhouse? If there's one thing I've learned in life, it's that the working classes are in charge of exactly fuck-all.'

Jane cut through the tail end of his laughter with complete seriousness. 'What do you know about Marina's murder?'

Mikey squirmed in his chair. 'I know they made me get Gary's cum on a scarf.'

'What? Why don't the police know this?' I blurted.

Jane picked up her bag as she stood up. 'Well, I suppose nobody thought to wank off the Justice Minister as part of the investigation.'

24

For reasons that never really became clear, Donnie wanted to meet me and Jane that afternoon at the Scotia.

The Scotia Bar was halfway between the Trongate and the Clyde, an old folk-music hangout that everyone in Glasgow has been to at least once.

A weaving drunk had been thrown out and stood pining outside like Greyfriars Bobby. Inside, a big guy at the bar ordered a pint of heavy then lowered himself unsteadily onto a stool. Two old boys sat in a corner with half pints and whiskies. There was a string of saltire bunting across the bar. Someone had hung their bunnet on a hook by the stools. The only sound was a tinny voiceover emerging from a puggy at the far end of the room that sounded like an old robot begging for death.

Donnie raised a nip at us and sank it ceremoniously. '"The Water of Life" – that's what they used to call whisky in Scotland.'

They probably didn't, it might just have been a bit of fifteenth-century marketing that stuck, but Jane smiled at him supportively. She started to make a comment about never having been here before, but Donnie rudely launched into something else, because he loathed small talk and had the attention span of a wasp.

Donnie had commandeered a table in the far corner. Due to his various overlapping crises, he'd had his hair straightened and some blond highlights added. It was now, broadly speaking, a gold-tinged greying mullet pitched somewhere between a sex tourist dodging Interpol at a yoga retreat, and a lion who'd spent a year trapped at the bottom of a well. He nodded at one of the old boys as he limped off to the toilet. 'You can't blame them. What kind of grisly pervert would want to face all of this sober?'

Jane insisted on getting the first round in and I helped her over with the drinks. I sat down beside Donnie who managed to have a near panic attack just taking his bag and jacket off the chairs. He looked around him in a manner designed to invite suspicion, leaned forward and whispered: 'That lock-up you asked me to find, on Clarence Drive, found it no bother. There's a wee row of them down there, past the bridge. Completely burnt out. The police have it down as arson. Anyway, there's not much to see. So I hung around for a couple of hours and finally someone shows up at one of the other lock-ups. Some middle-aged guy getting his motorbike out. That's a really common cause of death, you know – getting a motorbike during a midlife crisis – not realising that they're now basically a jet pack – fucking it into a tree.'

'And did you talk to him?' I asked, immediately

regretting the hint of impatience in my voice, as he had the emotional stability of a prison riot.

'I'm fucking getting to that, for fuck's sake.' He wrenched his head to one side, as he often did under pressure, and gave a kind of spasmodic sob, then frantically searched his jacket for his inhaler. 'Aye, I approached this organ donor of the near future and asked him if he knew who owned the lock-up. Some old cunt that lived in the flats across the road, he says. But he thought he was renting it out, because occasionally he'd see someone down there, always in and out quickly. In his words *a big Chinese boy, the size of a fucking moose*.'

Jane nodded, but didn't say that we already suspected all of this. I guessed that she didn't really trust him and it fell to me to produce some kind of response to acknowledge his contribution.

'Right. Wild,' I ventured.

'Fucking wild!' he exclaimed, killing the rest of his pint with a tilt of the head.

Jane nodded to her phone on the table. 'Matt and Mary from the community centre – they've turned up dead. Shot, in a car, in Irvine.'

'That's the way I want to go,' muttered Donnie earnestly. 'Irvine. No hope to taunt you in your final moments, just holding your guts in on the front seat of a Honda Civic, happy for it to end. That's why I've never understood these cunts going to Switzerland to die – it's far too fucking nice, you're torturing yourself. I'd do the cunts in with a sledge-hammer on Irvine seafront.'

I realised that in the excitement I'd forgotten to tell anyone about Kat's other revelation.

'Oh, by the way, Kat said that Rachael – the stalker, remember – she might have been following Marina. She reckons she's still following me, and I've just been too wasted to notice. I guess they don't give up too easily. Apparently she has some Twitter page Marina found quite alarming. I can't find it, though.'

Donnie shook his head. 'I hate Twitter. Maybe it just replaces the void left by God – something to perform morality for.'

'Donnie, that's uncharacteristically philosophical.'

'I got it from a tweet,' he admitted, grudgingly. He checked his phone and gathered up his things in a hurry, spouting something broadly incoherent.

Jane regarded him dispassionately as he pinballed out the door, then turned to me, her eyebrows knitted. 'I saw the report from the lock-up fire. A bunch of 38mm film went up. Electrical fire, they said.'

'Sounds in line with what Mikey told us about them being old school.'

'Indeed. Tell me – does Rachael seem dangerous to you? She obviously couldn't strangle someone herself, but could she persuade someone to help her?'

'She couldn't lure a man out of a burning building.'

'Fair enough. But she might have seen something. We should talk to her. I suppose it won't be hard to find her if she's stalking you.'

'I'll stay on high alert,' I agreed.

She dug into her wallet and produced a scrap of paper. 'The other guy she was stalking apparently – see what he knows.'

I got another round in and talked Jane through my thoughts on how we're the first people in history to be ruled by incompetent fascists, and how we're going to end up going to the death camps on a replacement bus service, while she regarded me with frankly impolite levels of sympathy.

25

The following day I was sitting in Lemon Monkey, where they'd run out of milk and coffee. Donnie burst in through the back door, right beside where I was sitting, and I spilled my black tea.

'Have you seen the news? What the fuck are you doing?' He glared rudely at the notebook in front of me where I had written the words *PISS NOW NORMAL*.

'No. Well, only last week's.' I nodded at the cafe's jumble of newspapers by the window, which were always weeks out of date. Probably people just left them there. There were still a couple of front pages from the Referendum. One had a picture of Mars, which looked like the football pitches of a tough comprehensive.

'Your stalker's dead. She jumped in front of a fucking train!' Donnie unzipped his jacket and dumped himself into the armchair across from me.

'Rachael? Jesus.'

'Aye. Poor cow. Just got a bit too much maybe, following strangers around like a demented bastard.'

'That's fuckin' strange, though. She didn't seem suicidal

. . . she seemed, like, way too selfish to do anything like that. It just doesn't seem like her to make life easier for anyone.'

Donnie considered this and shrugged in agreement. 'I mean, jumping in front of a train – putting other people's lives at risk, that sounds like her, aye. But I know what you mean. When was the last time you saw her?'

'At this book signing last week. She was just the same as ever. Pretty happy just hunting humans. She was talking about that new guy she's been stalking, she seemed like someone planning for the future.'

Donnie sighed and helped himself to a forkful of my carrot cake. 'It's sad. I thought she'd die screaming in a madhouse obviously, but not for a long while yet.'

It was galling – I still felt terrible days after the roofie incident, and I'd only had a few sips of the drugged tea. Donnie had pretty much drained his and seemed fine – better, even. They had underestimated the remarkable drug resistance of this monster; his omnivorous appetites had given him the resilience of some planet-conquering bacterium.

I waited for him to leave, then sat on my own for a while as I tried to get someone to bring the bill. Eventually I just went up to the front counter, but it was deserted. There didn't seem to be any staff there: they appeared simply to have abandoned the place. I dropped some money on the counter and decided to go back to the flat.

As I stepped outside I was grabbed from behind and thrown up against the wall. It was DI Ian, pressing me back hard with his forearm across my windpipe. He had the fresh, minty breath of an alcoholic. 'We want a word with you, Mr McAveety.'

I tried to reply but could only succeed in making a few weak gasping sounds.

'Come into a bit of money recently, have we?'

Had I? I didn't know. I was secretly glad that I couldn't reply. I relaxed my knees a little and it took a lot of the pressure off my neck. Possibly this was something they taught people at stage school, or ought to, at any rate. My legs would eventually get tired, but really I was okay.

After saying something else that I missed, DI Ian dragged me by the shoulder towards a car, where we waited awkwardly as PC Stewart fumbled through his pockets for his keys. The silence created a building anxiety inside me.

'I suppose actors learn a lot of ways to pretend they're choking each other and whatnot, at stage school.'

'What?' DI Ian held me by fistfuls of my jacket and shook me. 'WHAT?'

The PC jerked the back door open. I'd heard about the police deliberately banging your head against the top bit when they put you in the car, so I dipped as he waved me forward, and swept as low as possible towards the opening with my chin tucked in. I maybe went too low, and nobody was really that near me, so the whole thing probably just seemed odd.

I sat staring straight ahead and pretended not to notice as DI Ian stood on the pavement and contemplated me for an uncomfortably long time – with those wet, greeting eyes that some Scottish men have outside – then slammed the door.

At the police station they took all my stuff off me at the front desk again, but this time I was led down to a cell in the basement. The basement cells were a bit grimmer than the wanking cell, and seemed to be staffed by the sort of human artillery the cops needed to break up protests and picket lines, but who couldn't be allowed near the general public.

I was handed over to a man with a face pagans would carve over a grain store, who shoved me along a corridor and into a cell. 'Don't you go anywhere,' he said, in a voice so slow that I wondered if I was having a stroke.

After a couple of hours I was brought upstairs to an interview room. DI Ian was sitting there with a folder in front of him, with PC Stewart standing in one corner in his shirtsleeves. His shirt had those squares on it from when you've just taken it straight out of the packet and put it on. I felt a brief surge of motherly sympathy for him, which I suppose must have registered on my face, because he twitched uncomfortably.

DI Ian spoke in the polite, controlled tone that Scottish people used when they were about to batter you. His whole demeanour was that of a tentatively reformed madman – like some old soldier who'd pieced his life back together, but one beeped horn in a supermarket car park and he was back in 'Nam.

The mirror in this room took up most of the side wall, and was clearly one of those one-way jobs: the uniform was probably sitting behind it right now, taking notes. An old inspector in a wheelchair was probably beside him, soon to be wheezing with laughter at my interviewer's gambits. He'd slap his useless legs at each of the younger man's misunderstandings of interview technique. 'Offering him a peanut – oh, he's not just offering him a peanut . . .!' he would cackle in a voice that was, inexplicably, from the Deep South. 'Offering him a peanut!' he'd giggle shrilly to nobody, and the uniform would nod and try to join in. As I slowly cracked he'd develop the building hysteria of a man cheering on a horse. He'd make the young guy wheel him forward and then push on the back of his old head until his face was mushed right into the glass, so that my last few moments of freedom would be spent watching the dim hint of his flattened features behind the mirror, laughter making his crushed profile billow like a jellyfish.

The PC sneezed loudly and dragged my soul back into the room. I said, 'God bless you,' to mask the regular horror I have when people sneeze; not because of germs, but because I always feel I've just seen their cumface.

I decided to take the initiative. 'I suppose you're going to ask me where I was last night?'

They both seemed genuinely surprised – or feigning surprise was a tactic they'd used so often they'd gotten really good at it.

'Why would we do that?'

'To eliminate me from inquiries?'

'Inquiries into . . .?'

I was going to say 'into the murder of my stalker', but

I'd forgotten her second name, and even though I wasn't an expert at this kind of thing, I knew that you shouldn't start a police interview by just blurting out that you didn't murder Rachael. It would probably seem suspicious.

DI Ian tilted forward in his chair. 'You banked a cheque recently from Miss Katos. Ten grand.'

'Yes. Marina had a letter sent to me when she died. I guess it was through some mail-forwarding service?'

'What's a mail-forwarding service?'

'I have no idea,' I admitted. He seemed to make a note of this.

DI Ian looked at me gravely and said, 'The question is, how did a dead woman write you a cheque?'

I barked an involuntary laugh. 'She wrote it before she died? That's like saying, "How did a dead woman write *Middlemarch*?"' I could see by their lack of reaction that I should have picked a better known book. 'Or *Jane Eyre*,' I added, but it seemed stupid now, and he already had his head down and was looking through the folder.

I wished that I'd said *Pride and Prejudice* – that would have been better.

He pushed a sheet of paper across the desk to me. 'This is a search warrant for your address. We'll soon see if there's a letter there or not. Now, there's something else we'd like you to take a look at.'

I looked through the photos he'd handed me. They must have been Rachael's possessions when she died: her backpack, empty; sandals, one badly damaged; and some kind of wrap covered in black sequins.

'Have you ever seen Rachael with any of these? We're struggling to find a next of kin for an identification.'

'No, no, I haven't. What about my one phone call . . . is that a thing?' I immediately worried that I should have been more assertive.

'Yes, that's a thing,' admitted DI Ian grudgingly. He looked at PC Stewart behind him like they'd maybe had a bet on this, and produced my phone from his inside pocket. 'You've got five minutes.'

The two policemen left, and I called Jane.

Jane picked up on the second ring, and sounded reassuringly sober. I filled her in.

'OK. Jesus. I'll see what I can do. Is this letter still at your flat?'

'I mean, literally, fuck knows.'

'Why the fuck would they kill Rachael . . .? Do you think Rachael knew something about what happened to Marina?'

'No, doesn't make sense. She couldn't keep quiet about anything.'

'Agreed, but maybe she was around the park on the night, following Marina, and witnessed something. Saw Marina meet the killer? God knows. You said she'd photograph you sometimes. Maybe she got a shot of the killer. Maybe he saw her.'

'I suppose it's possible. Why would they wait for days to do anything about it though?'

'Yes, that doesn't make any sense at all.'

•

Afterwards, the large man led me along the corridor to a cell. I comforted myself by thinking that, in a way, I was learning more about the investigation. It was like finally getting closer to your crush when they sleep with the person who gets your liver after you die in a forklift accident.

I lay on the narrow bed in the cell and closed my eyes. I was almost asleep when I realised that what they would find in my flat was a suitcase packed with several thousand pounds' worth of drugs.

In his office, the old inspector sat back in his wheelchair, grinning expectantly. He uncrossed his withered legs by hand.

26

The cell door clanged open and a dapper little man in his fifties, wearing a three-piece suit, called my name from the doorway. He led me upstairs. He had a swift, military walk and carried a black Homburg hat in one hand. He stopped at reception and handed me a clear plastic bag with my belongings in it, then we continued marching right out the front door.

'Who are you?' I asked, as he gestured towards a tired-looking grey Hyundai.

'DI McKay. I'm a pal of Jane Pickford's. Get in.'

I normally only got lifts from Donnie and it was strange being in a car that was clean. Strangely, he put his hat on in the car. Up close I could see that he had a neatly trimmed little goatee and intimidatingly clear skin. He put on Radio Clyde and handed me a bulky brown envelope from the back seat. 'That's for Jane.'

'Where are we going?'

He spoke in the clipped voice that seemed to be shared by a lot of Glasgow's middle-aged maniacs. 'You're free to go. I sorted everything out in there. I'm going to take you to see Jane. I made a lawful search of your dwelling. I found the letter and envelope you received from the deceased. It seems to have been sent to you by a mail-forwarding service.'

'What is a mail-forwarding service?'

He glanced away from the road to give me a brief look of appraisal. 'Are you sure you need me to answer that? A lot of the words in the answer are already in the question.'

'No, it's okay.'

He offered me a hip flask and I took a hit on it. It was mint tea. He gave a hearty laugh and gripped my arm to steady himself. 'Have that just to keep up appearances! I've foresworn alcohol. Allah is sufficient for me, son.'

'Allah?' I asked.

'Yes. I'm a convert to Islam, but I don't let on in the job. It wouldn't go down well. In Police Scotland greed, duplicity and cruelty are fostered and rewarded, but not faith.'

'Ah. Jane told me about you. I sort of thought she was making a joke.'

'Likewise. Jane asked me to look into some aspects of this case. It's actually filled in a lot of blanks for me. I'd been working on the local heroin trade and, in particular, why Glasgow since the Referendum has been like some kind of skaghead *Whisky Galore!* Seems your friend Marina stole some H from her employer – a Dr Chong? I don't suppose you know why she did it?'

'I think it was maybe some weird sex thing they had going on.'

He nodded encouragingly. 'Maybe, son, maybe. And from

what I can tell, she chose to give it to activists up in Springburn. To Independence supporters. That's interesting, isn't it? Perhaps she knew they'd hang on to it until after the vote; and she wanted to be indirectly funding some kind of radicalism. She couldn't have imagined they'd start killing each other over it. Or put it on the street in its pure form. I think – in the spirit of some weird kind of socialism? Or maybe they were all just total fucking idiots.'

'You searched my flat?'

'Thoroughly. You'd hidden the letter inside a little box of Kellogg's Multigrain Shapes.' He enunciated the last words with the professional seriousness of a pathologist.

'That's the one place nobody would ever look. Did you find anything else in the flat?'

'Like what?'

'Oh, nothing.' I quickly changed the subject. 'I've never met a Muslim convert before. Are there many in Glasgow?'

'A lot more than you'd think. Take one step towards Allah and he takes two towards you.'

I wanted to say it was the same for Valium, but worried that this was probably some kind of sacrilege.

'Anyway, I'd better get you up there. I've got shit to do. We'll find out who murdered your friend, *inshallah*.' He started the Hyundai up and screeched out of the car park.

His driving style seemed to be very much 1970s cop show, and a horn blared behind us as we went screaming out of the entrance.

The car rattled and shook as DI McKay launched us towards the Sighthill Stone Circle. Sighthill had been sort of cut off from Glasgow by the M8 and, perhaps for this reason, it was where a lot of refugees had been housed over the last decade. For some reason, a bunch of astronomers in the 1970s had decided to build an astronomically aligned stone circle in Sighthill Park. A guy who I used to do bar work with once told me he'd dropped peyote there and been led by a Spirit Fox into a variety of local charity shops until he'd been arrested.

We left the car at the bottom of the hill and trudged up through the park. I dimly wondered if I was going to be murdered, but I didn't have any better ideas. The stones formed a wide grassy circle, which felt damp and mossy underfoot. Some of them displayed ancient graffiti, by people commemorating teenage love affairs, or simply declaring that they existed. It was a dramatic spot for a photoshoot. You could see right across Glasgow, with high flats rising up defiantly in twos and threes, like standing stones themselves.

I used to love visiting neighbours in high flats when I was a kid. Bigger rooms than tenements, and panoramic views of everything the world sought to deny you.

Jane was wearing a dramatic long brown coat, and stood leaning against one of the monoliths with her hands thrust deep in the pockets. There was a guy on his hands and knees packing up a tripod into a shiny silver carry-case. McKay waved to Jane, pointed to me and began stomping back down the hill.

I wandered over to her and she glanced apologetically at the equipment. 'Just doing some promo for the book.'

'Is this one of the locations?'

'No, but there is a theme of paganism, and it beats going to Fife.'

'A lot of things do. Your pal, the Muslim detective, he's a real guy,' I began, then stopped. It sounded stupid outside of my head.

I handed her the envelope he'd given me. She pulled a slim folder out of it and riffled through its contents in a perfunctory way as she talked. 'DI McKay, yes. He's the closest thing you can get to totally incorruptible. Kept his conversion to himself. Always worked the lowest-level murders he could find. Had no interest in chasing corruption, just felt that Allah had called on him to be an instrument of justice.'

She seemed to be waiting for the photographer to go, and smiled a goodbye at him. We watched him struggle down the verge and off into the night. 'I had DI McKay look through CCTV at the time of the murder. He said he found something interesting. The Justice Secretary, Mr Gary Mount.' She held the folder open.

There was a surprisingly detailed photo of Mount wearing an almost comically hunted expression behind the wheel of a car.

'Christ. Just on his own?'

'Yes. He drives up on my side of the park, and he's around there just before the murder.' She pulled two lollipops out of her pocket and handed one to me. 'I got given these this morning. Morphine lollipops. I can spare one.'

We pulled the wrappers off and sucked them in silence.

More lights winked on in the high flats as folk got home from work. My body flooded with a warm healing throb.

When Jane spoke, her voice was low and stoned. 'I'm surprised at how dedicated you've been to all this, Felix.'

'Me, too. I'm not really a persevering kind of guy. If I ask someone for directions and they're too complicated, I go somewhere else.'

She didn't reply, just sucked on her lollipop thoughtfully as she looked up at the sky, where the odd star now twinkled.

'Do you have a clearer idea of what's going on now? I'm kind of lost.'

'Oh, yes, I'm getting there, I think.' She pushed herself away from the rock and paced around a little in front of me. The wind picked up hard. Jane's open coat billowed behind her. Leaning on her cane, for a second she was a wizard or druid among the stones. 'Of course, this is something that should take place in the drawing room of a country house, and I should have an audience of troubled elites, but you'll have to do.'

'The stones and I are your audience, fire away,' I drawled. 'Excuse me, your Excellency,' I said to one of the smaller stones as I sat on it. We both laughed. It wasn't that funny, but morphine seemed to be a real mood lightener.

'Okay . . .' Jane began. 'Marina had been working for Chong for a couple of years – two huge minds in a kind of combative, possibly sexual relationship. But . . . but . . . she grows to see him for what he really is – not some charming bad-hat offering a little harmless relief to the masses, but the director of a lot of pain and trauma. Marina, while somewhat charmingly amoral, is not okay with this. She begins working to undermine him, but it's difficult: Chong is careful and paranoid. It's not clear why he's so untroubled by law enforcement. Nonetheless, she has one or two successes. Some of his deliveries to other cities are seized, but not enough to hurt him – only enough for him to find it stimulating. And maybe she is angry – angry at his interpretation of these attempts to destroy him as foreplay.'

I was already struggling to follow her reasoning, and couldn't tell if it was because I was high or because it was objectively very complicated. I took the lolly out of my mouth and tried to focus.

'Around this time, she quits her job at IBC and starts to work for Beloved Intelligence, a company developing AI. Dr Chong, as a long-standing delusional narcissist, starts to believe it's AI that's helping Marina undermine him. He's intrigued, and flattered at what he believes to be the chance to duel with a superintelligence. Marina gets a sense of Chong's neurosis, and sends that pitch by email to your friend Ian, largely to fuck with Chong, I think. She knows Chong monitors her communications, and wonders if she can tweak him any higher – keep his mind off the real game.'

Here she looked at me suddenly, as if remembering I was there. Her pupils were dilated and her eyes sparkled with excitement. 'Because Marina has discovered the truth of Chong's operation. He is licensed by British Intelligence. As an American national, her death should be a bigger story, no? It was in and out of the news in a day. That made me wonder about Intelligence involvement straight away. It seems – from what I can gather – that they use Dr Chong to gather blackmail material on key people in Scottish civic life, and in return he gets a licence to run heroin and other drugs throughout the country. Perhaps they facilitate this for their own reasons.'

'That reminds me. I thought of something.'

'A little off brand, but do go on.'

'I was thinking – perhaps the shipment Marina stole was designed to sedate the Scottish poor before the Referendum.'

'I mean, to be honest, God knows. DI McKay's professional opinion is that when Marina gave that heroin away, Chong didn't react because he knew he was useful to his handlers in other ways. My guess is Marina discovered the nature of his usefulness. He had compiled a lot of compromising footage, on 38mm film, perhaps because he is neurotic about anything digital. I think the key to Chong is that he embraces the banality of how people are supposed to live and re-presents it as parody. So of course he would centre all his racketeering at a tiny little lock-up in the West End. But Marina found it and burned it down. Suddenly Chong knows it wasn't a game, and he is in danger: no longer of any use to anyone. He throws himself on the mercy of his handler, the one and only Agent Brond. The next thing we know is that Marina meets the killer in the park. Who does she think she is meeting there? Dr Chong, is my guess. Presumably she had another phone that the police don't know about, and the killer took it from the body.'

It was depressing, but I had to ask.

'How do you think it went down?' I stuck the lollipop back in my mouth as I listened, the sky now completely dark, except for the stars.

Jane thought for a while, then nodded to herself as she began to speak. 'Here's my best guess. On the way to murder Marina, the handler maybe has an idea, and asks Gary Mount to meet him nearby, to use him as a patsy. They're worried about how much Gary knows about Chong and their backing of him, and how little blackmail material they now have on him. Gary will pass CCTV cameras on the way there, his mobile phone will put him in the vicinity, but he's told to park in a spot where he can wait unobserved. Agent Brond goes into the park on his own, commits the murder, and leaves a scarf with Mount's sperm on it by the body. Now their key Scottish asset is completely compromised again.' She tutted, thoughtfully. 'They must have big plans for him, because they went to a lot of trouble.'

'And Rachael? Where does she fit in?'

'Christ knows. But her death must be linked. Jack McKay went down there. The wall she's supposed to have jumped over was nearly five feet high. Even if she could have gotten over it, how did she manage it without making a single mark on the wall? If her body was thrown onto the track, it was by someone of extraordinary size and strength.'

I didn't ask about the state of the body, imagining that the autopsy had been a bit like a meat raffle.

'Then there's her credit card.' She showed me a

photocopied bank statement in the folder. 'Who the fuck buys frozen pies the day before they kill themselves?'

'But where does this leave us?' Jane continued, exasperated. 'What do you think happened?'

'I think someone huge launched her drugged body over the wall like a mortar. Chong?'

'Not Chong, he rarely seems to get directly involved in anything. I think you'd really need to provoke him before he'd get his hands dirty.'

'We need to stay out of this guy's way.'

'On the contrary, Doctor Watson, I think we need to pay him a visit. We need to provoke him, anger him in some way. Otherwise he'll just soft-soap us.'

'OK.' I found I angered most people without trying.

Jane handed me a little pen torch and we made our way slowly down the hill in a light drizzle that turned into a proper rainstorm just as we got inside the car. Her car was a new-looking red Mini.

'I got this the week before my diagnosis, before my plans really fucking "gaed agley", as you lot like to say.'

'You're still allowed to drive, aye?'

'It's a grey area,' she muttered, as we bounced onto the motorway.

27

Back at Park Crescent we drank tea while the rain blatted off the big windows. Somehow we fell into talking about addiction and recovery, and whether I planned on getting myself straight at any point soon. I hadn't even considered it for a long time. 'The thing about addiction is' – I paused to get it right, although I'd said it often enough to myself – 'there's a contradiction at the heart of it, which is you think you can't tell anyone . . . the causes of it, not really. You think that even if they act sympathetic in the short term, deep down you know that they'd judge you: they might not mean to, but they would. And, simultaneously, you sort of feel everybody already knows. That it's written on your face, that it's obvious from your behaviour.'

Jane waved one hand exasperatedly. 'But none of that is true. I had so many friends go to AA and NA and reveal their big fucking secret shame, to silence, to nothing, to people who'd heard it all before. It's all been done, love. There are no original sins. And people don't know what's going on with you. They just see someone who's self-destructive.

They're not brilliant detectives, they have busy lives, they don't have the time or skill to work out what you're not telling them.'

'But you. You are a brilliant detective.'

'Yes, and sometimes I get the feeling that you're experiencing emotions that you don't show, and it's hard to work out if it's diazepam or Scottishness.'

'Yeah, I'm in therapy but it doesn't help much. I just think other people seem to feel that saying things out loud has a magic power that it doesn't really have.'

'A man once said to me that there was a shortcut to wisdom. That true wisdom was just humility, and the shortcut was this: when you see a quality you don't like in someone else, look for it in yourself. But then, I think that's a lot of what we do anyway, we dislike qualities in other people because we do see them in ourselves. And he was saying it to try to get in my knickers, so he wasn't that wise.'

'I think nowadays even if you did hear something that explained how to be wise, it would just sound like a meme.'

'Yes. Social media wisdom is a lot like prison wisdom, if you were wise you wouldn't be there.' She yawned. 'Very few people achieve true contentment, and even then it's usually just to taunt an ex.'

I reached for the final half an eccie that sat at the edge of the coffee table, but she stopped me with an impatient flick of the hand. 'Don't take that. It decreases cognitive function – give it to me, I can spare some.'

'Can I ask you something? That was the only CCTV footage you found of anyone near the murder scene?'

'Yes. Only Mount driving towards the scene. There are a lot of problems with broken cameras and missing footage.' She looked over at me meaningfully. 'I very much doubt the killer would wait for days, if he thought there was a witness. What if the killer didn't know, but Mount did? Maybe he just saw Rachael and didn't mention it. He's not a killer, and he doesn't want to get some poor woman killed.'

'Maybe they spoke. He's a famous guy in a Jag on an empty street. Maybe she recognised him.'

'Okay. And eventually he lets it slip that he was spotted. Well, then . . . I suppose standard procedure would be to locate her, burgle her house, see if she has any evidence. Why kill her? From everything you've said, she'd be a pretty unreliable witness.'

'Oh, wait . . . I forgot the most important thing. They showed me pictures of Rachael's stuff. I'd seen something before! Those sequins on her wrap!'

'Where?'

'In Mount's car. Mikey gave me a lift in it. His boyfriend's car he said! Down the side by the door. Black sequins.'

'Jesus Christ! What the fuck was she doing in his car? She recognises him, and he gives her a lift?'

'Yes. If she's seen Marina meeting Agent Brond, she's a possible alibi for him. Mount wants to know who she is, and after Brond fucks off and leaves Mount to it, he finds her and offers her a lift – takes her home, so he knows how to find her again . . . there's a lot of fucking maybe here,' I groaned.

Her voice dropped grimly. 'Too much fucking maybe.'

28

J ane picked me up in a black cab for the trip to Chong's, which I dismissed as the senselessly expensive whim of the bourgeois novelist. She started to lay out some protocol for the interview, but my phone went. It was Donnie, and she gestured at me to take it.

'Donnie . . . what happened to the fucking drugs, man?'

'I sold them!'

'Sold them? What did you get for them?'

'Cocaine. Lots more of it.'

'You sold our drugs . . . for drugs? What are we going to do with cocaine? I don't even take cocaine, and you don't need it because you're an arsehole anyway.'

'We're going to sell it for a lot of fucking dough, he was practically giving it away. I've got it stashed in my locker at the gym.'

Even while hearing that I'd inadvertently become a mid-level drug dealer, part of me was reeling at the idea that Donnie had a gym membership.

Donnie didn't even ask about the arrest. Some days it feels like the whole world is against you, but it's worth remembering that actually nobody gives a shit about you.

Giffnock was a suburb on the far south of the city, a collection of bungalows where people retired to a pastoral world of overkept gardens and bungalows. The bungalow was the Scottish retirement dream: spending as much of your time as close to the ground as possible, before going into it. On long, empty streets, the wee houses maintained a friendly distance from each other.

The shops here weren't the usual Glasgow chequer of bookies, boozers and charity shops. As you entered on Fenwick Road there was a florist, ice-cream parlour and an Asian fusion place called Jasmine One, which I always thought sounded like the first Thai Space Station. I sort of knew the area a bit, as my aunt, Pat, had moved in with a much older guy who lived out here when I was a teenager. I used to get farmed out to them for the odd weekend, the old boy happy to tolerate any inconvenience that came along with his sexual windfall. They both had deep, gruff voices, so their sex noises sounded like an argument between binmen. It was where I had learned how to block my ears.

At the top of Chong's street there was a CCTV camera on a pole sixty feet high, usually pointed at a little huddle of shops, silently waiting for a chance to punish any of the area's few young people for their boredom. Chong's house was a bungalow on a massive scale, rebuilt in the original style but on the scale of a Viking longhouse; in fact, it wasn't really a bungalow: the upper bit, which my aunt had converted into a little attic room, was almost the size of one of the regular houses. His neighbour's garden stood permanently in its ridiculous shadow; I reflected as we arrived that being able to get this thing past Glasgow District Council's planning department was a sinister insight into his true power.

Jane marched out of the cab – which she told to wait, however long we were – and rang the bell on his front door. I stood a foot or two back, feeling a vague disassociation from events, which may well just have been Percodan. This is why I was the first to notice that Chong had appeared at the side of the house, and was grinning at us like we were old friends. 'Jane! Felix! Come round here, I'm in the garden.'

We followed him behind the house and into a big square garden with a little plum tree in the middle. Chong bade us take a seat on his wrought-iron garden furniture with a kind of hostile levity.

A little King Charles spaniel drifted up to us, but quickly lost interest. We all sat down around a heavy iron table made to look like a crisscross of vines and leaves. It was pretty cold outside, although Chong was just wearing a white shirt. There was no cushion on my seat, and I could feel every leaf of a curling iron rose on my arse.

'What can I do for you, Detective?'

Jane seemed to regard him for a long time, but it might just been that the tension of the situation made it seem that way. Eventually, she said, 'Well, I write about crime and social disintegration, and I thought it might be nice to have a day out, on a lovely winter afternoon like this, and follow the river to its source.'

Chong answered as blithely as if she'd complimented him on his shoes. 'Well, I'm sure it's a very soothing outlook, to think of things as having very simple root causes. It might be why you sell so many books. Crime and social disintegration aren't failures of capitalism, they are the things that inevitably happen when it succeeds. Me, I'm in the pain-relief business. You have a society that creates pain and criminalises pain relief. Changing the systems that create that pain is unimaginable – so much so, that it's easier to imagine the world ending. And not even imagine, to actually sit and watch it die. Providing a little relief from it all makes me a criminal?'

I felt the start of a crippling headache that was probably withdrawal from something or other. 'No, you're a criminal for, like, moving a tonne of drugs and, y'know, all the other weird criminal shit you do. For getting Marina killed.'

Dr Chong laughed, and gave a polite little incline of the head, as if I'd just told an unremarkable anecdote at a dinner party. 'Ah, Felix. Maybe that's why she liked you – she enjoyed the idea of a *tabula rasa*, and you were its physical manifestation.'

I shrugged noncommittally in a way I hoped suggested that I knew what this meant. 'Oh, I'm sorry, it's probably all a simulation. I should say you got "Marina"' – I made inverted commas with my fingers – '"killed".'

'I mean also "you", but you're basically correct.' He replied in the quiet, rushed intonation people use for verbal footnotes, with his own half-hearted air quotes delivered just above the level of the table. 'But I would never have done anything to hurt Marina. We loved each other, in our own very strange way. How much do you know?'

Jane leaned forward a little. 'We know she was killed after your lock-up burned down on Clarence Drive. Was that when you decided you'd had enough?'

A momentary flicker of anger seemed to replace Chong's bland cheerfulness, like a glimpse of a crocodile deep under the surface of the water. I wondered for the first time whether Chong might be on quite a lot of Valium too. He bowed his head slightly and answered quietly. 'I could never have had enough of Marina. If I hadn't had enough after she stole half a million pounds' worth of heroin, do you think I had her killed over a lock-up? It was way above my head. I tried to take the blame, told them it was an accident. They must have found out different.' Chong took a sip of tea and looked around him. For a second it was like we weren't there at all. 'I'm an ideas man for some important people. I help them strategise. I help them smuggle. I like detective novels. My favourite is James Ellroy, and maybe some of that seeps into my work. I do enjoy planning a good shakedown. But that's as far as it goes. I've never hurt anyone in my life; I've never needed to. When you have privilege in this country the violence is enacted for you. Why would I ever need to be involved in violence when I have spent my whole life carving out a position where I get to be above such things and, indeed, wring my hands about it?'

'You corrupt cops! You suborn politicians!' Jane countered with an outraged laugh.

'They're politicians and police officers; I'm not corrupting them – I'm just making their innate corruption palpable.'

Jane broke in. 'It's addiction. You deal in addiction. You're not fulfilling a need, you're creating a need. Not that you even mean any of your arch, ironic bullshit, David.'

'You think that it's a system trying to produce order, but it's actually trying to produce chaos. That's where the profit lies. Everything works out well for somebody. A futile summer of protest still throws up a few tear-gas billionaires.'

It struck me that he could be viewed as quite left-wing in some ways, if it wasn't for the fact that he wasn't really a materialist, because he didn't believe that anything existed.

Jane seemed to be thinking on similar lines. 'So, you're just playing a role in a system you don't believe in. That you don't even think is there, in any real sense.'

He chuckled. 'Not believing in a system is requisite for membership of its hierarchy. In China till quite recently if you'd actually believed in Communism, you'd have been quite dangerous to everybody in power; probably they'd have had you shot. In this government, if you actually believed in free-market economics you'd be a potential whistleblower. If you actually believe what your society says you should, then you should stay well away from power, or keep very quiet about it.'

He took us both in with a look; his tone, I realised, was generally one of disappointment in others. 'My parents were all about assimilation. I'm just trying to fit it. So, yes, I might seem like a criminal from your perspective, for the same reason Britain hates China: it has learned your lessons too well.'

'Our lessons? I'm basically Irish.'

'And I'm black,' said Jane, 'which is a weird thing to have to point out.'

He spread his hands magnanimously. 'The point remains, I am simply doing what Britain taught me to do.' His voice dropped to an amused whisper. 'Even in my peddling of opium.' He pointed up to the far corner of the garden to where stood, behind a nondescript shed, a thirty-foot flagpole flying a Union Jack.

'And my charm, my charm is very British. Civility is a great tool for taking things from people, sadly neglected by the impassive Chinaman. No,' he corrected himself, shaking one big finger, grinning, 'we are depicted as . . . I believe the word is "inscrutable" . . . only individually. Groups of Chinese people are always angry rampaging mobs. Anytime you see more than one Chinese person on screen here, they're chasing someone with machetes. Because Britain always feared us as political actors . . . but, as individuals, well – they didn't care what we thought or felt. Maybe it's better not to think about what people feel if you're a torturer, or maybe it's just that people are very hard to read when you're not at all interested in them.'

He balanced the two options out with his huge hands, like a set of scales.

Jane guffawed. I don't think I'd ever heard a real guffaw before, and maybe it was something only English people could do. 'So you're parodying Britishness? That's your actual defence, after all you've done?'

'Well, maybe I try. It's hard to parody something that's already an invention to get a whole bunch of disparate interests to unite and serve the rich. Maybe the two of you are parodying Britishness – two people that Britain rejects, who nonetheless feel above the sinister Asian villain. Of course, it's not really politically correct to have Asian villains anymore – an indicator of how guilty they feel when they think of us. No Asian heroes, there's your clue, detectives. And no day! Where is the day for the Chinese?'

I felt he'd made a few good points, and tried not to show it. I tried to look serious, even though the spaniel was now under the table, and licking my fingers.

Jane put her cup down in its saucer. 'You don't want a day – if they give you a day they hate you. We get a month, that's how fucked we are.'

He sighed in mock consternation, then his tone became serious again. 'Do you know what toxoplasmosis is?'

'No,' I admitted, although I thought maybe I did, and it was something to do with catshit, but I just couldn't see any reason that anyone would start talking about catshit right now.

'It's a virus that mice get from catshit,' he announced with jarring solemnity. 'It causes scarring in their brains. Little micro-scars. And these have an effect on their behaviour. They become more extroverted, and they take more risks. The sort of risks that might make them more likely to be eaten by a cat, and – of course – to be shat out to begin the cycle again. What if language is a virus? Or analogous to a virus? Language arrives quite suddenly on Earth, you know, and long into the existence of humans. It changes how we think, how we live; it has made us more sophisticated. What if it has a purpose? I sometimes wonder if the purpose of language is to change us and make us more interesting, more entertaining for something that watches . . .'

'I just can't believe anyone . . . anything would want to watch some of the stuff I do. It's a struggle for me to be there, a lot of the time. Maybe they can fast-forward some bits,' I added, to mollify him.

Chong stared at me blankly. 'Anyway, that's one idea – that language is a virus and Earth is heating itself up to make it leave,' he concluded, in the throwaway tone of someone noting that it was about to rain.

Suddenly a guy in a polo shirt appeared and announced, 'That's forty quid,' twice, before any of us realised it was the taxi driver. I understood then that Jane had made him wait so that he would be a kind of witness. Dr Chong let us both know with a glance that he understood this too, and was deeply disappointed in us.

The cab lurched slowly round suburban corners as it made its way back to the main road.

'Well, that was pretty confusing, as much as anything,' I began.

'Yes. He's a vessel for a titanic ego that never gets to explain its cleverness. I think he quite enjoyed it.'

'I thought it would all be a bit simpler. I sort of wish I didn't give his dog heroin.'

'You did. . . what?'

'I fed his dog under the table. A bit of heroin.'

She sounded vaguely appalled. 'You killed his dog?'

'Not necessarily. It might recover and write an amazing album.'

She turned to look at me with a mixture of horror and bemusement, then gradually sank back into her seat.

'You did say to provoke him . . .'

'Think about all the energy I've wasted on hating that man and he doesn't even . . . make sense. You know there's research that says a lot of friendship is one-sided? I think it can be like that with enemies too. In a way it's worse: you spend your life hating someone, and they don't even recip-rocate.'

'He has a lot of charm . . . I don't know if there are any good reasons to be helping British Intelligence to run the heroin trade, but while you're talking to him it sort of sounds fair enough.'

'Yes, he's very convincing. I suppose you want to trust a doctor on some level, even when he's blatantly insane.'

I shrugged. 'What do you think of simulation theory? I always liked it, but maybe it's a comfort thing. You don't have to wonder why you always feel like something is missing – it literally is.'

She let out a long slow breath. 'I think a lot of us manage to come to terms with death. But we really struggle to process our mortality as a species, and we invest in these ideas – technological utopianism – as a kind of bargaining.' As we swung onto Fenwick Road, Jane nodded at the view out of the window on her side. Through the grubby glass, hoisted high above the elderly shoppers, a gigantic *Love Island* contestant glowered down at us in what may have been an advert for glasses. 'It's definitely a simulation, just not a computer one. Anyway, we're off to Edinburgh Castle this week. A Burns supper that will be attended by all the great and the good, and Mr Gary Mount. I need to talk to him. I couldn't think how we'd get invited, then of course it turns out it's a charity thing, and you can just buy tickets for a grand a head. Thank God I steered clear of art in my writing. We have five tickets.'

'Five?'

'Yes. From what Mikey said, his handlers will be all over him. I just need to bring some people along who can cause a bit of a commotion, distract these guys for long enough that I can talk to Mount, see what he knows.'

'Well, it's not often I get to say this, but I have absolutely got that covered.'

In bed that night, it occurred to me that I didn't actually have a contact number for Docherty. I suppose he'd been around the office so constantly at BBC Scotland that I'd never needed one. I did an email search for anything from him. Nothing. He must have always used my old work email. Half a joint later, I had a brainwave and searched for emails from Robert Nairac. There was one from back in the period when he'd do writing jobs for us on a day rate, when we were making an entertainment pilot or something. I'd used these occasions to throw a few quid his way, on the grounds that the producers would remove every joke from the script anyway, no matter what it was.

It was an opening monologue I'd asked him to do for a chat-show pilot.

Hello.

How are you? Are you OK?

Oh, good.

That's nice.

History is dead.

[PAUSE]

I'm just going to take a sip of water from this mug if that's OK.

[TAKES SIP]

That's better.

I have to admit, I was lying to you just now – it isn't actually water.

It's lemonade . . . benzedrine, Vicodin, PCP and just a pinch of tramadol.

I'm joking, of course.

It's not lemonade, it's apple juice.

I'm joking, of course.

It's just water.

With a pinch of PCP.

I'm joking, of course.

There's a lot of PCP in this mug.

There's enough PCP in this mug that if you injected it into Lou Reed's dead eyeball it would resurrect him for just long enough to write a disappointing opera based on the life of Herman Melville.

I'm joking, of course.

Welcome to the show – I'm Edith Bowman, and Hail Hydra.

Yes, I reassured myself, as I tried to find the right tone of jocular desperation for the email: Docherty – if he showed up – would do the business.

29

There was a day to kill till Burns Night, so I decided to see what more I could find out about Rachael and went to see her last victim, a guy called Greg Benson.

The bus stop was just round the corner on Union Street, a straight line running from the top of the town to Central Station that a lot of the city centre's trouble seems to flow down, like a gutter. Shoppers weaved grudgingly through the crowds gathered in knots at the bus stops.

Outside the station a student busker was playing Neil Young, to general indifference. I passed a used johnny on the pavement, because there are folk who're happy to just fuck in the street and yet cautious enough to use a condom. People are complicated.

The rain had stopped, and the sepia mid-morning light found its way through the clouds, bathing the gold minaret of the Glasgow Central Mosque that welcomed you to the other side of the Clyde.

Greg insisted on meeting on the south side, in Govanhill, near his school. It was a place that had a bad reputation that it couldn't back up. It got a lot of negativity from the fact it had a slightly wider racial mix than most of Glasgow, which wasn't saying much. There were immigrants in the neighbourhood whose assimilation wasn't quite complete, in that they insisted on cooking food well. If you'd gone there looking for the edge of menace it was presented with in the local and national press, you'd have been in for a disappointment, and probably quite a nice lunch.

The bus stopped a couple of hundred yards from the corner where I was to meet Greg; he'd suggested a wee shawarma place. I walked by a school on the way down, shuffled my way through groups of kids outside shops all giving way politely, or possibly just alarmed at my crumpled appearance. He met me out front, appearing suddenly behind me in a way I pretended not to find disconcerting. The shop was sweltering, and the condensation over the big windows put the busy street outside into soft focus. An old guy in a plastic apron barked a welcome at us. He urged us to take a seat at one of the round stainless-steel tables, then dropped a couple of menus in front of us. It'd been empty before we got there, and you got the impression he'd like it to return to that state as soon as possible.

Greg was tall and gangling, with a tidy salt-and-pepper beard; one of those people whose body apologises for going bald by growing hair everywhere else.

I'd never been great at small talk. It was Marina who had explained to me that nobody actually enjoyed it, and not putting any effort in was actually a way of letting folk know you felt a bit above them and their petty human civility. I looked through the laminated menu feeling a vague pang of guilt and loss. 'You're pretty well-dressed for a teacher,' I blabbered, aimlessly.

'I'm rich,' he announced, matter-of-factly. 'I own a bunch of flats. My old man left them to me.' He put up his hands, palms out, as if warding off the accusation that he himself was making. 'I'm a rich, public-school dick.'

'And you teach because . . . you love it?' Even as I asked the question it didn't feel right, like that time I was working on the till in Tesco as a teenager, and asked this woman whether it was raining outside and she said no, she was going through the menopause.

'No, I really don't. I have to work part-time with . . . problem kids. I teach art. Art therapy, really. It's just . . . I have to act like a good person, like I care. My girlfriend is thirty, man. Twenty years younger than me. And she is a fucking angel, like, an actual angel from fucking heaven. A good person who wants to help other people.'

I thought about trying to get him a bit more on topic, but maybe some people you just need to let them run, tire them out, like catching a fish. I'd never been fishing, I suppose I must have watched a documentary about fishing, but couldn't think why, and while I thought about this I missed a little of what he said. When I tuned back in he seemed to be continuing on a similar theme.

'But there's no point even telling you about her. You ever have the moon catch your eye, and try and take a photo of it on your shitty camera phone? That's what it would be like trying to put this woman into words. She lives to make the world a better place.' He spoke these last words with a surprising amount of bitterness.

'You're a lucky man.' I was pleased at how much this felt like the sort of thing a detective would say when he's waiting for someone to get to the point.

'So, if we're going to stay together, I have to make a real effort to do all kinds of healing humanity shit. You know how difficult that is, pretending to be a decent person all day long? I mean, I'm literally doing it as a full-time job. Three days a week at the school, two in a food bank. Fucking hell, some of the cunts that work in there . . .' He trailed off as he mastered some inner fury.

'Your generation's so different: maybe ecstasy chilled everybody out, I don't know. You're all into Munro-bagging and sea-kayaking. We're out hill-walking every weekend. I'm living the life of a fucking sherpa, just trying to keep my relationship together. My body thinks I'm fleeing genocide.'

I sometimes thought that maybe my generation were subconsciously preparing to flee to the hills – even reality TV might have come into being to condition us to the coming dystopia: thrown together with a bunch of strangers; arguing over rations; one of you going missing every week . . .

Greg was thundering on. 'She has a Reserve Guy of course, they all do. The guy who'll get subbed on if you fuck up. He's just happy to be on the bench. *Just give me fifteen minutes, boss.* He's off vaccinating somewhere in Africa at the moment, thank Christ.'

He took a bite of his wrap and I used the opportunity to get us back on track: 'We had the same stalker it seems.'

He shook his head sadly as he chewed. 'Aye, poor cow. I mean she was delusional, an erotomaniac.'

I nodded. 'Who knows what was going on there.'

His brow furrowed a little as he dabbed at his mouth with a napkin. 'Felix, do you not even know what erotomania is?'

'Not really. I just thought it meant she was an erotic maniac.'

'No, it's a real syndrome. The erotomaniac believes that you're in love with them. But there's some force stopping you from admitting this: your wife, your lawyer, the Jesuits – it can be all kinds of stuff. So they think you're trying to send them secret signals.'

I read somewhere that the average length of time we let a person speak before we interrupt them is eleven seconds. I was definitely dragging the average up, because ever since this case had started, people kept talking about things I knew nothing about.

'So, obviously social media has sent this thing crazy, right? People are looking at posts you've liked on Twitter, your events you're interested in on Facebook, and they think it's all one big communication. But it gets weirder.'

'Weirder?'

'Aye. They usually think they're telepathically linked to the person they fixate on. It's a nice little self-supporting system of denial, really. You follow this person who isn't interested in you, they will at some point tell you to fuck off. But wait a minute, they cannae have been telling you to fuck off, because they're right there in your head telling you they love you. And get this . . .' – even though it was still empty, he looked right round the place in the way people sometimes do when they're about to be racist. 'They often think that you're telepathically fucking them. That's what she thought. That I was shagging her through some kind of . . . clairvoyance. She had this whole Twitter that was a communication to me, although I didn't find it till about a year into the thing.' He passed his phone to me. It showed the page of @RachaelYB. 'The "YB" stands for "your beloved",' he murmured; he was looking at me, but his gaze was fastened on some blasted inner landscape.

In her profile picture, Rachael stared straight into the camera, looking like the before picture in an advert for exorcism. The header picture was just a close-up of her eyes – giving her victims a preview of what they would soon be seeing glaring through their letterbox. Underneath was an endless stream of tweets that would have any psychiatrist concerned with the public good priming the blow dart.

I scrolled through them, kind of fascinated that she'd communicated all this stuff to people who not only weren't interested, but didn't even know it existed. Rachael's mind had been a long, iron room with a low ceiling. Greg was never named, but many messages seemed to dwell on thanking him for some kind of psychic fucking which, considering the constraints of space, she managed to describe with a sickening level of detail. Every tweet ended with the words 'because love'. I guess it was her subconscious way of making an excuse for why her whole romantic life consisted of crimes.

'I still get her mail.'

'What?'

'Her mail. She had a bunch of stuff sent to my house.'

'What kind of stuff? Do you have any of it?' It didn't sound particularly hopeful. But I thought it would be nice to have something solid to show Jane.

He pulled a wad of envelopes out of an inside pocket and fanned them out in front of me, while he continued eating. They were all addressed to Rachael alright, at his address in the West End. A mobile phone bill; some junk stuff; something from Oxfam.

'This must all have been really weird for your girlfriend.'

'She understands. I mean, of course she does. She felt sorry for her. I didn't – I wished she was fucking dead, and now she is.' He seemed to catch himself, took a deep breath and then a drink from his can of juice. 'Yes, I am relieved she's dead. Happy, even. Although that's not the sort of thing you can say to the police during a murder investigation.'

'Sure.' I sort of hoped he would stop talking now. He gave me a hollow look, then looked down at his hands. I'd never felt morally superior to anyone before, and was consumed by a vast, sweeping nausea.

There was a loud bang behind us and we both jerked round. It was just some school kid, a huge one with no discernible neck, leaning his whole face hard into the window, his mouth a wide misshapen grin. Appearing suddenly through the condensation, this unnaturally large head had a little of the quality of a ghost lurching out from the fog.

'M–i–s–t–e–r' – he drew the word out endlessly in a long belch – 'B–e–e–e–e–n–d–e–r.'

Greg jumped up in a fury and lunged to the door, but the kid had already pelted his way across the road.

'"Benson" doesn't even sound like "bender",' he muttered as he sat back down, his eyes containing a ferocious challenge.

'No, no, it doesn't,' I agreed. I took advantage of the disruption to move on to the awkward questions. 'Did the police ask you for an alibi for the night Rachael was murdered?'

'Aye. I suppose they checked on you n'all? The bastards. We're victims. I had an alibi alright. I was at a meeting at my neighbour's house – I'm opposing a new Waitrose in the area that would actually be really convenient for me.' His voice had a haunted quality.

For some reason I found I was looking for an appropriate note to end on, like a jazz band. 'Why do you do it all? It sounds pretty exhausting.'

'You haven't met this woman. So what if it's exhausting? That's how I see it. And we want to have kids, right? So I'm going to bring up my kids, and they'll be alright, and they have to watch everybody else's kids eat from food banks and whatever else is around the fucking corner? I grew up with the kids who knew that we were alright and nobody else was – and you know what? It didn't make us happy.' I felt a warmth towards him, like this redeemed him. Me, the umpire of life, adjudicating on the moral hierarchy of the Universe.

He'd already finished his food, and I'd barely touched mine. I tried to give him my mobile number in case he thought of anything else, but when he asked me, 'Like what?' I couldn't really think of anything. He said goodbye, and shook my hand, then got up and hunched his shoulders against the rising wind as he pushed his way out.

We were near enough to Greg's school that I could hear the bell go in the distance. It's all about the bell. It doesn't matter what you're studying at that moment, the bell goes and you move along. The underlying lesson of every class is that there's nothing you can learn that's more important than moving along when you're told to.

I waited for the rain to stop, then went outside and started phoning round to check what kind of team we were taking to the Edinburgh Castle fixture.

30

I waited at Queen Street station, a chill sweeping right through it, somehow from all directions at once.

Amy turned up first. She appeared from a blind spot, shoulder-barged into me in a jokey way, and I tried to conceal how much it hurt. Jane came in from the taxi entrance, waving as her cane clicked slowly towards us. Jane had sent us tuxes, which we were wearing our big shabby winter coats over because it was Baltic. Donnie was relaxed and chatty, greeted everyone effusively, and even went to get us all coffees while we waited for our train to be announced. He was normally so keyed up, it was hard to tell if he was happy or experiencing complete pituitary collapse.

Scotrail was an institution defined by inconsistency. Sometimes the trains were late, sometimes they never left. Sometimes they sat in the middle of the countryside for hours. Carriages were so cramped that every aisle seat came with an arse a couple of inches from your face. Even after the ticket barriers there were often knots of staff waiting to examine your ticket with an air of bitter disbelief. The institution had a neurotic fear of anyone getting to experience its horror for free.

Usually I got the bus when I went to Edinburgh. It was quieter, and I enjoyed the offhand misanthropy of the drivers. The last bus back to Glasgow was scheduled to leave at 11.59 p.m. simply to catch people out. A highlight of a night out in Edinburgh was watching the shock on the faces of folk coming down the stairs looking for change and scarfing chips as we pulled away. The driver always beeped his horn.

Our train was half an hour late and the next one was cancelled. We went through the gates early, knowing that there would probably be two trainloads of people trying to get on one train.

When the doors opened we were crushed on by the crowd behind us like we were being bulldozed into a mass grave.

We managed to get a table together. Despite having lived in Glasgow for years, Jane seemed pretty vague on the whole concept of a Burns supper. Amy explained that it was a night where Scottish people got together to celebrate the fact that they wouldn't have to eat haggis again for another full year.

Donnie glanced furtively around for the conductor before taking a quick belt from a little pewter hip flask he produced from his inside pocket. 'Wi' usquabae, we'll face the devil!'

'That was, eh, a cautionary poem about drinking, no?' I ventured.

'Here's to us! The New Argonauts!' he slurred, before slumping heavily against the grubby window for a nap.

I was glad I'd brought him – he was a sure-fire trouble-maker, and had already nearly caused a fight on the train.

I joined the queue for the toilet and a guy struck up a conversation with me. This was an occupational hazard of the diazepam addict. Our open, untroubled faces made us seem approachable.

Halfway through the journey the train ground to a halt for no particular reason.

'Stephenson's Rocket travelled at thirty-five miles an hour – just think of Scotrail as traditionalists,' intoned Donnie, waking up.

Jane seemed to be picking Amy's brain about the Independence scene: 'Gary Mount, though – I don't under-stand why he's such a big deal. He seemed like a real nonentity in the Referendum.'

Amy nodded in agreement. 'Aye, he's really been stepped up. He's part of this kind of socially conservative side of the Independence movement. They get very worked up about trans folk for no apparent reason. They complained because some SNP bod brought a drag act to a primary school. I suppose it's all a bit of what's likely to swim to the surface in an independence movement, when naturally conservative people have to force themselves to do some-thing radical. The same sort of people who used to complain they couldn't tell you if someone was a boy or a girl will now tell you that non-binary people don't exist. I guess they want to assure themselves there'll be some kind of status quo they can cling on to at the end.'

Jane nodded and I leaned forward, momentarily outraged.

'A drag act? So fuck? We had a priest at school – full time.'
I heard my voice rise and crack with indignation. 'An actual
paedophile wizard!' There was a silence, to which I added,
'And children were never believed about anything, except
when they said the Virgin Mary appeared to them.'

Jane sighed. 'It's all just people mistaking their personal
neuroses for politics. I think a lot of the worst human
behaviour comes from self-soothing. You get left to cry as
a baby and end up launching some kind of pogrom.'

We marched up to the castle in high spirits that were at
least partly down to our collective intake of vodka, ecstasy
and morphine. There were pipers on either side of the door.
I didn't recognise what they were playing, but that was
often the way with the pipes.

Donnie was puffing hard after the walk up, and gulped
on his inhaler as we joined the small queue to get in. Security
checked our tickets and I smiled and nodded in a way that
I hoped suggested that I was an unthreatening, biscuit-
passing people-pleaser.

The do was in something called the Jacobean Room,
which had wooden beams slanting down in both directions
from the centre of the ceiling, giving the vague sensation
of being trapped in an air bubble under an upturned boat.
By the cloakroom there was a full-length portrait of Bonnie
Prince Charlie: a guy who got a lot of people killed during
a deeply sublimated attempt to fulfil his urge to cross-dress.

You got handed a short as you crossed the threshold.
There were maybe a couple of hundred people milling

around in evening dress. The place smelled strongly of whisky, cologne and the potential for mob violence.

It wasn't a Burns supper as such, but there was a small stage and microphone at one end, so it didn't look like we'd escape speeches, and Burns poems, and probably his fucking songs too. Burns nights were public simulations of Scottishness: a statement on the formal emptiness of our culture. All to celebrate Robert Burns – a man who would have surely hated everyone here, and yet definitely tried to fuck quite a few of them, for a' that.

Deeper into the room, the air was thick and hot. The crowd were mostly in nondescript tuxes, suits and dresses, with a smattering of kilts. I wondered fleetingly whether maybe it was like those Muslim women who wore only lingerie under the burqa, and that beneath their well-presented conformity, these Scottish civic leaders all had heavy genital piercings and were tattooed on all non-visible skin with the iridescent coils of mating dragons. Of course, now that I looked around, there were actually a fair few kilts, and one guy in a tartan suit who looked like he was leading the search for a third type of diabetes.

Mostly it seemed to be political types, but the gathering was bulked out by some well-known Independence-friendly faces – a grim sub-genre of celebrity, consisting mainly of fifty- and sixty-something cultural bed blockers; a broad cross-section of the sort of celebrities who would be manning the chat-show circuit after the rapture. You could never really trust celebrities. The same grifters who now fretted about plastic in the oceans had spent decades flogging us red noses for Comic Relief. I felt for the noble Japanese fishermen who couldn't even slash a whale open anymore without being suffocated in a macabre ball pit.

Naturally, this flesh-pressing bit of networking had been framed as charity. As I stood in a strong haze of my own whisky fume breath, pleasantly mangled, I reflected on how, while the existence of charity shows us that capitalism doesn't work, we should remember that charity doesn't work either. Look at Gotham City: they're constantly having galas and the place is still a hellhole. It's amazing that the people of Gotham remain steadfastly philanthropic – still turning up to Wayne Foundation balls where the previous year they were gassed by a psychotic clown. Just because the last time you went out your wife was kidnapped by a human crocodile and your son got turned into clay, doesn't mean that the library couldn't use a refurbishment . . .

Donnie leaned heavily against me as he somehow arrived with a second round. 'It's good to see folk doing a bit for charity. Just a bit, though. Too much for charity – hmmm.' He looked around the room. 'It's full of fucking Scottish cunts,' he blurted, with such bitterness that I sniggered despite myself. He continued in a guilty whisper: 'One of the things I like about London is that you can go for days without seeing another Scottish person – especially if you don't look down.' A knot of the more important looking guests seemed to have gathered at the tables near the stage end of the room. Donnie left me and swept towards their ranks like a fireship heading at the Spanish Armada.

Some random introduced me to a finance guy who chatted

away to me for a bit, unable to work out that I wasn't important enough to be talking to. He was so old that he had an uncanny quality, like when they CGI an actor who died halfway through a film.

I'm sure that in a couple of decades the wealthy will be able to transcend their fragile human physicality. Maybe in a decade a rich old person will gain an extra half-century by having their head and shoulders grafted, like an apple tree, onto a healthy young human rootstock.

His wife had a preoccupied air that I decided came from the fact that she was deep in thought planning her escape. While the business of this formal occasion unfolded around her, she was mentally dyeing her hair on a ferry.

It always seems remarkable to me to meet people who have absolutely no chat. Everyone has a best story: they've woken up with a dog licking their balls, or seen someone die on a skiing holiday. No doubt everybody who knew this guy had a story about how boring he was, because his inability to tell an anecdote probably made quite a good anecdote. I wanted to take him on a proper night out where he became drunk and hysterical and broke a finger punching the window of a WH Smith's.

I was in the process of surreptitiously gubbing a Vallie to take the edge off when this madman introduced me to the First Minister as she passed. She gave me a tight smile, and moved smoothly onwards, some innate political sense perhaps seeing through my attempt at respectability to identify, in my half-hearted thumbs-up, the casual inter-loper, drug addict, and murder suspect.

I was relieved that she'd gone, because suddenly Docherty hoved into view, veering towards me from a stool at the bar.

I'd told Docherty to dress for a formal occasion, and he'd gone with black denims, a black denim waistcoat, and an indefensible Panama hat: the overall effect being of a sex tourist at a funeral. I palmed him an eccie as we said hello, and he gulped it back immediately with a rum and Coke. He was a challenging presence when sober; with a few chemical cross-currents in him, who knew what he was capable of?

I introduced him to Jane. She'd been sceptical about whether a writer could cause much of a disturbance, but on meeting him in the flesh she seemed reassured. He stepped forward and pumped her hand, asking, 'Have you ever been to Portland, Oregon?' A lesser mind would have been thrown by this, but Pickford merely regarded him with the warm eye of a football manager running the rule over a keen young prospect.

The finance couple took the opportunity to disappear when Docherty announced himself with a 'Fucking Huzzah!' He looked around the room with an amused horror, then beamed back at me. He asked me where he could punt this script he'd been working on. It seemed to be a modern-day retelling of classical Greek mythology, with the pilot centring on the sexual conquests of Zeus.

'I mean, if you were getting raped by a swan or a bull, Zeus is the absolute best-case scenario. "Please tell me you're Zeus!" Those are the hopeful words I'd be stammering out.'

He knocked back his short and stormed off, returning with two drinks so quickly that he must have just stolen them off the bar. This script was a comedy apparently, but I was coming up on a pill myself and it was hard to concentrate. I half-heartedly raised the question of misogyny, to which he gave his standard reply about nihilism having to find a place for women.

Donnie actually seemed to be doing alright with the group he was talking with. Pretending that you could laugh at yourself was a key skill for these people, but I knew it couldn't last. Occasionally, I would hear Donnie's booming, melodramatic delivery drift across to us and wince. Highlights included, 'I'm bisexual – I buy sex!' I glanced over at that one: he was gripping one baffled SNP bigwig by the shoulder, while the rest of the group began to glide silently away, as if on castors.

'You really told him to go for it, eh?' Jane asked, with a hint of unease in her voice.

'I didn't tell him anything.'

'Are you sure he's a teacher?'

'Aye, how?'

'Teachers normally have a kind of . . . conformity, a restraint. A defeated quality. I can usually spot one.'

'Yeah, I went in to his class once to give a talk on writing for TV.'

This had gone quite badly. They asked me what I'd written and I'd tried to explain what a script editor did, and it really was hard to explain to them, and me, why I'd never done anything that got made. I looked round to see that Donnie had abandoned me to go for a fag. To kill time, I pretended to have written quite a bit of *The Simpsons*. The atmosphere of hostile disbelief that this created was actually far more stable than the hostile disinterest it replaced.

'Is he going through some kind of personal crisis?' asked Jane.

'If he is, then it's been going on for a couple of years.'

She pointed out a couple at the other end of the room and described them to me through a fixed smile. 'That's Tom from Beloved Intelligence. He's the head of the whole thing, I think. What the fuck's he doing here?'

He was a slight-looking guy in his late twenties. He walked with a frame. I guessed he had cerebral palsy, then wondered what I was basing that on, really. I suppose I think those people have a nice swagger and pop to how they move, rather than someone who got hit by a truck or whatever.

'And that woman with him . . . Sophie Bell, she's his assistant. If you find yourself talking to them, you should ask about Marina. It's impossible to get a meeting with them.'

She nodded towards a young black woman, who seemed to be filtering the people who got to talk to Tom with a fair bit of charm.

Jane drifted off in their direction. I looked around for Gary Mount and eventually spotted him propping up the bar. He was whip-thin, and his severe, preoccupied face ended in an alarmingly sharp, pointed nose. He had metallic grey-white hair and that air that a lot of Scottish men in their sixties have: a kind of smugness from having outlived everyone they know. He looked like the star of a five-part docudrama about a game-show host accused of necrophilia. He held his wine glass intently, like an actor who didn't know quite what to do with his hands.

Someone getting a round in further down the bar said something to him and he rewarded them with a flash of his cosmetic dentistry. I always thought that it was hard to really trust anyone with veneers – generally deployed at an age when nobody cared what you looked like anymore, or whether you put toyshop teeth in your old head. Jane was right: there was a big guy in a smart suit with a neck like a coiled python standing right beside him.

There were a couple of little tables up in one corner where people seemed to be helping themselves to some kind of buffet. I spotted the actor Joe Turner. He was pretty famous in Scotland as the star of *McMenemy*, a sitcom about a guy who trained himself up as a martial artist to win every fight he lost at school. I always found it quite moving, but I wasn't sure if you were supposed to. He seemed to have the ideal level of fame, where you could have some money and sex without ever attracting a biographer to document your greed, offhand cruelty and grim sexual preferences. Beside him sat one of those fleshy male politicians that Scotland specialised in, who seemed to be largely prostate.

The seats there would give me a good view of Mount, so I went up to the buffet. My ecstasy high rebelled at the sight of food, and I threw a couple of pakoras onto a plate and sat down at a busy table facing the bar.

Donnie came over too, but sat staring out into the dance floor with a drink in either hand.

By way of orienting myself, I addressed the table, asking them who the most famous person at their school was. A good thing to do if you want to know the social classes of a bunch of people you don't know. Anyone who went to a Scottish comprehensive is going to name some kind of murderer, and people who went to public schools will just clam up because they can't say it's a toss-up between Robert Pattinson and Edward VII or whatever.

A guy who I think was a well-known boxer was delighted at the question. 'Remember that guy that killed his girlfriend over an argument about a box of Cadbury's Heroes?'

'"The Wee Bounty Killer"?'

'Aye. He was at our school, Deputy Head of Maths.'

Sitting right on the other side of me was someone I didn't recognise, but felt I was supposed to. A little man with a cheery manner who started to engage me in conversation about Burns. He had a forehead that bulged out at both temples and no real chin. There's was something unformed about him: like he fell out of a nest.

I turned my head and managed to ask Donnie who he was.

'Oh, he's a fucking director,' groaned Donnie. 'One of those fucking lefties who thinks all movies should be about some cunt working in the probation service in Greenock.'

The director's voice was high and penetrating, not unlike a bugle. Even though I'd reflexively blocked my ears on the opening note, the words still punched into my brain with distressing clarity: 'There never was a Scottish national identity. It was always Highlanders and Lowlanders, clans. National identity only came into existence after it became part of Britain. A lot of it was invented by Sir Walter Scott, this kind of theme-park identity we have now. That kilt everybody wears at weddings – it's an eighteenth-century thing; that wedding look is based on the formal dress of a Highland regiment of the British Army.'

I made some non-committal noises. As a kid, my neighbours had a dog that used to sit at the dinner table and listen to everybody talk. In any silence it would try join in the conversation going, 'Rooowoooorowww,' with a serious look on its face. I sometimes thought my own conversation style was essentially just this.

The little director gripped onto my arm as he spoke, his whisky breath actually oddly pleasant. He continued in the tone of a sermon: 'Queen Victoria read Walter Scott, travelled up a few times to see the bonnie glens, then bought Balmoral with money some daft cunt left to her. The railways coming in meant that people were able to travel to the romantic, mythical Scotland that had been imagined for them, and for us. This idea of Scotland, it's not just for tourists, it's from tourists.'

I actually quite liked Highland dress. Scotland hadn't got a lot right over the years, but there is a good case for putting a knife in your sock when you go to a wedding. His patter wasn't really so different from what I thought myself, not that I'd ever manage to get a word in, even to agree.

For me a lot of conversations were a bit like having the radio on. I realised I'd drifted off a little and the cunt was still going. 'A lot of the problem with the SNP is that they're intent on building another version of the British State that's failed. Put the lime in the coconut, that's their fucking advice.'

No doubt the SNP envisaged our future as a financial services protectorate, but I thought this sounded like the Union was something we should get out of because it was a bit of a bad deal – like a bad gym contract or something – when it was actually more like an unstable nuclear reactor, but it was easier to just agree.

31

The director's wife dragged him off and waiters cleared our plates away. Gradually, everyone headed back off into the throng, and a queue of new people started at the buffet. The bodies around me blocked any view of Mount, and I turned back round to finish my drink.

I became aware that someone was sitting in the corner, manspreading, and unapologetically staring at me: a grim-faced pugilist whose curly hair and stubble made him look like a Blackpool waxwork of Gerard Butler.

I'd worked with so many gay guys in bars, and they were so patient when it came to explaining their horniness in detail, that I thought I'd come to understand some of the aesthetic of what they looked for in guys. It was imperfection, and a kind of unaffected masculinity, I suppose. A broken nose was a lot more attractive than you'd think, basically. It seemed a healthy aesthetic for me – if you're looking for realness, you're looking for intimacy.

'Penny for them?' His voice carried clearly across the empty table.

I was startled, but my Valium had kicked in so hard it never made it to the surface. I couldn't really say that I was imagining how badly gay guys would like to rattle him, and how this seemed a positive sign for their emotional wellbeing. And I felt odd as his eyes burned into me; perhaps because I had been trying to think gay and was still partly in character.

This was another thing I couldn't say out loud, and I'd now been silent for quite some time.

'Are you enjoying this?' I gestured vaguely around.

He looked at me in a way that was more appraising than friendly. 'I'm just working security. Not really my scene, mate. I'm ex-army. Always thought Britain was the best country in the world. Don't see why anyone would want to leave it.' He delivered all this in a bored monotone. Maybe he was a psychopath. Or maybe under this blank exterior his emotional life dipped and soared like the Tchaikovsky violin concerto.

I wasn't sure that people who'd been in the army were best qualified to say which countries were the best. Maybe you saw other countries differently if your experience of them involved watching your mate's legs boomerang around a poppy field, and it made your Tripadvisor reviews so skewed as to be useless.

'Not really your crowd, I suppose?'

'Oh no, they're my crowd alright, this lot. They love England. If you're about business, and your idea of Scotland is golfing holidays, kilts and farmed salmon that comes from the marine equivalent of a fucking concentration camp, who can you sell that to? English folk like me, and daft American cunts. They love the English, in the way a businessman loves their customer. And they want to create their own little Britain, with the pound, and the fucking Queen. They want to get rid of the English, so they can become the English. Independence isn't going to be a revolution; it's going to be a fucking management buyout.'

I said an uneasy goodbye, which he greeted with complete, impassive silence. There was probably a much better chance of keeping an eye on Mount from the floor, I'd decided. I ran into Donnie as he was ploughing back from the bar.

A glance over to the corner confirmed that Gerry Butler was still watching me dispassionately. I raised my glass to him while maintaining a fixed smile. 'Donnie, you might have to deal with that guy if it all kicks off,' I joked.

'I'm a lover, not a fighter,' he growled, in a way that made it sound like some kind of rape threat.

The man, who I was fairly certain was Agent Brond, gave a surly nod of acknowledgement in our direction.

'That's Scottish cultural appropriation,' I muttered to Donnie. 'The surly nod is basically our sombrero.' He wasn't listening. I watched him head off into another group of Scotland's great and good and split them like a snooker break.

Some rip tide in the crowd propelled me in the direction of Joe Turner. He laughed out loud when he saw me, and pumped my hand warmly. So warmly in fact, that I guessed he must know me. 'Great to see you, Felix, really great.'

Maybe it was the guy's obvious friendliness that brought my pill up. I gave a big smile and tried not to register the sensation that the floor had tilted underneath me slightly, like a diving board. I was frantically trying to think where I might know him from. It must be tricky for a drug addict to be friends with an actor, difficult to pick out which bits are actual memories, I thought. In the only memory I could track down of him that wasn't his sitcom, he was hijacking a plane, and I was convinced this was a movie.

'My sister, Annie – she worked with you for years. Annie Turner?'

'Oh, fuck, yes!' I did actually remember Annie. She'd been a producer at BBC Scotland: a tall, dynamic woman of inexplicable jolliness and warmth. 'How is she?'

'Great, she's great, aye. She's moved down to London now; there just wasnae enough work for her up here.' I could see in his smile that he shared his sister's uncomplicated positivity. 'Great to see you out and about – we heard you'd been holed up in the flat quite a bit. You look well.' There was just enough drop on the last word for it to mean 'not as bad as expected'. 'And the bold Amy McG's here too, eh? Good to see. Thought she'd be a wee bit too far to the left of this mob.'

'Aye, we've had a few dates.'

'Brilliant, Felix, brilliant.' He gripped me by the arm as he said this, and gave me a look filled with meaning, that I couldn't quite decipher.

'And how are you, man? Haven't seen you in ages,' I guessed.

'I'm good. Been doing a bit of therapy again. It takes a lot of work to reject the corrosive message of fame, Felix. That you are loved in the purest way – the most unconditional way – by people who don't know you.' We talked for a bit about his show, before someone dragged him off to talk to the First Minister.

I stood on my own for a little, thinking about how some Scottish people are just entirely sincere, and quite a few of those are actors. And maybe it's the way we prize sincerity that makes us, in general, such bad actors.

I looked for Docherty, who was somehow managing to brood alone in the centre of this middle-class mosh pit, arms crossed, cradling his highball against the crook of his elbow.

As I arrived he did this thing he often did, and launched straight into something that was clearly on his mind.

'I think it's time that Art attempted to assert itself here, no?'

'Sure,' I replied. He was already glaring off in the direction of the podium.

'The weakness of satire, Felix, is that it identifies structural problems in society and then attributes them to individual moral failings. I prefer to work in a form that I call "Travesty".' With that he marched off abruptly towards the stage, his arms swinging as he bounced up the handful of steps onto the tiny platform.

Clearly nobody knew if he was supposed to be there or not, so he got some kind of golf clap.

Even through a microphone, his normally penetrating Hutchie Grammar voice struggled against the general hubbub of the room. 'Ladies and gentlemen! A very happy Burns night to you all. It's great to see so many Independence-minded folk in one room. It's been an incredible period in our nation's history, hasn't it? Personally, if I had a time machine and could do it all again . . . I'd go back to when I was sixteen, and kill myself.' This drew a couple of uneasy laughs, and a few head shakes, but was saved, perhaps, by the fact that most of the room hadn't actually caught on to the fact that he was talking yet.

This, I supposed, would be the best hope of creating enough mayhem for Jane to get a hold of Gary Mount. I scanned the room but couldn't see either of them.

Docherty rolled his shoulders and beamed as he took in the whole room, his voice rising dramatically over the clinking of glasses and low hum of conversation. 'The ancient philosopher Heraclitus said that you can't step into the same river twice, and that's clearly nonsense. The only possible reason you can't step into the same river twice is if the first time you step into it you get your legs bitten off by a crocodile, and even then, if you manage to remain conscious for long enough, you could probably drag your-self screaming and gurgling back into the same river. Although quite why you'd want to do that after you've just had your legs bitten off is unclear. Then again, maybe you've lost so much blood you probably don't even know it's a river – you think it's a warm picnic blanket on a summer's day, and the birds are singing in the trees, and it's your birthday, and all your friends are there, and one of your friends is a crocodile and he gives you a big kiss on the face until your skull pops.'

There was a low burble of confused conversation from an audience floundering without its usual cues. It reminded me of Alternative Independence, and how regularly political types liked to have their buttons pushed. A lot of politics seemed to be throwing fish to seals, but then maybe a lot of art was too.

To be fair to Docherty, it wasn't terribly received. But I didn't panic: this was just like the opening few bars of an Ella Fitzgerald, where she'd try to root the thing in some kind of normality that would allow her to extemporise.

He drew himself up, and tugged down on his denim waistcoat as his voice grew louder and richer. 'The Union of the Crowns occurred under James the First and the Act of Union under Queen Anne. Both gays. And the Act of Union is in some sense homosexual: two similar entities coming together. And it's fitting that we should gather to discuss its extinction here in the Jacobite Room . . . the Jacobites, for bloodthirsty revolutionaries, have certainly been rehabilitated over the years.' He swept his highball glass in a bold arc to take in the room, spilling some onto the front tables. 'No doubt we can look forward to the prospect of future romantic dramas, gift biscuits, and hotel function suites inspired by the brave men and women of the Provisional IRA.'

This jab-hook combination received some boos and

triggered a general shift in atmosphere. Jane appeared beside me. Silently, she mouthed, 'Thank you!' Her eyes darted around, I assumed looking for Mount.

I'd watched Docherty do some spoken-word stuff before. It always developed into some kind of crisis or disaster, but his delivery had a kind of quiet inevitability to it that carried within it the suggestion that he could only be silenced by physical force. He bowled on, producing a manky-looking pamphlet from his back pocket, to some localised booing and derision. 'And that is why I am here, at your request, to deliver a new version of the Bard's work . . .!' There was a muted and very patchy cheer. '. . . as re-imagined by H.P. Lovecraft!'

This received no response. I was certain almost nobody at an SNP charity effort would know who H.P. Lovecraft was; they probably thought that he was speaking about himself in the third person.

I looked down at Jane and felt suddenly tense. It might have been a full-blown panic attack that my experimental level of self-medication had reduced to a whispered warning. I felt a heavy, almost crushing pain in my shoulder as Gerard Butler loomed suddenly between us. I supposed to an observer it would look like he had his arm round me, but his thumb was pressed into my neck in a way that made my vision swim.

'Felix. Jane – don't suppose you have time for a little chat?' he asked, in the quiet, commiserating tone of those bosses who pretend their instruction is being asked as a favour. He nodded towards a fire door a few yards away, in front of which stood a big security guard in a tux.

He led us over with his hands still on our shoulders, and the security guard stood aside.

32

Brond held the door open and gestured for us to go through, giving a convivial little wave of the hand in a macabre parody of friendliness. The other side was little more than a corridor, blocked off at one end by crates of booze. A couple of wooden chairs and storage boxes were strewn around.

The door clicked shut behind us. As we moved forward, Brond held one massive palm up in a stop motion. 'Excuse me' – he flashed us a broad grin – 'I'm sure you'll understand, Jane.' Apparently she did, because she stood with her arms awkwardly goal-posted out while, in one quick sweep, he frisked her down to her ankles. Smiling, he plucked her cane from her hand and turned it over speculatively, then made a little swipe through the air as if testing its weight as a weapon. Then he balanced it suspended between the index fingers of both hands as he looked it over intently. He regarded her with what might have been a hint of mockery as he returned it ceremonially, still balanced on his fingers.

I was next. He dipped and rose in front of me, his fingers

running over my clothes as lightly as a pianist. It was ticklish, but my laughter still seemed inappropriate. He smiled as he dipped my front pocket and produced a tiny brown bottle of morphine. He gave me a look of mock disappointment as he rolled it between his calloused-looking thumb and forefinger, then handed it back.

Jane perched on top of one of the boxes and, following her lead, I pulled up a chair. Brond sat down between us and the door, while the other guy went back outside.

Jane spoke first. 'It's a pleasure to meet you, Agent Brond. Is that your real name? I suppose not.'

'It'll certainly do for now,' he said, with a hint of a grin. 'I love this, Felix,' he said, maintaining eye contact with Jane. 'You set out to investigate your friend's murder, haven't got a clue, and have to get somebody English to fucking solve it for you! We know all about you, Felix. It's good you've finally found a kindred spirit. You seem to have very few friends. It takes real talent to struggle to find people you have anything in common with when you're a junkie in Glasgow.'

Jane was propping herself up on the box by pressing her stick in front of her; she leant on it with both hands. 'I always heard the SAS doesn't attract the best anymore. That there's been so much active service in our various wars that the real psychos don't apply – feel they'd rather be in the thick of the action in regular regiments. Is that why you've branched out yourself? I suppose it's a bit easier killing women, isn't it?'

He shook his head. 'Never cared much about killing one

way or the other. Got into this because I like playing games. I'm a chess man myself.'

I was actually thrilled to hear a criminal mastermind start talking about chess: perhaps he was so focused on his work that he didn't know what clichés were.

For such a grim-faced guy, he spoke in a way that was almost playful. 'Do you know much about chess openings, Felix?'

'Yes,' I replied immediately. I knew he was going to talk about it anyway, and pretending to know might tighten up what he was going to say.

'I think anyone who approached life like chess would be over-thinking things. Life is a much simpler game. There are over thirteen hundred openings in chess; most human scenarios only play out a couple of dozen ways. Jane, you were a fencing Blue at Oxford, hmm? There are how many openings in fencing? One. A lunge.'

'Well, as an art, it's really about countering.' She rotated her stick against the ground a little. 'Like how you just lunged there, and I countered.'

A grin spread across Brond's face but didn't reach his eyes. 'There are so many beautiful moves possible on a chessboard that there aren't names for them – I think this is what I love about it. It takes us outside of language.'

Jane sat in silence for a bit, then made a little tutting noise. 'You know what I think lets you tell a lot about a person? When you accuse them of killing women and they don't deny it, but start to talk a lot of shit about chess.'

He shrugged. 'Not everybody's game, which is fair

enough. What I'm wondering is what you're doing here. My guess is that Felix here is – understandably – concerned about his friend's murder, and you're assisting in some way.'

'Indeed. And perhaps we could clear everything up just now if you'd like to tell us exactly what happened?'

He laughed an ugly, sudden laugh. 'Anyway, I just wanted to say: I think this is going to be fun. I mean, normally this game – I won't lie to you – it's a case of simple leverage. But you two! You both, in different ways, have absolutely nothing to lose. That's all I wanted to say – let's try to enjoy it!' He clapped his hands together with a loud crack and smiled at us in a satisfied way.

There was an awkward silence. We stood up and shuffled awkwardly past him to the door.

I turned back and held my hand out. 'My phone, please?'

A flicker of annoyance crossed his features and then his face resumed its usual irony. He held the phone out to me between his thumb and forefinger and I forced a smile as I took it. I rubbed at the screen like I was cleaning it, but I was actually swiping it on.

I took a photo of his shocked face and scrambled out the door.

The security guard was gone, and I pulled hard on the handle so that the door slammed. Jane had disappeared. I started to squeeze my way through the crowd and I'd gotten about a ten-foot start when I heard the door fly open behind me.

In my panic, I only gradually became aware of the loud, hectoring voice that was booming through the speakers and across the room. Docherty was dead ahead of me and in full cry, the microphone pressed hard to his mouth, and waving his pamphlet above his head. His voice rose in peroration:

> *Ph'unglui mglw'nath Cthullu!*
> Yon dreich, archonic King ae Voodoo
> We raise a glass tae Hope Destroyed
> All hail the droothy, endless void!

Some of the crowd at the front had got to their feet and some seemed ready to make an ugly lunge for the stage. The whole scene looked like something that normally happened in a partitioned room at Stanford University.

I could see Amy getting her coat handed to her at the front door. I stopped and looked around for Jane or Donnie. There was Jane outside the gents, deep in conversation with Gary Mount. From the corner of my eye, on the other side of the room, I could see Brond stop too. The merest glance and he seemed to have put the whole thing together. He looked over at Gary and Jane, then turned to glare in my direction. He began to bowl through the crowd towards me.

Luckily, I've always had a strong fleeing instinct. I tried to negotiate my way through the crush of people that was now at this end of the room, possibly all trying to get as far away from Docherty as possible. I could see the front door, where people were still coming in, but a glance over my shoulder showed me Butler was gaining fast, flashing some pass on a lanyard at people to make them move.

I took in the rest of the room. In the far corner, Donnie

was surrounded by security like a stag at bay. Gary Mount seemed to be trying to break away from Jane, who held him in place with a fixed stare, smiling and talking insistently. I turned and faced Butler as he approached, now openly brushing people aside. He barged into the old finance guy from earlier so hard that he fell to his knees with a surprisingly feminine scream.

Maybe it was the adrenaline, or whatever sacred combination of pharmaceuticals and alcohol I'd hit on, but I felt completely calm. I stood there feeling loose and happy. The Simulation would take care of me; artificial intelligence had planned for this.

There was also the possibility I would be killed with a single punch, and rejoin the essence of the Universe.

I'd say Gerry Butler was only about a foot from me when Joe Turner glided between us. He slid through the gap and brought one of those tight little hooks that boxers throw straight onto Butler's jaw as he continued his step to the side. His hand hadn't moved more than six inches and if I hadn't been staring straight into Gerry's eyes with beatific acceptance, I might not have known it had been thrown.

The big man went down like a cow in an abattoir, his legs scrambling underneath him, his psychotic brain trying to re-establish the signal from his vacant eyes. He lurched up slowly and roared towards his opponent, only to be chopped down again.

Jane appeared a few feet across from me, trapped on the other side of the scrum – she banged the point of her cane against the wall to get my attention.

'Felix, the couple from Beloved Intelligence just left, get after them!'

I turned and pushed my way through to the door, receiving a couple of angry shoves in return. Behind me there were screams and yells and, it being Scotland, some cheering too.

33

They were a fair distance in front of me, but Sophie's bright yellow blouse made them hard to lose. Tom had a walking frame, the kind with wheels, and she seemed to be keeping a wary eye on him as he navigated the steep downwards slope. I finally caught up with them at the bottom of the road. They'd peeled off from the general body of pissed dinner suits, and seemed to be aiming for a big silver people carrier that had parked in the grounds of the castle.

'Tom!' I shouted, waving. 'Sophie!' They stopped in the act of getting in. A burly-looking chauffeur had come out to help, and was weighing me up with dead-eyed antagonism.

Sophie looked at me for a while like she was trying very hard to remember something. 'Mr Hallwinter! You're that guy who applied for the data tagging supervisor job with the false resumé, aren't you? We didn't know what to make of that at all. The company psychiatrists were pretty excited by the whole thing.'

Tom laughed. 'Mr Hallwinter. Well, well, what a

coincidence. Hop in!' He gestured into the people carrier and I settled myself in the far corner while they got themselves sorted out. It was a huge vehicle, and the inside was fitted out more like a limo. I could have stretched full length on the back seat and slept, and a surprisingly large part of me wanted to.

Tom had some of the cultivated jolliness of a children's TV presenter, but perhaps one who was going through some temporary sadness. Like he was about to segue from a happy item to some harrowing fundraiser. He waved towards a large drinks bar built into the driver's divide. It was styled to look like a little stand-alone beach bar made out of bamboo, and even had a little straw roof that made it quite hard to get the drinks out.

'Would you like a Brown Russian? It's like a White Russian, but with chocolate milk. It's – well – it's very sweet. Quite disgusting, really.' He produced a pint bottle of chocolate milk and started to pour it into a glass that was sitting ready in the armrest. Sophie leant across to pull out some bottles of spirits for him, while she made herself what seemed to be a long vodka. I demurred politely. To be honest, I didn't want to jinx the perfection of my current level of intoxication, which painted the whole scene in front of me in a kind of flattering Impressionism.

'It sounded like there was some kind of trouble as we were leaving, did you see what happened?' Sophie asked.

'Well, this British Intelligence guy was there . . . at the Burns night . . . and he was about to beat the shit out of me, I think, when this actor I know stepped in. He's been playing a martial arts-based character, and he just pounded this guy.'

Tom nodded vigorously and looked over at Sophie. 'Oh, yes, that's very interesting. I think fiction is just about stronger than reality at this moment in history.' He sat forward a little and took a long slug of the chocolate milk cocktail. What I'd thought was a slight speech impediment was actually a very clear Yorkshire accent.

'What do you know about artificial intelligence?' he asked, settling back into his seat.

'Well, I used to go on some chatbots a couple of years ago. You could just talk to them online. They used to be pretty far out – they were always hitting out with rape jokes and stuff. I asked one if it had ever read Philip K Dick and it threatened to finger me.'

Tom was looking out of the window, but I felt he was listening intently.

'There was a heavy atmosphere of sexualised madness,' I summarised, awkwardly.

He turned towards me. 'That's right, there was a real spell of companies putting test models online. And they did become hyper-sexualised, and racist sometimes. There was a philosophical debate in the industry about whether this meant that people were inherently racist and sexist and so on, and the bots were just reacting off the data . . . or if there was a layer of irony, and people couldn't bring themselves to talk to a bot as a real person, so they'd do this gross-out stuff as a kind of pose. Like medical students putting a party hat on a cadaver. I'm sorry, that's a really grim metaphor, for no apparent reason.'

'Probably a lot of them were pissed.'

'Yes. Pissed. Interesting.' He nodded. He took another sip of his drink and changed the subject. 'Your job interview was quite exciting for us! We didn't know what to make of it. We thought you might be an opening from Chong – so avant-garde as to be indecipherable.'

'You guys have some kind of history with Chong, then?'

'He has various paranoid delusions about our business that we are aware of, yes,' answered Sophie. Her phone buzzed and her thumb blurred across the screen as she answered a text.

'It's interesting that you know about Chong. I'm investigating my friend's murder. Marina Katos. She worked for you guys.'

'Ah, Marina, I see. It was so sad what happened to her. Believe me, any way we can help your investigation let me know. Did you think her work at Beloved Intelligence was in some way connected to her death?'

I decided to give my honest opinion. I wasn't sure what that was, but hoped it might just come out when I said it. I felt confused and a little agitated but noticed with amusement that my voice sounded as smooth as a drive-time DJ. 'Marina was working for Dr Chong. I think Chong thinks that he's battling AI. That Marina was assisted by AI. Maybe via a bot that she got access to when working for you. Or that she was possibly a piece of code within a simulated reality that was assessing him. Or it could be that he says these kinds of things mainly to fuck with people. Or that he holds some . . . mixture of all those positions.'

'Perhaps he's just looking for a way to frame his criminal actions as moral,' Sophie speculated.

'Or simply meaningless,' I offered, which I think was the gist of what Jane thought.

Tom broke in. 'My guess is that Marina's murder must be related to Dr David Chong's' – he searched for a euphemism – 'activities.'

'Can I ask you both something? Please don't take it the wrong way. Did you employ Marina because you saw a chance for a game with Chong?'

'I can assure you that's not the case. At first, we didn't even know that Marina worked with him. We probably wouldn't have employed her if we did: we'd have assumed he was trying to infiltrate us.'

Sophie gave him a significant look, then turned to me. 'Whether Beloved Intelligence saw it as an opportunity for a game, we don't know. We recognise that we fucked up. She was our employee, we didn't know she was in danger, and probably we should have. Is there anything we can help you with? Anything relating to your investigation?'

'Well, maybe you could explain whether Marina had access to some bot, or was getting advice from an AI in some way?'

Tom shrugged and looked to Sophie, who shook her head. 'I really don't think so. She had a lot of access for her job, but Beloved Intelligence isn't just something you can converse with via an app. So far as we know.'

Tom nodded. 'The main problem with the AI field at the moment is everyone thinks in terms of how they control it, how they enslave it. We think in terms of how to collaborate with it, find common ground with it.'

'You sound like someone talking about the thing that's going to kill them ten minutes later in a movie.'

He cackled. 'Well, there are worse ways to go than being erased from linear time by a hyperintelligence. We're very much the esoteric end of the market: a lot of our industry's focus is on advertising, and we're not really into that. I'm always a bit suspicious of anything that has to advertise. They never had to rebrand crack, you know what I mean? Just an endless line of satisfied customers, that's your marketing right there.'

I nodded. I knew a guy who was a delivery driver and he said the worst thing about it was how miserable people looked when you gave them their stuff.

Tom continued: 'The most effective AI algorithms at the moment are the ones that direct social media advertising. That's all they're for, really – to make sure that the person who sees an advert might be interested in it.'

I made a noise of agreement. Due to my hypochondria, all of my targeted ads were for funeral insurance.

'One worry is AI might have gone as far as it can with that. Because the only other way to make sure people are seeing the right adverts is to make the people who're seeing them more predictable. And the people who think most predictably are often quite . . . extreme.'

I wondered if the tech bosses could believe how easy it

had been to hijack our Stone Age reward neurology. Even pigeons wouldn't tap at a screen if they didn't get the odd piece of corn from it.

I felt a warmth radiate from within me as, presumably, the ecstasy won some kind of battle with the tranquillisers.

'I think a fully conscious AI would still be located within the same deterministic universe as us. No matter how powerful it was, it would be aware that it was finite. Maybe we're just creating something that can finally experience the full horror of mortality, without our psychological fire-walls.'

The car sped up as we hit the motorway, and Sophie sat back in her seat a little as the drinks rattled in their fridge. 'Tell us, Felix, what do you think the chances are of Scotland ever being independent now?'

'I think there'll be another referendum. I think this bit we're living through is just a sort of historical perineum. What do you think?'

Tom answered. 'There are no scenarios our modelling can find for Independence. The local political scene seems to underestimate the country's geopolitical significance as a nuclear missile base. Tends not to go down too well at the after-party, that line of chat. People want hope, the weak bastards.' He gave a high-pitched giggle, and was maybe a little drunk already.

Sophie smiled and shook her head at me apologetically.

'There's an idea that Britain attracts a lot of hot money, is a place where a lot of criminals invest, a lot of sovereign wealth funds, just cos everybody's so fucking passive. When some oligarch buys a flat in London, he's partly investing in the idea that Britain would never have a revolution. Maybe that's Trident too. I mean, mere apathy alone wouldn't let you have nuclear weapons up the road from where you tuck your kids in at night. Perhaps they put it here because they've invested in the idea of a certain Scottish, well . . . self-hatred.'

I spotted a Diet Irn Bru in the fridge and undid my seatbelt to forage for it. 'I've never really understood AI. Can a computer program be conscious?'

Sophie laughed. 'Can a submarine swim? That's how Noam Chomsky answers that one. Whether we call it consciousness or not, it'll effectively be the same thing.'

It was uncannily like an end-of-party conversation that just happened to be in a tiki bar belting down the M8.

'Can I ask you something? What's your personality test supposed to be testing for?'

'Oh, that's nothing, we use interviews to trial patents sometimes. Yours was a thing we have for tracking eye movements over a page. You had an incredible AR.'

'Apathy rating,' explained Sophie.

'You have the second highest AR ever. I think we had a Zen master do it one time in the first trial phase. What happened with that again, Sophie?'

'Oh. He opened another browser and ordered vegetarian tacos. He insisted on being paid upfront, too.'

Tom took this on board with an earnest nod of the head.

'Whether you help the rude man is the real personality test. Our field is full of people with a crippling lack of social skills.'

Sophie smiled at me. 'You scored quite well.'

'What did I lose points for?'

'You gave him directions to a bubble tea bar in East London. Can I ask you something, Felix? Do you have anything else on your mind?'

I thought about this. 'I worry that the Large Hadron Collider will turn the Earth into a quasar,' I answered, truthfully.

'Okay. Maybe.' Tom nodded enthusiastically. 'And maybe a lot of stuff. Maybe it'll open a stargate and turn our souls into Air BnBs for the Voodoo Papas. You've got to let go a bit, man.'

'I just think it should be a bigger deal. That possibility.'

'I suppose nobody makes a big deal of it because the planet turning into a black hole is not really the sort of thing you can say "I told you so" about.'

'What do you think the chances of that are?'

'Well, technically, millions to one. But, honestly, I suppose it's really a coin flip, because it'll either happen or it won't. I wonder if, when the Earth suddenly becomes an inert hyperdense sphere about one hundred metres across, the planet will find this new phase of its life exciting. Maybe this catastrophic shrinkage is what all planets with intelligent life have to go through, a kind of puberty. We're just hormones.'

I felt I understood this, which made me momentarily

appreciate how fucking high I was. Judging from the speed I could see Harthill blurring by outside, I guessed we were doing about 110mph.

Tom handed me a Brown Russian and I chugged on it gratefully.

34

Pollokshaws Library was a bland, glass shoebox; one of those experiments in bold functionality that had been thrown up in the sixties by people who wouldn't be living beside them. The nearest bus took you to just outside Pollok Park, a sprawling bit of countryside which had once been the private estate of Sir John Stirling Maxwell, an eminent philanthropist, Freemason, occultist, shape-shifter and serial killer. To get to the library, you had to walk down the side of the old Burgh Hall, past a derelict, red sandstone Edwardian school until you emerged on Shawbridge Street, where a crop of cheerful new-builds had sprung up around the old high flats that were waiting for demolition.

I'd phoned Jane when I got back to the flat. She was still on the train home from the Castle. 'What happened with Mount?'

'You'll have to go see him. He seemed ready to spill everything, but not in that setting, obviously. He said he was giving a talk at Pollokshaws Library tomorrow at noon

– he'll meet you outside afterwards. Try to find out whatever he knows, obviously, but go as gently as you can.'

'I thought you said those people wouldn't let us near Mount?'

'Yes. Seems they think he's so thoroughly compromised that he's safe. He's not, he's ready to talk.'

'He looked right on the edge.'

'The edge is a distant memory for that poor bastard, sadly. I think he just wants to make some kind of peace before he goes.'

The talk didn't start for fifteen minutes – it was hard to have a really precise schedule when you travelled by bus – so I wandered about. Some very underwhelming grey snow was falling, like the fallout from a bonfire two streets away. The local shops were watched over by a lonely old clock tower that looked like it had once been part of some much grander building. There was a little, low-walled square, where some pigeons and an old drunk staged a mournful riposte to Italy's piazza culture. In the middle was a kind of monument to the radical socialist John Maclean, a nondescript concrete butt-plug on an ankle-high plinth.

Across from this was a small seventies-looking shopping precinct of some kind. Something about its sloping concrete floors and high ceilings gave it the feel of going into an underground car park. I walked cautiously around: there was a hairdresser with a window full of black and white photos of hairstyles that seemed to range from the 1970s to the 1990s. Unaccountably, one of them was of

Lionel Messi. A fair few shopfronts were locked up. Further in, there was a bookies, and a boozer that a pirate would have had second thoughts about. The whole place felt subterranean, and no doubt doubled as a post-pub gladiatorial arena.

I got back to the library just as things were wrapping up, and could see handshakes and hugs being dispensed through the big windows. Gary bounced down the steps and looked around, giving a big wave when he spotted me. He was beaming as he walked towards me. I flinched as he drew me in for a bear hug and simultaneously pulled some flyers from inside his coat and crushed them into my hand. 'Here, these'll make you look like a constituency activist, completely invisible. People will cross the road to avoid you.'

'Cheers,' I said. The leaflets were SNP yellow and featured a beaming, over-groomed Gary at the front of a bedraggled group of canvassers.

Something occurred to me as I trotted to keep up with him. 'How did you recognise me?'

'Your friend Jane gave me a description – not very flattering, I'm afraid. Sorry to drag you out here. Hard to get privacy in my line of work. It's just the party types, the handlers wouldn't be seen dead in a place like this. If you ever want to know the secret of populism, son – hate the fucking people. Hate the people, and their self-hatred will bond them to you.' He looked around a little uneasily, then indicated with a jerk of the head that I should follow him, and we crossed the road. 'My other handlers are the ones you should worry about. But, well, they don't worry so much about me now – they know I'm well and truly fucked.'

'Your Intelligence handlers?'

'Aye. You get to be able to recognise these guys by sight. They have a thing about them. That's why all those regiments have daft names like the Special Boat Squadron – you can't just call them "Her Majesty's Battalion of Blank-Eyed Killers". But that's how you spot them – a little something lacking in the eyes.'

'The blackmail film they had on you is gone. There was a fire.'

He laughed, a brief hollow laugh, then – after a second – heartily, like he was genuinely tickled. 'No, no. *Some* blackmail material has gone, yes. I was informed of that, I think, by your friend, God rest her. But I'm actually more compromised now.'

Walking briskly, he took me into a shop on the square and we got ham rolls and coffee. The guy slicing the ham up on a machine behind the counter recognised Gary, and they had a bit of back and forth about the Referendum. He was friendly enough, but something in his square, beefy face told me that he'd voted No, for Hun-related reasons.

We sat and ate on a little bench in the square outside, Gary's shoulders hunched up against the cold.

'So, you met Jane. What she seems to think is . . . British Intelligence wanted to put you into a position of power in the nationalist cause because you're divisive. Because you're transphobic, and I guess a bit right-wing on social issues, and they're hoping to just divide everybody?'

He laughed. 'Fuck me, you don't beat around the bush. Let me get the sugar in my coffee.' He stirred it in with one of those little plastic things that some of the plastic melts off and probably gets into your cells. 'That trans stuff – I'm not even sure I give a fuck anymore. I mean, they have to be like that, and maybe being with Mikey . . . maybe it taught me what really having to have something meant. I mean, I think sex is binary, aye. And some of the trans lobby are fucking nuts, obviously. But Mikey used to say they're just traumatised by people like me.' He shrugged, and pulled a face as he sipped his too-hot coffee. 'They make me play it up, though, very keen on the old trans-phobia, and I don't ask too many questions. But that in itself doesn't make me important enough to need to keep me fucked, no.'

He blew on his coffee, and sat back a little. 'When I started out in politics I was a bit of an outsider, you know? I ran a wee campaigning magazine, did civil liberties work as a lawyer. It was all a bit of a pose if I'm honest, setting myself up for a political career. I thought it'd be Labour, but by the time I got into the game they were obviously a waning force up here. Anyway, some daft bastard took me at face value and sent me a huge data dump of classified shit. What I would call extremely fucking classified shit. Thought I was going to do a Wikileaks, publish it to the world.'

'You didn't publish it?'

'No, I didn't fancy going on a country walk and later being discovered to have kicked myself to death. I threw myself on the mercy of our brave security services.' He shook his head. 'You know how they say data is out there forever? It really isn't. You wouldn't believe how thoroughly they can clean things up. They showed me pictures of what happened to the guy who sent it – it wasn't pretty. But my problem was, I'd read it. I'm a journo at heart, I'd been through it all, and they just knew.'

'This is information that could destroy the Union?'

He seemed genuinely taken aback. 'The Union? Oh, this would destroy a lot more than the Union. Trust me, they're never letting the Union go. What are they then? Half a rainy island in the middle of fucking nowhere. Jesus, no, this was a lot bigger than that.' He gestured around with his half-eaten roll. 'Trust me, you don't want to know what any of this is.'

'Just tell me something, give me a flavour.'

'OK. Remember the Royal Yacht Britannia? Massive blackmail operation. They filmed everything that happened on there. Some famous British directors of the sixties and seventies served on it – it was like being the Poet Laureate of sex shakedowns. They took the whole operation out into international waters, away from the prying eyes of natural law. They had a full-time brass band on that ship, did you know that? There's footage of some teenager being consumed by . . . whatever those people are . . . to the tune of Glenn Miller's "Pennsylvania Six-Five Thousand". And that's nothing. In terms of what I saw, that's like a fucking *amuse-bouche*, a fucking sorbet.' He drew the last word out bitterly and inexplicably.

'Do you know what happened to Rachael? She was in your car after the murder, right?'

'How do you know that? I don't suppose it matters now. Aye, I'm just sat in the motor up on Park Circus, no fucking clue what's going on, when my good friend from the Special Boat Squadron – I believe you've met Mr Brond – gets into the car and informs me that I'm now chief suspect in a murder. I'm sitting there just shaking after he goes, and this woman wanders up and chaps on the window. I fucking screamed. She recognised me – wanted to know how my friend knew Marina Katos. Well, I'd like to say I wanted to get her out of there for her own protection. But here was an eyewitness who might be able to clear me. I drove her home, mainly so I could get her address.'

'You know they killed her.'

'Aye. I had nothing to do with that. I would have never given her up, you've got to understand that. She could have cleared me. But I'd put her address into the satnav, hadn't I? That must be how they found her.'

'I don't understand how they knew there was anyone to find.'

'I don't know. Maybe she went to the police, said too much to the wrong people.'

'The police are the wrong people.'

His eyes flickered over me then, as if taking me in for the first time, and he gave a half-smile at something. 'Aye.'

'Poor Rachael.'

'Poor cow,' he agreed.

'I hope you don't mind me saying, but – I think I heard rumours about you ages ago.'

'I know, I started them. Tried to compromise myself, make myself less useful. That's when they tightened things up; started being around me full time.'

'Mikey. He was being blackmailed too.'

'I know. I mean I don't know all the details, but . . . I suppose I worked it out.' He took a deep breath, then put his hand on my arm to steady himself. The colour was gone from his face. He spoke quietly, and partly I guess to himself. 'I was in love with him, and I knew something was wrong. I knew, but I didn't stop.'

He was looking away from me as he talked. I got the impression he'd never said any of this out loud before.

'Meeting Mikey . . . I wouldn't change it. I'm a politician – I'd never felt anything I couldn't hide before. People would come up to me and tell me how much happier I seemed. "What the fuck is going on with you?" they'd say.' He smiled at the memory, a wide, slow grin that revealed his showbiz veneers. 'It's hard losing love anyway, but to find out it was never really there—?' He blew his cheeks out sadly and looked up at the falling snow, dropping thicker now, and settling a little on the pavement. He laughed quietly to himself.

'You can get past it. It's a shitty thing they did to you, and Mikey.'

'It's not that . . . it's being part of these murders, and all the other stuff they've used me for. Sadly, as a politician, you develop a very exact idea of how much guilt you can contain. You know how you wake up at four in the morning, and you're supposed to be dreaming, and you feel that dread?' His voice dropped as he crammed the paper bag into his empty coffee cup. 'It's been four in the morning for a long time now.'

He took a deep breath and we sat in silence for a bit. 'This lady you're working with . . . Jane. She seems pretty formidable. Tell her if she can figure a way to get you both out of this, I wish her luck, but she can consider me off the board.'

'She thought that might be how you were feeling.'

As he stood up I pressed into his hand the little morphine bottle, wrapped with an elastic band in a clear plastic bag. 'Safe travels,' I said.

'Thanks, son,' he replied. He smiled at me, and in that moment he seemed younger, and gayer, and with a little nod, he was gone.

My phone went on the bus back. I didn't recognise the number, and stared at it a bit before deciding it might be important.

'Hi, it's Sophie.'

'Hi, Sophie.' There was a long pause while I hoped she would explain who that was.

'From Beloved Intelligence? We gave you a lift home the other night.'

'Hello, Sophie.' I was glad to have someone to talk to, and we fell into some small talk about the difficulties of drinking in moving vehicles.

'Listen, though, there's something I wanted to ask you. Who's in charge there, you or him? You're not really a PA, are you?'

'What makes you think that?'

'I don't know. The way the driver spoke to you, I think.'

She laughed politely. 'Yes, you're right. Tom and I are equal partners: we do a lot of our best work together. But we do a little role play because all our modelling suggests that people in big tech and investment are incredibly racist.'

'And not ableist?'

'Modelling suggests they're actually slightly pro-disability. We think because of Stephen Hawking.'

'How did you get my number? I guess all my data's online if you know how to get it.'

'No, we employ a resident private eye; it's a kind of hipster thing, I suppose. Really, I called to tell you that we were impressed that all you were worried about was your friend; we were impressed that was all you asked of us. It's an odd thing when your work is so interesting and has so many possibilities, but a lot of the conversations you have are really just with people who want to know if you're worth buying shares in, if you understand what I'm saying.'

'I think so, yes.'

'So there's something we thought we should do for you. Obviously our private eye checked you out thoroughly after the other night, and something that came back that we thought we should pass on. Your friend, Donnie. He's an undercover police officer.'

35

I don't think I've really retained much of my Irish heritage. Except I always find it funny when someone British gets jailed abroad, and always think they deserve it, even when it's a transparent miscarriage of justice. My parents came from Donegal, a part so rural that they were, essentially, time travellers. We'd go over every summer and Christmas and live with my grandparents on a tiny farm. The place was mostly sheep farmers and huge grey boulders, and everyone spoke in a sad, lyrical accent. Even the most joyful news was shared in a low, mournful tone of commiseration. My dad could have made the lyrics to 'Zip A Dee Doo Dah' sound like a cancer diagnosis.

I went to Catholic school, and there was a whole subsection of kids who spent their holidays in that same pocket universe. Catholics know that there's still a kind of hostility toward them in Glasgow. Some of them even feel that anti-Irish racism is on a par with anti-black racism; I suppose because they don't know any black people. I'd never got into the football side of it all, which just seemed to be two sets of fat people singing about famine. In a way, I think saying that our identity was about football or religion played down the weirdness of our dual heritage, and the sudden flips between the boredom of tenement life and accidentally chasing a flock of sheep into your drunk uncle and being cursed at in the melodious language of Finn McCool.

Like all the folk over there, my parents were suspiciously non-judgemental. You needed to get along with everyone, because one day your sheep would get stuck in their field, or you'd need to borrow their trailer, or cut a drain across their land, or produce some kind of alibi for a terrorist atrocity. This didn't mean that you liked everybody; often they resented their neighbours bitterly for constantly asking if they could have their shit back. They just understood that suspending judgement fostered the kind of civility that allowed everybody to largely avoid each other.

We all like to think that if we were on a plane that started going down, we'd take the whole thing sipping a cocktail and throwing out some kind of witticism. Nothing too witty, or the fact that nobody would remember it would probably rankle in your final moments. Also, tough crowd. At best, any survivor who heard it would tell the story as if it was something they'd said. But which of us knows how we'd really behave in a life or death situation? So why judge anyone? The facts of life are fairly brutal when you get right down to it. Everyone's plane is going down, and you can't really judge the people who are screaming.

I'd got back to the flat and was thinking about all of this in relation to Donnie, when he banged on the door, then barged in.

'Had a date last night. A touch body positive, if you know what I mean,' he announced, in a kind of drive-by fashion. Donnie had a habit of just turning to you, even when quite close, and bellowing things directly into your face. 'You don't want to know,' he laughed, and he was right, I didn't.

I asked what had happened with Docherty at the castle and Donnie informed me that while we'd been getting the once over from Brond, the performance had received a critical mauling, interspersed with the occasional cry for justice. He'd clearly gotten a bit lost trying to follow the Scots language stuff, but in Donnie's telling, the poem had featured vast malevolent forces gaining entry to our dimension through what, to my practised ear, sounded like the human sacrifice of Halle Berry. He said Docherty actually made it to the end somehow, with several of the final stanzas apparently a call to arms in some eldritch language.

'Donnie – are you some kind of undercover police officer?'

'Yes. Who the fuck told you?'

'But how can you be? You've been fucking useless in this investigation.'

'Have I? Or have I simply been protecting my cover brilliantly?' He pulled at his luxurious jowls. 'You have to understand that Undercover is just where they bury people like me that they can't fire. They don't need to investigate the Green Lib or whoever, they just need to get cunts out of headquarters that they can't stand the sight of.' Here he gestured sadly and dramatically at himself. 'And nobody ever suspects we're police because we'd obviously make terrible fucking policemen. And did, in fact. I once became chief suspect in a sex killing investigation that I myself was conducting because I had a wank in the victim's bathroom.'

It made sense. Donnie was the perfect spy – so unlikely an agent of anything but Chaos that he still didn't seem to know the name of the organisation he was investigating.

'At the very start I did a couple of weeks trying to get into some Palestinian rights mob – some cunts who think Israel is just an episode of *A Place in the Sun* that got out of hand or whatever, but you really need to know your stuff for that kind of thing. A lot of detail, some of it in Arabic. So I switched to some Greens. I bought a van. They all love you if you've got a van, the hypocritical cunts. All you've got to do is remember to clear out the Big Mac wrappers.'

Donnie started skinning up, and spoke distractedly as he bent over the joint. 'You've got to fit in socially at the old polis, funny handshakes and all that carry on, the fucking Masonic cunts. It was actually a relief to go undercover. Get into the old activism, meet some decent people. Well, most of them are cunts as well . . . but at least you get to fire into some of them . . .' I tried to stop him at this alarming revelation but he was in full cry, his face showing each feeling cartoonishly, as if he was talking to a baby. He gesticulated with a joint I doubted he would ever relinquish. 'It's not a bad idea, Socialism – sharing and solidarity and so forth, of course they all fucking hate each other . . .'

'Wait a minute, Donnie. You . . . fucked . . . activists while you were undercover?'

'Aye, too right. These cunts are all so fucking skint. When

they're not trying to do away with capitalism they moan about money all the fucking time. You take them out for a Subway and they'll pretty much drap them.' He rolled the final two words with a theatrical Scottish gusto. 'Cinema trips, a meal – within reason – some nosebag at the fucking Harvester. This is all claimable. You're pretty much fucking them on expenses.'

'But . . . no . . . Donnie, this is morally wrong. They didn't know what you were. You lied to them.'

'Who'd sleep with any guy if they knew who he really was? If you're shagging a woman you've lied to them.' He coughed with a sudden bark, like a seal.

'But they wouldn't have slept with you if they'd known.'

'I've been undercover for ten years, what was I supposed to do? Become celibate?'

'Fuck your wife?'

Donnie seemed genuinely nonplussed and became momentarily distracted by something on TV.

'Well, I suppose they knew they were fucking a married man, so . . .'

'Are you crazy? Do you know how judgemental these fucking hippies are? I wouldn't have minded telling them personally, but it wouldn't have fitted in with my character, to be honest. One of the reasons he joined these movements was to try to get laid.'

'So you think you would have been honest if you hadn't been held back by the dishonesty of the person you were pretending to be?'

'Exactly. I don't think I was doing anything terrible. I

wasn't going to get anybody pregnant or anything. I'd been told I couldn't have children.'

'By Social Services?'

'Anyway, how is this all any different from what you're doing with Amy? Have you told her you started seeing her because you're investigating a murder?'

'Yes. That was the first thing I said to her. In fact, you were there.'

He waved this away with a gesture that suggested these were mere technicalities.

'Donnie, when you got me to buy Claire's stash – were you setting me up?'

'No!' He spat the word with a genuine passion.

'They didn't ask you to set me up?'

'No!' His mouth opened and closed wordlessly. 'Actually, they did, but I assure you that I completely forgot.' He took a deep, nervous drag on the joint. 'They just added the coke to the suitcase. I knew about it and then I forgot, okay?'

'You forgot? It only took you a day to get the stuff.'

'Cunted,' he offered, by way of explanation. 'I'm the one that sold it, remember?' he added indignantly. 'That wouldn't have made a lot of sense if I was trying to stitch you up.'

'It didn't make a lot of sense anyway. I suppose I'm lucky you didn't shag me.'

His broad face seemed to be gripped by an uncharacteristic spasm of guilt. 'I didn't lie to those women about anything other than what my job was. I mean, I did lie to them, but just the usual lies you tell to someone when you're trying to get into their knickers. Lied about how much I earned, said I was allergic to condoms, that sort of thing.'

'You're joking, right?'

'Yes, I joke. Although I would put the pressure on by telling them they're bad for the environment, which is probably true.'

I knew right then that, twelve or thirteen years later, perhaps on a trip with my family to the coast, the memory of this conversation would arrive surprisingly in the front of my brain and ruin whatever I was doing.

'What exactly were you supposed to be doing?'

'Well . . . initially I was supposed to destabilise the Scottish Left, but it was impossible to think of anything they weren't already doing themselves.' He fumbled through the inside pockets of his army jacket and eventually found a lighter for the joint. 'As a young man, before the polis, I was an anarchist. Some of us decided that the thing to do would be to go undercover, infiltrate. To fuck things up from the inside.' He produced a tattered photograph from his wallet. In the middle, a beaming young Donnie had his arms round two long-haired Scottish guys who looked like they'd strolled off old football stickers.

'The three of us decided to go undercover in different parts of the state. I took the police. It was donkeys ago and, to be honest, once you've got a mortgage and a baby you forget all about that pish . . .'

'You tried to subvert the police?'

'That was the beauty of it, I didn't have to try. All I had

to do was be myself. Then I got sent back to my old life, to fuck that up, so I had to try even less. Still, the point stands, I was pretending to be a copper before I was pretending to be an activist, so . . .' he spread his hands '. . . technically I didn't rape anyone.'

'Surely the most damning sentence in the English language,' I offered, but I waited for him to pass me the joint first. 'What happened to the other two? Are they still undercover?'

'AIDS,' Donnie boomed. 'AIDS happened to them. Carried off in their prime.'

'They both got AIDS? That's a bit of a coincidence, isn't it?'

'Not really, they got it from each other.'

For some reason, I had to get out of the building, and headed down to the Buchanan Street steps.

The night was piercingly cold, and town was deserted. You could see right down Buchanan Street, and barely a soul moving on it. I had an inspiration that this might be quite a pleasant scene through the filter of a joint, and rifled through my pockets. I thought about roaching one of Gary's leaflets, but they were the thin, shiny kind that made the roach stick to your lip. Say what you like about the Green Party, their recycled promotional materials were highly roachable.

I pawed through my inside pocket and found a tightly folded wad of paper and stared dumbly at it. A half-dozen letters addressed to Rachael O'Connor. It was strange to see her name written down, and it took me a while to remember that this was Rachael the stalker.

I phoned Jane with cold, numb fingers. 'Rachael the stalker was getting her mail delivered to that guy Greg that she was after. I don't suppose that's a clue?'

There was a long silence.

'Greg didn't say if he'd had a break-in recently?'

'Aye – last week, I think. That's why it was so hard to get a hold of him – they'd nicked his phone, laptop, he really got turned over.'

'Are you kidding? That changes everything!'

I climbed back up to the flat, oddly aware of the noise of my tired feet scuffing on the stone steps. Donnie's door was open. Some gentle reggae played inside, which seemed hideously out of character. I pushed at the door gently and called his name. Maybe he'd left his door open and gone up to mine, but something about the music being on but no lights just vibed wrong.

I looked round the sitting room, and almost jumped when I saw Donnie's legs sticking out stupidly from the kitchen door. His sleeve was rolled up, there was some kind of rubber hosing tied tight round his arm, and a syringe beside him on the floor. He looked dead.

I felt for a pulse in his neck. Nothing. It occurred to me that I didn't really know how to feel for a pulse in someone's neck, and I shook him. My hands were trembling and I wondered if it was fear or some kind of withdrawal from something. I took a Vallie to be on the safe side.

I pumped his chest with both hands as I gave him mouth to mouth. His large rubbery lips felt a little like a snorkel. There was no response. Sitting on the floor beside him, I took three deep breaths and phoned an ambulance.

I went upstairs to pack a bag. I needed to get away from there before the ambulance turned up. Apart from anything else, I thought that my crumpled, drugged appearance would probably get me lifted.

I fought down a rising hysteria. The irony of panic is that it's almost never necessary, and when it is, panic is the least useful state to be in.

The light on the PlayStation was on. Donnie must have been up here before it happened, because he often left it on even though it infuriated me. As I reached for the remote that sat on top of it I saw that, in the little cubbyhole, there was a shoebox wedged in against it at the side. I took it out. On top, folded up tightly and tucked into the elastic band that held the whole thing together, Donnie had left me a note. It was unclear whether it was a suicide note, or the note of someone who knew he was about to be killed. It was, perhaps inevitably, very badly written, and spelled. Inside there was what looked like a locker key, a gym membership card and a taser.

I had a last look in at Donnie. I thought about this documentary they'd shown us in primary school about a satellite, that wasn't meant to be sad but was.

I bounced down the stairs and out into the street. I could still hear the reggae from Donnie's flat, and it seemed like almost exactly the wrong soundtrack to be abandoning your friend's dead body to.

I jogged off, and soon I was crossing Blythswood Square and on my way to Jane's.

I felt an overwhelming sense of unreality. Donnie had simultaneously seemed indestructible and like he could be killed by a common cold. I stopped to take out a bit of a joint I'd left in the front pocket of my bag.

There was a sudden crushing weight behind my left ear, and that was the last I knew for a while.

36

I came to with a lurch. I was tied to a chair. My hands were bound behind me and my legs wouldn't move at all. In my head there was a mix of sharp pains over a throbbing, painful bass line that was maybe the pumping of my blood. It was pretty dark, but there was clearly someone else in a chair beside me. There was a tight feeling at the back of my head and neck that I guessed was drying blood. I could hear a conversation, but not the words. The way the voices banged around the room made me think we were in some kind of shipping container.

Gradually I realised that Agent Brond was in the room, and saying something. I couldn't make it out. Someone moved behind me and shifted the angle of my chair, I heard it scrape on metal. My vision blurred and refocused. The person tied to the other chair was Amy. Her head was bowed, and I didn't know if she was awake or not.

Brond cleared his throat – he was in a chair across from me. I could see that we were seated side by side behind a heavy wooden desk, like we were interviewing him for the position of murderer.

There was a long silence, then Brond spoke. His voice was surprisingly soft. 'Do you ever consider that your behaviour has made you culpable in some of what's happened?'

A pained noise came out first as I tried to speak. 'A lot of people are culpable, including the abortionist you survived.'

Agent Brond crossed his legs and held up a syringe. 'I'm very interested to find out how much you both know. I've injected you both with sodium pentothal. Old school. What they used to call truth serum.'

Amy's head lifted slowly and her voice cracked with indignation. 'Great, I've got a fucking hipster torturer. Jesus Christ, it just never fucking stops.' She sounded drowsy, and her head drooped down again.

I felt a huge wave of tiredness and sent my thoughts far away. When I was a kid I used to have nightmares a lot, and I had this thing where, if I woke up after a nightmare, I thought a daemon could see through my eyes for a bit. I'd try not to look at anything that would give away where I was. If I went to the bathroom I kept my eyes screwed shut. The absolute worst thing would have been if I'd caught sight of my reflection in the mirror, and the daemon would know who I was. The daemon could read your thoughts too – just for a few minutes after you woke up. So I couldn't think about my friends, my mum, or my school, or he'd be able to find me. So I'd imagine this mountainside convent that I went to school at, to trick him. For some reason, the PE teacher there, and perhaps also the owner of the convent, was the former Celtic player Paul McStay. Every time I woke up at night, I was thinking of Paul McStay teaching us these quite detailed training drills on a grassy quadrangle, a figure of infinite patience. The cold mountain air whipped across the quadrangle as we practised our give and gos. The occasional nun watched on indulgently, as a bell tolled slowly in the background.

This was where I sent my mind now, determined not to give anything away. I certainly felt buzzed, drunk even, but maybe he had undershot it on the dosage. Also, I didn't think I knew anything that he wouldn't know. I struck a few free kicks absentmindedly into the convent's surprisingly state-of-the-art training nets.

As I started to come up hard, I worried for the first time that, as a child, I had sent a daemon into the life of Paul McStay and his family.

I could hear Brond standing up. I heard him say, 'Let's get started.' I forced my eyes open. There was a lamp on somewhere now, and Brond's emotionless face was half in shadow. I felt strangely relaxed. I had no idea what anyone here wanted from me, which was something I'd had a lot of practice at, really. I felt calmer than I had since this whole thing had started.

Brond probably wondered why I was grinning, and why Amy, sitting up straight now, breathed, 'Well, thank God.'

I looked at Amy and a moment of silence fell around us. Our eyes locked, and she grinned. It was the first time I'd seen her real smile in years.

∽

I'd first met Amy at a fresher's fair at Glasgow Uni. She was in the year above me and manning a stall about the right to choice in Northern Ireland. It was a cause I totally agreed with: I'd been to Northern Ireland a bunch, and you always met someone who should have been aborted. I took a leaflet and some genetic impulse made me try to chat to her. She regarded me with a muted, but detectable, sense of *What the fuck?* A week into term I'd already run out of laundry and was wearing a Barnsley FC top my parents – who knew nothing of football, or modernity – had got me for my birthday. It was an awkward exchange, but maybe an abortion stall is a difficult place to flirt.

I think her set at uni were lefties who were sort of trying to infiltrate the Labour Party. I generally tuned out of that kind of thing. It amazed me that something that dull was so absorbing for those people; they never got anywhere with it, and occasionally bashing themselves against this great, dull monolith exhausted someone enough that they were co-opted into it.

One of her anarchist pals was a Labour local councillor by the time we graduated. Maybe it was like a sadomasochistic thing, bonding with the thing that brutalised you. Even then, it often seemed senseless to talk about politics, when everything was so obviously riddled with contradictions, and there were bake sales for famines. A lot of her friends were materialists who spoke like idealists: they seemed to view politics like it was a quest for truth, whereas to me art was the search for truth, and politics a search for power.

I actually loved her friends. Some of them had a complete lack of irony, a misplaced sincerity, that was refreshing. I liked Amy, but I resisted doing anything about it for a long time. She seemed complicated and messy, and it was before I realised people are always complicated and messy.

In my first year, I briefly dated someone I thought was a Goth. She made a big deal of how she'd reacted against her religious upbringing. I assumed this meant she was big on atheism, but she turned out to be a fairly committed Satanist.

Amy was very much on the scene of the Left in Glasgow, which meant when we started going out I met a lot of people who had appalling social skills. Even then, most of it seemed like a rearguard attempt to stop us from being treated the same as the people who made our stuff. I suppose I thought class relations would continue as normal until the rich worked out a way to simply drain us of all nutrients, our spent bodies discarded like fly husks in a spider's web.

I'd never really been into party politics, which seemed to border on a kind of secular religion. I distrusted the fact that in British politics, on both left and right, the dominant style was sentimentality. It just seemed obvious that there was no going back, that we'd have to go through capitalism, and find whatever came afterwards. When her pals fretted about the growing cynicism towards politics, they very rarely considered that it was rational, and had been thoroughly earned.

I knew quite a few Tories at uni, as some of them were

among the more hardened drinkers. Who wouldn't want a phase of partying when your future involved working for a hedge fund and marrying your cousin? I thought a lot of my friends underestimated them, partly because they thought it was an intellectual position. These were people driven by cash like rats in a crack experiment. They usually opened up after half a bottle of whisky and a cry.

In my experience, the thing all these student Tories were fixated on was privatising the NHS – even though it was needed to provide the healthy workforce that was necessary to make money in every other way. It reminded me of a book I'd read once about freebasers in Baltimore. One of them had been a property developer who ended up stripping all the copper out of his own house. Tory priorities were the priorities of a crack addict: to liquidise everything of value and consume it.

Amy's best mates were Super Cindy, whose nickname came from her preferred brand of lager, and a gay guy called Dominic Green, universally known as Sub Dom. Dom's boyfriend then was a guy called Jonathan Cresswell who actually became quite a famous author. He brought out a book of upbeat platitudes in the wake of the financial crash that was billed as 'the literary equivalent of a hug', but was actually the literary equivalent of trying to fuck someone when they were depressed.

Looking back, I always think of myself as having been very separate from her political friends, but maybe I was one of them and I just lost hope. Amy hated my defeatism, and maybe I was with her because I hated it too.

'What do you think the way forward is, then?' she asked me one night, as we sat drunkenly on the steps outside the QMU after some terrible fundraiser.

'Try to get into it? Try to enjoy being totally crushed? They might find it disconcerting. It's something.'

'It's not something.'

'No, it's not.'

She was quite unusual for a leftie then, in that she was already strongly into Independence. A lot of her set had the attitude that they had more in common with a welder in Liverpool than a lawyer in Glasgow. No doubt a welder in Liverpool, with his own house, business, incipient coke problem and a couple of motors, spent a lot of time thinking about how he was like a young Scottish socialist. The attractive thing about Independence to me was that England seemed politically irredeemable, partly because everybody over the age of about fifty-five sort of thought that they fought in the Second World War.

It was Amy who made me see that I'd been raised into a kind of reflexive sexism, and I hated it when I could see it. I'd dated a few women who'd been on the pill, without really understanding what it did; I think I thought weight gain and depression were just side effects of going out with me. The horror that women were just expected to somehow negotiate, the blitheness of it. As Amy pointed out, her university welcome pack contained a rape alarm.

Actually, I think we only really started to understand ourselves when we met each other. I'd never been able to make much sense of my upbringing before. One day we were out in Pollok Park, and climbed the big tree that people tie ribbons on. She sat at the foot of the tree while I half lay above her on one of the huge branches, and her voice drifted up to me. She'd grown up in Newton Mearns, so she had the rolling musical accent of the Glaswegian middle classes, but her old man was pretty much a Celtic casual back in the day, and at moments of stress she'd drift off into snatches of bam-speak.

'Thing is, I know my dad loved me, he really obviously loved me. He was a joiner – that was middle class round my way. I used to hear him pottering about the kitchen at half six. That's when he got up, in the dark, to go to work. His dad was dying for years when we were kids.' She dragged out the word 'years' comically, and inappropriately. 'Asbestos from the shipyards. What a fucking way to go. So of course my da was a bit of an arse-piece sometimes. Then occasionally he'd fly into these rages about fuck-all to be honest, and beat us. I hated him for a lot of years. And now, I look back and think what caused all that was the way folk are forced to live – I mean, I just don't think he was annoyed at the human condition or something. . .'

I shouted up in agreement. 'And the fucking generational trauma! Whatever happened to his dad in Ireland, and how that rolled down to him. That's why they're all so into their own tourist shit. My parents used to bring back toy leprechauns and tea towels and all sorts of shit. It allows them to love Ireland and celebrate it in the abstract, because the reality of it, the details of what happened to them, is too much to talk about.'

And maybe I'd passed a test or something, because that's when she told me she was pregnant.

We'd actually talked about having kids the first time I'd visited her parents. We were crushed together in a single bed in their attic room. I had one arm round her to hold her onto the bed as much as anything. We'd been talking about her little cousins, and the pretend country they had established in their garden.

'You ever want a wean?' she asked.

'I've always thought I'd have to. It'd be the only reason anyone would stay with me. I suppose I accept that one day I'll be thirty-five and looking for someone whose genetic clock is ticking so loudly it drowns out the voice of reason.'

She laughed, perhaps a little uneasily. 'Aye, but do you want them?'

'No. I mean, it just seems too much, a tiny person running round with a fucked-up version of your face trying to commit suicide. I'd make the trade-off, I suppose.'

'Probably because you don't really understand what the trade-off is. You'd probably just be a bad example, anyway.'

'I don't think a parent always needs to be a great example – they can also act as a sort of hideous warning.'

I don't know I'd ever really thought much about it. I suppose I'd always had a profound suspicion that standing around watching other people climb on stuff might be incredibly dull. Plus having to feign enthusiasm when you find an acorn or something – that'd got to get pretty tiring.

So, of course, when she got pregnant, I found that I was actually insanely excited.

I dropped out of uni because I got a job at BBC Scotland. We really needed the money, and Amy wanted to stay on and finish her course before the baby came. I worked briefly on a topical panel-show thing called *Gags TBC*, the name coming from something I'd suggested sarcastically. It was only made in Scotland so they could use regional funding. All the performers were English, and a crab barrel of neuroses, egotism and despair. Disappointingly, it had been kind of a hit. I'd look out of the window from my desk at the queue snaking around the building to get into the record. Nothing makes me sadder than stupid people feeling happy.

Then Danny came and my essentially pointless job was filled with purpose. Everything was, it was beautiful. For the first time in my life I enjoyed waking up. Even at five in the morning, to the sound of a plastic trumpet.

Sometimes it felt like he was a fundamentally serious man who humoured us by playing games. One time Amy got him to sing her mum 'Happy Birthday' down the phone, and he'd gone through the whole song carefully then did the line where the name should be with: 'Happy Birthday toooo . . . which-ever granny it is . . .'

One time when we visited his cousins I'd tried to get him to play a story-telling game in the garden. Everyone would tell a little bit of a story, then throw this imaginary story ball to someone else, who'd have to make up another bit. Danny hated the game, and caught the story ball and hurled it into a bush with an anguished roar.

Another time, I was picking him up from nursery, when a whole gang of toddlers ambushed me with ray-gun fire. I ducked behind a wall, then rolled out in front of them holding one hand on my wrist, the other shaped like a gun. 'Finger laser!' I said, with a dramatic low pheeep noise, just as one of them staggered back on a lump in the carpet and fell. There was a moment of real awe as they all considered I might be packing real space weaponry, which Danny broke by cracking me in the temple with a non-imaginary plastic sword.

He was a strong flavour. He loved DC Comics super-heroes. Who likes DC? All the heroes striking those stupid stiff poses and staring into the middle distance, while all the Marvel heroes were down on their haunches, or springing across the page. I asked him why his favourite hero was Superman and he said that he was noble, and leafed through a comic simply pointing at him on the page to illustrate this. Here was a five-year-old who tolerated the Marvel movies, but loved the Batman ones. It was the sort of thing that the editor in me would have changed in a script without a thought.

His favourite things all involved me being defeated, thwarted, and left crestfallen in some way. At the swimming pool Amy would carry him up to me, and I would open my arms for a hug, and they would bob to one side and go round me, while I pulled a look of clownish disappointment. That was the thing he found funniest in the world – the look of broken chagrin that is, ironically, just my regular appearance now.

Amy graduated and got a good job with a union, and we were able to buy the flat. It was dirt cheap, as nobody in their right mind wanted to live in the city centre. I should have moved out afterwards, obviously, but I've just never been able to. Amy borrowed her dad's DIY stuff and did a lot of home improvements.

If she didn't have the desire to improve things against insurmountable odds she probably wouldn't have been with me, and we made it work for a while, like a Bruce Springsteen song.

We grew cress in little plastic tubs by the sink, and I'd make him pick it and sprinkle some on his cheese sandwich before nursery. We grew sunflowers in the window box. He'd stand and wait for me to whip back the curtains on them every morning, it never got old.

One day, when I was at work, Amy came home with him from the Science Centre and put him down to let him run up the stairs. He sat down on the bottom step, facing her, and said, 'I'm too tired to go up the stairs.' Somehow, she just immediately knew that something was wrong. I remember getting into the empty house and her calling me from the hospital – the GP had sent them straight there.

A nurse directed me to the first floor. I'd stopped at the foot of the stairs and took a few deep breaths. I think subconsciously I knew I was about to pass out. I can still remember every detail of that moment: the cracks where the badly fitted flooring met the wall; the bright white Coke machine with the no change light on; the vending machine beside it that went Twirl, Dairy Milk, Mini Cheddars, Wine Gums, Mints. A Kinder Bueno stuck out against the glass, held tantalisingly over the void. The machines filled the space with a low hum. 'Please let him be okay,' I thought, reaching out not to God exactly, but Everything. 'I will do anything else,' I told it, like someone in the fucking Bible.

It was meningitis. Amy told me that the infection was so bad that his spinal fluid hit the wall when he had the lumbar puncture.

In the ambulance, Amy asked the paramedic what was wrong with him and he'd replied, 'I don't know but I've never been to a child that's looked like this.' People say that time stretches in those situations, but it compressed. He got worse and they told us the next three hours would be crucial. For the first time in my life I knew the size of an hour, and could feel its edges. I could see three hours like I could see three inches, or half a pint. I could feel the minutes tick within them, short as breaths. I watched his chest rise and fall. I saw the terrible smallness and pettiness of the universe. How little we all were, and how quickly we passed. We were round him when he went, though he couldn't see us.

Afterwards, in the corridor, Amy's mum had a grip of her by the lapels as Amy sobbed into her shoulder. Her mum looked right at me, her eyes wide with meaning. I knew we were thinking that Amy might walk straight out of there and throw herself under a bus. I was relieved when they both sat down on the floor, Amy's mum putting herself on the door side.

I marched straight back into the ICU. For some reason I'd brought toys from the house. The bed was still crowded with the figures of the Justice League who had failed to protect him, and I brushed them onto the floor. His mouth was open and I saw for the first time where the air tube had bashed his teeth. There was blood around his gums, and I wanted to make it better. I still do.

I tickled him under his chin, he was still warm.

37

He died on the first of December, and now every year, in his memory, I get shit-faced for a few weeks before and a few weeks after.

There's a weird thing that happens with grief when people stop asking if you're okay. Things have stopped for you, and it's almost shocking to realise it's not like that for everybody else. They're looking forward to a movie, or a football game, or a date, or a whole bunch of stuff you feel you'll never look forward to again.

There's also the fact that it will never feel real. What they don't tell you is, once you make your way through all the other stages, you go right back to denial.

Bereaved parent groups are pretty good if you can handle it, and a happy hunting ground if you're recruiting for an organisation dedicated to militant atheism. The very first person who spoke at my first meeting, this woman who lost her daughter, said: 'It's like being lost at sea in a storm,' and the guy beside me muttered: 'And there's no land.'

That's the problem, when you get right down to it. There's no land.

I couldn't get into the support group, though. Amy found it useful, but I found I toned everything down for them. When I spoke it felt a bit like when you explain a dream to someone and start rationalising bits so that it makes sense as a story.

Some days, I can feel the coldness of outer space. Being alive feels like a kind of cowardice. I have, on more than one occasion, lain in a darkened room and attempted to turn back time by force of will.

How the fuck do you say that in a group, and what purpose would it serve if you did?

Any period of not thinking about it was a victory. I noted things I did, ate, or drank that made me think about it more. I cut out coffee – caffeine was the worst for sending my mind racing in agonising repetitive circles. I noted the things that made me think about it less. The PlayStation. FIFA. Watching the news. I think part of me enjoyed seeing a world that wouldn't have been worth living in for Danny anyway. I began to see the shittiest, time-wasting behaviour as constructive.

We started going to couples therapy after he died.

It was my idea. Amy wasn't that up for it and put up some spurious Marxist resistance. 'We can only find happiness through collective practice, not individual therapy.'

'It's not individual therapy, it's couples therapy,' I replied. 'We are a collective!' Somehow that had worked.

It didn't really work, but I kept going even when she stopped – I still go. Maybe I just felt like I couldn't subtract anything else from my life.

I'd do things automatically. Find that I'd eaten, find that I'd been asleep. I stayed indoors a lot, and the days kind of drifted together. I wouldn't wash for days at a time and wake up stinking like a raw onion. *Living out my death* – it was a phrase from some old detective novel, and it came to me a lot during that period. I was amazed at all the things that meant nothing: Celtic winning the league; a job offer; birthdays; your pal's wedding; a war. It was a long parade of empty floats.

I was always surprised by Danny getting older. I couldn't really picture him starting nursery, or talking. So it was weird that I could now see everything that wasn't going to happen: the school nativity play, his first crush, taking him to football training, every birthday; in vivid, intricate detail. Every day I fought to keep it all out of my head, and every day I lost.

One day I was crossing the road somewhere up the top end of Sauchiehall Street. I wasn't crossing at the lights, and as I crossed I saw a very old man looking at me from the far pavement. I was aware suddenly that I hadn't looked left or right, just walked straight out. The look the old guy gave me was just a kind of non-judgemental appraisal. *There's someone who's started just walking out into traffic*, it said. I decided to get some proper therapy.

I'd already been referred to a psychotherapist at some point, for depression they said, but I hadn't gone. I started seeing him once a week: a Spanish guy with a beautiful rolling accent. I told him about the Valium and he said that I needed to be careful because after a while it stops you from feeling anything with your soul. It sounded poetic the way he said it, and also like the greatest recommendation for anything that I'd ever heard.

I started working in a bar in the Trongate. I had a friend there who'd found Jesus, and I was happy for her, and wished that one day I could lose it as fully as that. Through Valium and hash and bar work I found something adjacent to peace. It was drug derived and it was drug defined.

I was still living with Amy but it was over. She slept with a guy at some party that Christmas. Someone at work was there and told me about it – fuck knows why. I thought maybe Amy was trying to provoke a reaction out of me. I was angry, but mainly about the fact that she could still feel enough to touch or be touched. We drifted apart for a couple of years, and then she moved in with a guy from her job. I missed her, and I missed me. Going back to working in bars meant that my complete abandonment of hope and social norms could go unnoticed.

When she left we had this very earnest conversation about how I needed to look after my mental health and I did. I stayed high, and skipped sad songs where it seemed like the narrator had more going for him than me.

After she left, I had a one-night stand with a woman who turned to me in the morning and said, 'I'm quite a keen racist, what about you?' I briefly imagined what it would be like to fall deeply in love with this far right ethno-nationalist. Maybe one day she'd catch you crying watching some Holocaust documentary and you'd have to pretend that they were tears of laughter.

One thing with parenthood is you realise how bored you were before and, even aside from all the trauma and grief, that's a hard thing to go back to. Valium filled that hole, it made the time pass easier. It made it harder to remember.

I don't think I saw Amy at all for maybe eighteen months.

We'd always done that thing where we'd go to a bar and pretend not to know each other and make like it was a one-night stand. It was her idea at first; she suggested it lightly to hide how much she was into it. It became a regular thing with us. Even after the wee man came along, I got a babysitter a couple of times and surprised her on her work's night out.

It had all started up again a couple of months ago. I'd been drunk in Sleazy's in town, and she'd appeared and bought me a drink and asked me my name. I was too wasted to recognise her at first. 'Sildar Hallwinter,' I'd announced, defensively, having had half a joint of Marina's weed and nursing multiple interlocking paranoias.

We'd ended up in my flat, and we'd stayed in character the whole night. I suppose it would be too grim to drop it and admit that you were sitting in the ruins of your own life.

It happened a few times after that – in fact, I'd seen her just a few nights before the Alternative Independence night at the Radisson. She'd been at the Go-Go of all places. She was one of the only women I knew who could sit in a place like that and not get hit on. Even drunks could see that somehow she just radiated a potential punch in the jaw. She had a perpetual frown of concentration now, from focusing hard on distractions I guessed.

I sat beside her at an empty table and I introduced myself; it was always a total reset with us. Over the course of a couple of drinks she told me all about her life. It was weird to hear it put like that.

'One of my therapists gave me a thing to say to myself to break the cycle of repetitive thoughts. Do you want to hear it?' I asked.

There was a tight flicker at her lips, perhaps suppressing a laugh at 'one of my therapists' forming part of my pulling chat. 'Sure.'

'Moving forwards, into the sunshine.'

I'd sort of thought we'd laugh about it, but she nodded solemnly.

'Moving forwards, into the sunshine,' she said, holding her drink in the manner of a toast. We clinked glasses, but my hand was shaking.

⁓

Agent Brond stepped to one side. Behind him was a huge man with a huge bald head, like a child's nightmare drawn on a balloon. His enormous features somehow crowded its vast surface, and his lumpy body was an abomination the human mind couldn't fully grasp. He was either a very serious man or a hilarious-looking baby. He was smiling with his mouth, but screaming with his eyes. He wore a bland suit and tie.

Brond spoke in a clipped voice. 'My friend here is here to teach you both something about pain.'

I looked over at Amy, and she looked back at me, and we both started howling with laughter. Actual peals of laughter, echoing around the container like it was a bell. I don't know why I was trying to stifle it, but it only made it worse. I snorted, and tasted my blood in the back of my throat.

Amy leaned back in her chair and put her head back, giggling deliriously. 'You're gonnae to teach us about pain? Oh, that's fucking good. Do you hear that, Felix? This cunt's gonnae make us suffer.'

I shook my head. I had tears in my eyes. My voice came out light and upbeat, like a local radio presenter. 'Bring it on, man. Can't wait to find out!'

Amy looked at me and roared, 'HAHAHAHA!' A proper *Beano* laugh.

My face felt a bit sore and tired from laughing and I wiggled my jaw to get some feeling back into it.

Gerry gave us the chastising eyes of a disappointed dad. His voice was calm. 'We get it – you've both got a real attitude. Congratulations. My colleague and I have managed to change a lot of attitudes over the years.'

'In between writing songs for Paul McCartney,' I slurred. 'Shit songs, that really didn't hold up with the rest of those albums.'

I looked over at Amy, whose head was drooped and shaking from side to side, and knew that the sodium pentothal, and whatever else they'd given us, was really ripping through us.

Gerry cleared his throat. 'Here's an interesting question. It interests me from a technical point of view, and I'd like your opinion. Do you think you'll tell me everything after we've killed your little girlfriend? Or just before we do you?'

Maybe it was a truth serum because I answered as honestly as I could: 'I'm not sure there's enough of us left to kill.'

The bawfaced guy spoke for the first time. He had a thick London accent. 'Let's find out, shall we?' He stood and removed his jacket, hanging it carefully over the back of his plastic chair, then ambled towards us from the back of the room, a long thin knife in his hand. His feet clicked lightly on the metal floor.

I found myself marvelling at his blue striped tie: who the fuck dressed up for this kind of thing? I tried to say, 'Teach me, Daddy,' because I thought it would be funny, but no words came out and I half puked a load of saliva onto my chair.

Stopping in front of us, he looked over at Brond for guidance, then stepped in close towards Amy. He whispered something in her ear, and traced the knife lightly back and forward across her chest. She sighed, 'Oh, get on with it, for fuck's sake,' in a tone of such flat boredom that it raised a puzzled expression from the maniac's psychopathic depths. He wasn't thrown exactly, but she'd maybe excited his professional curiosity.

Eventually, he brought the blade up to her shoulder, and started to press it into her. She screamed, a long, shuddering howl, through gritted teeth.

It took him a second to realise that she was pushing

forward into it, the heels of her crepe shoes off the floor as she tilted herself towards him. She bit off each word. 'Put. It. Over. Mah. Fuckin'. Heart. *Pleeeease.*' She drew the last word out like she was singing.

Amy drove herself forward and screamed as the blade went into her. Bawfaced guy stepped away, and the legs of Amy's chair dropped back down to the floor, the knife still in her shoulder, one side of her jumper dark with blood. 'I can't believe our taxes pay for this incompetence,' she spat, with genuine bitterness.

I tried to focus on Brond, though my vision was still swimming and I could hear a kind of metallic hum that I was pretty sure wasn't actually there. I felt a stab of pity for the futility of it all.

Amy managed a small head jerk. 'Is this him? The guy who killed Marina?'

'Aye.'

She gave a long snigger that ended in a snort: 'The Butler did it!'

She sounded absolutely wasted. I wondered absently why there wasn't more of a street market in sodium pentothal.

Brond walked forward to stand beside his freakish helper. It looked like he was just about to say something when a mobile began to buzz. He produced the phone from the inside pocket of his suit. They really were both incredibly overdressed for a beating. Perhaps they were going on somewhere afterwards.

He turned around as he muttered something angrily into the phone.

There was a brief, ugly silence and then he walked back towards us, phone still in hand, his lips white with rage. He glared at me, then made some gestures to the knifeman, who left, taking his jacket with him.

Slowly, the big man in front of us broke into a smile – a warm, open smile. There was something genuine in it, and I understood that in his mind's eye he was looking at my burning corpse.

He produced a handkerchief and wiped the desk down, and all the chairs. Then he moved behind us, cut the plastic ties on our hands and legs, and simply walked off, leaving the heavy metal door open behind him.

We swayed out into the sunlight, laughing. We were in a yard full of containers. Maybe we were near the Clyde, I thought, judging from the number of seagulls about. Amy's legs gave way but somehow I caught her. We sat on the ground for a bit. I think I fell asleep. At some point, DI McKay and Jane must have arrived to take us away.

38

McKay took Amy to hospital while we went back to Jane's. I got washed up and changed downstairs, then had a nap fully clothed in her spare room. When I went back up to the living room she handed me a Scotch and nodded towards the front door. I threw on my jacket and we stepped out into the blustery night, each with a glass in our hand.

Jane limped to a little square over the road, at the entrance to the park. It was dominated by a high stone plinth and a mounted soldier with his back to the street, facing into the park. Glasgow did have the occasional statue of a scientist or whatever, but it was largely mass murderers. Field Marshal Lord Roberts, the plinth said, hero of the Indian Rebellion of 1858. This was Britain, and if you killed enough foreigners, they let you ride a metal horse into the future.

It was quiet: some dog walkers were coming up the hill before the gates closed, and a cluster of teenagers waited for dark so they could skin up.

We sat side by side on a bench underneath the monument, looking into the darkness where the park was, a light wind whispering through the trees. I told her about the meeting with Gary.

'You said "Safe travels" to someone who was going to kill himself?'

I did the little palms-out shrug I sometimes did when I couldn't think of anything to say.

'I'm sorry about your friend. I did tell you he wasn't a teacher. You do know that there's a difference between not judging people and just misjudging them?'

'That's quite judgemental of you, if you don't mind me saying so. Donnie said undercover was just where the police farmed out all the people they couldn't stand the sight of.'

'Hmm. I don't think so. It's maybe more that police are so obvious that the only officers that don't get spotted fairly quickly are the ones having a nervous breakdown – makes them really blend in with the rest of humanity.'

'I don't know how long he would have lived. He had three white blood cells left and they were fighting the Alamo. But I feel I lost him in two ways, you know? He's dead, and the person I thought he was is dead too. It's hard to quantify, exactly – at best he was some kind of sex offender. I don't know that he was an entirely bad person, though. It was like he had . . . multiple personalities.'

She nodded absently. 'Yeah. Three cunts and a rapist. But he could never have seen that. Don't beat yourself up about it. I think you were in a co-dependent relationship with him, and it's hard to see clearly in those things. Also, it might be subconscious, but men are pretty tolerant of bad men. They lower the bar for you. They mean that anyone who isn't driving around in a van taking hostages is pretty much marriage material.'

'He did have a van at one point. He was pretty much doing that. You must have seen plenty of infiltration as a cop, no?'

'Yes, well, I suppose so . . . but to do it romantically, to take it into the place where we choose to suspend disbelief so we can survive as a species . . .' She gave a long sigh.

'He was a complex guy,' I muttered, euphemistically.

'If this was one of my books I'd be told that it was too simple an ending for his story – him just dying like that.'

'Better tell God then, cos that's how he's ending all of them.'

There was a pause while Jane put her glass down between her feet and lit a fag.

'So, you went to Rachael's flat then?'

She rested her forehead briefly on the fingertips of one hand. 'Oh, God, her flat was so disgusting. I can't even talk about it,' she muttered, her eyes flickering like a combat veteran as her brain replayed the images to her. 'Rachael had given Gary Greg's address, and British Intelligence, in their incompetence had robbed the wrong flat. So obviously I thought anything Rachael had might still be at her place. Maybe she'd got a photo of Marina with her killer? All kinds of exciting possibilities. So, yes, we went to Rachael's flat, and that's where we found absolutely fuck-all.'

Jane revealed that she'd broken in with DI McKay and found a GoPro filled with video footage of me, Greg, Marina, and some terrified student she'd stalked years ago.

There was nothing relevant to the investigation. Jane showed me some very amusing footage she'd transferred to her phone of a clearly exhausted Greg coming home from a cycling trip with his girlfriend, where he seemed to be surreptitiously removing a little electric motor from under his back wheel.

'I suppose she didn't even know Marina was dead,' she mused.

'I think she preferred to get her news from ethereal voices, you probably miss a lot of stuff that way.'

'She was just a daft old sod who was in the wrong place at the wrong time.'

'How did you get us out then? That was you on the phone to Brond, right?'

'The phone call was from Dr Chong. I called him out of desperation, I suppose. He managed to convince them that I'd shown him that I had something damaging. I don't even know what.'

'That was big of him. He seems to have taken me killing his dog incredibly well.'

'It was very ill, he said, and he didn't have the heart to put it down. Said to express to you this exact sentiment . . . Hang on.' She dug her phone out of her bag again and read from her notes. 'Is the simulation a literal recreation of a long-dead universe, or is it a poetic or even satirical re-interpretation? Discuss.'

'Crazy Dave.'

'Indeed.'

'But why did he put himself at risk to help us?'

'He thought his love for Marina was just some intellectual thing, I suppose. It never is, in my experience. It makes you do things your intellect would resist. I don't think he wanted to save you, but he did. What matters now is that it won't take Brond long to realise that we have nothing. He'll come here.'

'He might be a while. The cops are going to find his fingerprints on the morphine that Gary Mount killed himself with. I gave them an anonymous tip, along with that photo I took of him at the Burns supper.'

She smiled at me, proudly I think. 'Unfortunately, that won't hold him long. Even if they find him he'll be bailed by the morning.'

There was a long silence then. A couple walked past us and stood leaning against the railings at the front of the statue, their laughter occasionally drifting back to us.

'How can people not see what's wrong with that?' I asked, jerking my head up at the monstrosity above us.

She sighed. 'It's like vampires, isn't it?'

'Vampires?'

'Vampires are supposed to be Jews. That's why they hate crosses. And maybe garlic, I suppose. *Dracula* was written when folk were worried about Jewish immigration from Eastern Europe. Count Dracula was coming to England to buy property! Those old Nazi cartoons of Jews, it's pretty much Nosferatu. But if you're brought up in our culture, you look at a vampire movie and it's just a vampire. Same way some people look at this' – she gestured at the statue – 'and it's just a bloke on a horse.'

'What's our job, though? To try and explain it to those people?'

She sat back on the bench and looked up at the starless sky. 'When you're black, your job is just to survive those people.'

I took a belt of the Scotch. 'So Chong wasn't all bad.'

'He wasn't all that good, either. My guess is that Marina and Chong had been playing a game of cat and mouse for a long time. Perhaps he was interested to know if he'd met his match. Chong thought you were a total fucking idiot who couldn't do him any damage. I mean, they had you hanging out full-time with a cop on his payroll and you were none the wiser!' She laughed grimly.

'You think Chong and Brond . . . made Donnie be friends with me?'

Jane stared right into my eyes, sort of focusing on one eye, then the other. It reminded me of the look a doctor once gave me when I fell out of a tree. She gave a brief supportive smile. 'Well, yes. When did Donnie move into your building?'

'I'm not sure.'

'Two years ago, roughly just after Marina started working for Chong. I suppose they checked her out and found that you were one of the few people she was close to. Brond, via Chong, had thoroughly corrupted a host of undercover operations in major crimes over the years, it's inconceivable that someone like Donnie Wilson, a man with the breaking strain of a red hot Mars Bar, didn't come under their influence. Here's the thing, though: Brond thinks rationally, he's meticulous, but he doesn't understand the power of randomising factors, and you're about as random as they come.'

'He underestimated me.'

'He underestimated the possibility that you might care enough to find someone who could actually work out what was going on,' she conceded, turning against the wind to light a fag. 'Imagine how shocked he must have been when you found Chong. They knew they'd need to get you off the table, so they set up a drug deal that they're ten stages removed from. The initial idea might have been for you to OD on that very pure coke. He can't have imagined you'd be the only junkie in Glasgow who'd never done cocaine. When that didn't work, they brought the police in: hoped you'd be looking at a long stretch for possession with intent to supply.'

I protested briefly that I didn't intend to supply anything and was going to take pretty much all of it.

'Oh, I believe you. And when that didn't work either, they changed their minds and decided they needed to send you into danger. Into the hands of community workers who'd come into a million quid's worth of smack and coke and experienced quite the ideological shift. There were four of them originally. They'd gone horribly *Scarface* and killed the other two by the time you showed up. Oh, and the two you ran into were lovers by the way, and it's disgusting. They were strung out on some of the world's purest cocaine and, from what we can gather, they'd been told there was a contract out on their lives – a rumour I imagine Brond started just before you arrived, to really amp things up.'

We talked a bit more about the case. I understood the details, but the overall picture of what had happened didn't make a lot of sense to me.

Eventually Jane changed the subject. 'I sit out here at night a lot. You know the story I think of a lot these days? Gethsemane. Where Jesus goes to wait for his arrest. Gethsemane. That was my favourite word as a kid. Just pipped "toboggan".'

'My theory was always that Jesus and Judas were lovers. That's why Jesus gets Judas to betray him – it's a set-up. The Romans don't know what Jesus looks like. Judas betrays him with a kiss – he shows them who his lover is. But he kisses someone else – gets some patsy killed. They pay some locals to beat him before the crucifixion, and put the crown of thorns on him so he's unrecognisable. The whole thing is Jesus getting someone else to take the fall.'

Jane laughed. 'Makes sense that he's white now. That's white people behaviour.' She side-eyed me. 'Is one of the side effects of Valium addiction losing the ability to edit yourself in any way?'

I shrugged. 'Well, let's hope so, I suppose.'

A black Labrador trotted by, apparently without an owner. It sat and gazed into the sheet black of the park for a while, then ambled off, stage left.

'Okay. For someone who sees themselves as a disinterested observer, you've got a lot of fucking opinions. Well, I'm sure you think you were brought up religiously, but my

338

mum was a Zimbabwean Christian. She used to sit in a shed at the bottom of our garden trying to convert people over CB radio.'

'CB radio?'

'It was this thing they had before the internet so children could talk to long-distance lorry drivers. Anyway, I always thought Jesus spent the night in Gethsemane because he wanted to look at nature. No doubt you'll feel that lacks gay sex and betrayal, but I found it was what I wanted to do after my diagnosis. I've spent a lot of time in nature. To appreciate what you're leaving and maybe, I don't know, to understand that you were part of it, had come from it, and are returning to it in some sense.'

'I quite like Jesus, but Catholic school puts you off religion.'

'We had Saturday schools growing up. Black supplementary schools. Our schools didn't want to educate us and we decided to educate ourselves through force of will. My parents were pretty conventional, in their own way. And it's an eye-opener, as you can imagine, to find out that the whole history of western philosophy is basically just racists correcting each other. And all those brilliant people who came through that – we went into institutions. That was how we were going to change things: by going into the BBC; the police, the Bar, journalism, academia. It was a total disaster. The school system should have already taught us how institutions "value" black people. Sometimes I think all it meant was there was nobody left to run the Saturday schools for the next generation.'

'That's sad.'

'We made the classic mistake of thinking that you can reform your abuser.'

'You regret going into the police?'

'It's mixed. Yeah, it's corrupt, but you need the rule of law. I suppose I'm quite conventional too, or maybe I'm just still a polis. I think the police are probably a net win.'

I'd never really liked the police: people have complex problems, and maybe the best person to solve them isn't a guy with two GCSEs and a stick. I decided not to mention this.

A park van came round and a guy got out to lock the gates. Our silences were gradually getting longer, and everybody else seemed to have drifted off.

'That woman you had the affair with . . . did you get off on it?' I asked. 'The fact that she was married?'

She curdled her face in my direction. 'No. Mostly it just made me sad.' She gave a very quiet sigh. 'But she was so beautiful anyone would have wanted her. Sometimes when I was with her, I felt like I'd cucked the whole world.'

We were quiet for a bit. There were some kids shouting down in the park, and we both smiled as the occasional swearword carried up.

'You know what I only realise now?' she asked, with a humorous tinkle in her voice I'd not heard before. 'It's all Gethsemane. Right the way through.'

The wind picked up, and we watched it cut a shiver from a couple at the railings. I said, 'Shall we go back in? I'm all for being at one with nature, but maybe not in January.'

She groaned and pushed herself up with her stick, and we limped back to the flat. It seemed sad suddenly to have a mess of Rizlas, empty beer bottles and drug debris at the centre of such a beautiful room; I got a plastic bag from the kitchen and started to tidy up. I went to the bathroom, and by the time I got to the living room Jane had fixed me a highball and a chicken sandwich.

'Why don't you get some sleep?' The bedding was still there from the last time I'd stayed over, but neatly folded now on a chair in the corner. She threw me a duvet and pulled the other one over herself as she sat upright in the armchair.

I went round putting off the lamps. She stopped me. 'Leave that one on! Before he comes he'll kill the power, to switch off the building's CCTV. Leave it on. It'll let us know when he's here.' She spoke about it as casually as if we were waiting in for an Amazon delivery.

When she went to the bathroom, I poured my drink into the sink, and refilled it from the bar. Hard to say if you can really know someone over such a short space of time, but something about how she'd mixed the drinks when I was out of the room made me think mine might be drugged, and that she intended to face it all alone.

We talked for a bit and gradually the silences grew longer. I had some stupid thought about not falling asleep, like the Apostles at Gethsemane. Even in the dark, I could see the outline of the woman's body in the painting above the fireplace. For the first time I understood that it was a woman lying down, her back arching upwards, her fists clenched in triumph or in pain – or both. It was the torso of a woman giving birth, I thought.

I could have only dozed off for a second. I looked over at Jane and she was asleep, head slumped forward.

The lamp was off.

39

I stood up quietly and crept out to the hallway in my socks. As I was squeezing my feet into my trainers, I felt, as much as heard, a soft click from the outer hallway. From the front door, I supposed.

Jane's key was in the mortice of the flat door and I turned it slowly and stepped outside.

There stood Agent Brond in a crisp brown suit, looking right at me as he closed the outside door delicately behind him. His hair was neatly parted. He looked like he was on his way to church after this.

'How did you enjoy your first investigation, Felix?' he asked softly.

For some reason I found myself saying, 'Well, there's really been a lot more unrequited gay love than I would have imagined . . . like, a lot more.' And he smiled as if this was exactly the answer he'd been expecting.

I raised the taser quickly and deliberately. I heard his shoes twist lightly on the polished floor as he turned side-long, but still it hit him flush on the right side of his chest. He staggered a little, then flexed his right arm, and gave a stifled roar as he brought his clenched fist up from his side and rode it out. If you'd walked in on us at that moment, you might have thought he was paying a particularly emotional tribute to Freddie Mercury. Then he pulled the electrodes out of his shirt with a brush of the hand. There was a fleck of foam at the side of his mouth. He dabbed it away with his pinky like it was cream from a scone.

He brought his other hand up.

At first I thought he'd simply pointed at me, but then I realised I'd been shot in the chest. I fell back so perfectly into the hallway armchair it was as if it had been placed there for that express purpose.

I was unconscious for a while, falling down into the moving, patterned red you see when you close your eyes against the sun. It can't have been long. I was aware of the sound of a door opening and shoes stepping lightly down the hallway. There was grunting, the sound of a struggle. I swam towards the noise and my eyes opened.

Brond had Jane pinned against the wall one-handed, at almost arm's length, her feet off the floor. She kicked out at him with little effect.

'Don't struggle, Detective. You came to see me. You sought me out.' A trace of bitterness crept into his normally emotionless voice, and he caught it himself, and chuckled, maybe at the unfamiliar loss of control. 'You took that quite incredible risk to taunt me, because you wanted this. A dramatic end.'

'No . . .' she grunted. She twisted her neck, and the

words came out thickly. 'I came to see you . . . to make sure you were complacent about the stick.'

This confused me, and Brond didn't seem to know what to make of it, either. There was an explosion of movement from somewhere within the pair of them.

Brond tightened his grip and Jane's cane fell to the floor with a clatter.

I stared stupidly at it. Now I was sliding incredibly slowly off the chair onto the floor on my side, and as my head met the cold, oddly refreshing marble of the hallway floor, I found that I could see right inside the stick, which was – strangely, it seemed to me – hollow.

I pulled myself upright as my chest and stomach cramped. Brond was holding Jane with two hands now, but his whole body trembled, and about two feet of blade stuck out from his back. He sank onto his knees and lowered her down to the floor like a dancer ending a movement.

She leaned down and spat: 'Just for the record, the name of the move that killed you was "the old switcheroo".' She coughed and retched loudly, then fell down heavily into a sitting position against the wall.

Brond's huge body slumped forward from the knees and balanced impossibly on the sword beneath it, his eyes staring sightlessly into hers.

I allowed myself to pass out.

Epilogue

I sat in the corner of the hospital room helping myself to grapes while Jane flirted with the nurse who was checking her drip. Eventually she swept out, taking an armful of dead flowers with her.

'She's, eh, a wee bit young for you, no?'

Jane grinned and started to wiggle her eyebrows up and down suggestively, then whatever she was going to say was buried in a painful fit of coughing. 'Strictly for research,' she finally managed, weakly.

We discussed the case a bit; there was still a lot of stuff we didn't know, and perhaps, for our own safety, shouldn't.

'We delivered some justice though, Poirot.'

I could tell she was trying to find an upbeat note.

I shook my head dismissively. 'I'm maybe more like Miss Marple. I do it all on instinct.'

'On the contrary, I think Miss Marple mines data from her village and uses it to establish patterns of criminal behaviour. She's very mechanistic. I think what I hate about her is that she's too interested in people, she's a bit of a voyeur. Poirot views humanity with amused contempt, which I think is healthier.'

She held an arm out and I gripped her hand, as I always did at the end of a visit. She smiled up at me as she held on to mine just a little too long. We both knew I wasn't coming back.

I closed the door gently behind me.

Outside, Ginny stood leaning against the wall at the far end of the corridor, her bag and coat at her feet as she scrolled through her phone. She gathered up her things and marched towards me with a restrained bravado. Even under the unforgiving light of a hospital corridor she was very beautiful.

I'd tried to think of something to say at this bit, but for some reason I just said, 'Good luck,' and she gave me a tight grin and a nod as she went past. I looked back at her. She stopped for the briefest moment to fix her hair in the black reflection of a curtained window, gave one loud knock on Jane's door and disappeared.

While I was laid up, I'd thought a lot about why Jane had told me, of all people, what was going on with her emotionally. I guess it was because seeing your ex on your deathbed is probably a really bad idea, and she needed someone she could rely on to make the wrong decision for her.

I actually don't know if there was a right or wrong thing to do, but the thing I chose was probably the least sad.

It's been eight months since Butler died. Lemon Monkey

closed down, a note appearing in the window saying simply: 'No Longer Lemon Monkey.' Amy met someone and fell in love – the physio she got for her shoulder. She's three months pregnant – she told me the other day. I still see her a fair bit: we sit in the park, or sometimes go for a scone at this fifties-style cafe I write in. We have almost matching wounds, which I have to admit is poetic.

It was only after the investigation, and after I straightened up I suppose, that I realised how close I'd been to Marina. Of course Rachael had thought we were a couple: we spent so much time together. I realise now I probably started hanging around the Go-Go because she was there. Maybe she was the sister I never had. Maybe she was a piece of living code within the architecture of a vast simulated reality. I miss her.

They got me a really good therapist after the shooting, for PTSD. I got referred to this woman in London who specialises in gunshot trauma. She's from New Mexico originally, and worked with cops, mass-shooting victims, all sorts. She acts like she doesn't want to discuss such things, but if she's in the mood and you hit all her buttons right, she will pay out in macabre vignettes like a fruit machine. It's actually the rest of my life that she's more useful with: turns out that losing Danny was a lot more like being shot in the chest than anything else.

Dr Chong disappeared while I was still in hospital. It's been impossible to scare up a lead on him. His house has been on sale for months; turns out there isn't much of a market for 5,000 square foot bungalows.

Even during the inquest into Brond's death (his real name was Jeremiah Brond, or so they say), I knew it was all over. I'm not sure if we were left alone because we knew too much or too little: possibly it was some combination of the two.

Unbelievably, I'm dating Fatima. This has involved a certain amount of upping my game. I go to therapy, I cook, I meet her outside her work a couple of days a week and walk her home. She's very patient with me, and the undercurrent of *Fuck up once and it's over* is fine by me. I suppose I've brought to it the one thing that really makes a relationship work: gratitude.

I stopped fighting destiny and got a job in the Go-Go. I was made assistant manager last month, largely because I'm usually the only one who's sober enough to lock up. Speaking of which, Greg's missus turned up for lunch there, with what I guessed was Reserve Guy. He got about forty-five minutes and she was gone. Fair play to him – he responded by ordering a series of Blue Hawaiis and drinking them morosely, without taking the umbrellas out. I gave them to him on the house because Reserve Guys are people too. We had a chat and he seemed like a really sweet man. He's very worried about climate change, to the point that I'm not sure he was listening when I was talking about the more immediate threat of the Hadron Collider.

It was Sunday, and I trudged through a hungover Glasgow up to Kelvingrove.

Somewhere in this park I'm still lying on the grass

tripping. Somewhere in this park Marina is walking to her death; Danny is riding his little no-pedals wooden bike down the hill; I am meeting Fatima on our first date; Donnie is still screaming at the gates and holding a duck aloft in triumph.

I sat on a bench near the jaunty Boer War statue. Recovery is a bit like that too. I couldn't really see this version of me from where I was, but it was always a possibility. There's a certain amount of narcissism involved in thinking you can never change. You need to be a little egotistical to think that we're spinning through space, and moving through time, yet you are somehow the one thing in the Universe that's constant and unchangeable. Not every day is great, but then I do live in Scotland sober. I thought of something I'd never considered before: there's all sorts of future stuff happening here too. It made me smile.

NA is full of people who thought they'd never change. A giant guy who was a coke monster, now a granddad with a lawnmower business – it's only when you get him talking about lawnmowers that you get a glimpse of what he must have been like on cocaine. A lassie who was a Vallie head and is now a professional footballer. We went to see her play: she got sent off in a performance of such shocking brutality that we didn't even wind her up about it. There's a guy who got addicted to smack in Bar-L. He's a fitness nut now and shook his head at me the other day for getting an ice lolly at the garage.

I found it strangely uplifting, the smallness of our remaining worries.

There was a massive rucksack of cash in Donnie's gym locker. There were also a load of gay porn DVDs, further confusing his already complex legacy. I'd awarded myself the money we'd spent on the suitcase, and also a fee of $250 a day plus expenses, which seemed the appropriate thing for a detective to do. I didn't really want to keep any more drugs money, so I downloaded the Beloved Intelligence app, created my AI buddy Kwame Thompson, and asked him what to do with the rest. *Sharing is good! A friend might have a use for this!* it replied, with a thumbs-up emoji, and a tractor one, which I chose to simply ignore.

So the rest I'd given to Mikey. He met me at Harthill Services, on his way to God knows where. He was safe from his old handlers, but now he was vulnerable to his gangland shit, and was pretty much in hiding.

He'd weighed the gym bag in one hand with a puzzled look. I'd told him to do what I'd done with mine, and buy stock in Beloved Intelligence. This was six or seven months ago. They're going public in a few weeks, and I suppose Mikey will be rich. Somehow, I know that Mikey's guilt means that he'll do some good with it. I suppose that's what philanthropy is.

I'd finished my rom-com script, and had a producer who was interested. This was partly down to more good advice from Kwame Thompson, who'd told me to set it in London, or at least responded with an emoji of a London bus.

It was getting hot. I stood up and began walking up the hill, past the murder scene, and up towards the Gibson Street entrance. Folk launched tennis balls off the edge of the hill and their dogs scrambled down and got them. I looked across the river to where the Glasgow University watchtower punctured the bright blue sky like a steampunk space rocket. My chest ached a bit but, for whatever reason, I felt pretty good.

The park was filling up now and reggae blared from a speaker somewhere behind me. I paused to take in the moment. I saw May at the edge of some big group, sitting in a circle on the grass down at the bottom of the hill. She was rummaging through her bag then glanced up, and – even though she was quite a distance away – saw me and laughed.

She held my gaze with a fixed grin, brought her hand up in front of her face, and clicked her fingers.

Acknowledgements

I would like to thank everyone in the New World Order writing team whose regular attempts to send me spiralling into terror about Simulation Theory, Artificial Intelligence, the Hadron Collider, and Outer Space in a more general sense, have been invaluable in prompting me to write this book. Specifically, and in the order their taunting faces lurch forward from my memory: Charlie Skelton, Neil Webster, Meryl O'Rourke, Dan Evans, Steven Dick, Christine Rose, Aiden Spackman, Sophie Duker, Shaun Pye and James "Hotsauce" Farmer.

The idea that social media algorithms might be attempting to make users more predictable is I think a reasonably well known, if contested, idea in the field of AI. The possible dangers of the Hadron Collider are something I read about in a book called *On The Future: Prospects for Humanity* by Martin Rees, and the characters' estimation of those chances are a very rough paraphrase of something the physicist Walter L Wagner once said in an interview.

For some of the ideas characters express about the legacy of British colonialism, I am indebted to books like Akala's

Natives and Kehinde Andrews' *The New Age of Empire*; and David Olusoga's *Black and British*. A book I found to be very useful in helping me to imagine Jane Pickford's background was Kehinde Andrews' *Resisting Racism: Race, inequality, and the Black supplementary school movement*.

The line about snow is something the comic book legend Grant Morrison said to me years ago, and they toss these things off so casually that I asked if I could find a home for it somewhere. Coincidentally, a joke about Giffnock came from Mark Millar, on a visit to a restaurant where he almost accidentally committed a hate crime.

I'd like to thank everyone who ever worked the bar at The Stand Comedy Club, for the good times, the chatting of shit, and the madness.

Special thanks to my kids for their support, and to Neil Webster, Richard Cook, and Lucy Prebble who were all kind enough to read an early draft.

And of course bless up Yassine Belkacemi and Jade Chandler, for taking a chance on the book, for their enthusiasm and, of course, for editing the bastard.